the home

Originally from the UK, Karen won the
Emirates Airline Festival of Literature
Montegrappa Novel Writing Award
2016 with her crime-thriller novel
and now has a three-book deal with
Head of Zeus. When she's not writing
novels, Karen is busy bringing up her
two young children and running her
communication business Travel Ink.

By Karen Osman

The Good Mother
The Home

the
home

KAREN OSMAN

First published in the UK in 2018 by Aria,
an imprint of Head of Zeus Ltd

This paperback edition published in 2018 by Aria

9 7 5 3 1 2 4 6 8

A catalogue record for this book is available from
the British Library.

ISBN (PB): 9781789540567
ISBN (E): 9781786699190

Typeset by Divaddict Publishing Solutions Ltd.

Printed and bound in Great Britain by
CPI Group (UK) Ltd, Croydon CR0 4YY

Head of Zeus Ltd
First Floor East
5–8 Hardwick Street
London EC1R 4RG

WWW.HEADOFZEUS.COM

For my husband, Fahad

'Everyone has two sides, good and evil. How you treat me will determine which side you will see.'

Unknown

Prologue

It was the smell that got me. They never tell you about that in training: how it gets under your skin. The lads at the station told me I was lucky to get such a case on my first day in CID. Once I'd finished vomiting in the nearby bushes, I didn't feel very lucky, I can tell you. After seeing the Jane Doe – or what was left of her, at any rate – I would have given anything to be back in uniform, working the traffic. The body must have been there since Bonfire Night, the people lighting the fire unaware of what lay beneath. I can only hope that she was dead before she was dumped. The body was so burnt there would be no chance of identification. You could almost imagine she wasn't human if not for the long strands of brown hair that lay as dead as their owner. But one thing survived the fire: a silver bracelet on the right wrist, its single chain home to a tiny hummingbird charm. I bagged it up, knowing even then that my first investigation was destined for the cold case pile.

I

Evelyn

Fifteen months earlier

Evelyn climbed the three flights of stairs to her flat, trying to ignore the thump of music that drifted down the open stairwell from flat 3A. Charlie, her beloved Yorkshire terrier, was trotting behind her. It was only half past eight in the evening but she knew the noise would go on to the early hours of the morning, as it had been doing since her new neighbours moved in a few weeks ago. If she were lucky, she would manage to get a few hours of sleep. She felt her teeth start to grind in irritation and her right hand twitched for a cigarette. She had done everything possible to get them to turn down the volume. Everything except calling the police, but she knew she was never going to get them involved. It was an unwritten rule amongst her lot to leave the filth out of it. Get in some muscle, pay a gang to rough them up a bit, but never, ever call the police.

Reaching the small landing of the third floor, she delved into her handbag for her key while shooting a murderous look at the flat opposite her own. The noise was making Charlie cower behind her legs. Picking him up, she held him close while unlocking 3B, where she had lived for over fifteen years. She slammed the door behind her, gave Charlie a comforting kiss on his head then put him down and watched him as he went into the kitchen, no doubt in search of some treats. Lighting up a cigarette, Evelyn followed, putting a few dog biscuits in his bowl before grabbing the ever-present bottle of vodka from the countertop. She drank it straight, letting the clear liquid soothe her.

Satisfied, she replaced the top and debated whether to tidy up a bit, but decided she couldn't be bothered. If she were lucky, she might just catch the second half of *Brookside* but, turning the television on, she heard the rolling credits sing out to her tauntingly. Evelyn swore. She loved her television shows. If she hadn't spent so much time listening to Joan go on and on about her errant husband, she would have been home half an hour ago, watching the drama in her comfy armchair, nightcap in hand.

The loud techno beats went up a few more decibels and Evelyn swore again. It wasn't even decent music – what was wrong with The Beatles, Frank Sinatra or Elvis? She knew that dance music was all the rage but to her ears there was no enjoyment to be had from listening to the hammer and clobber of a synthesiser.

Evelyn felt her patience finally snap and she stormed out of her flat across the hallway to 3A and knocked loudly on her neighbour's door. When nobody answered, she started banging, shouting every obscenity she could think of, releasing her frustration, tiredness and irritability with every thump of her fist.

'Oi! Shut it! You're making more racket than them, you silly bitch!'

Evelyn stopped abruptly and leant over the railing. Billy, who lived in the flat beneath hers, was standing in his doorway wearing only a pair of greying, saggy underpants.

'For God's sake, Billy, will you put some bloody clothes on? As if I don't have enough to put up with without you parading around in your undies,' shouted Evelyn.

Billy turned round and bent over, pulling down his pants. Evelyn rolled her eyes and ignored him. At the foot of the stairs, she saw a couple of druggies light up spliffs and she turned away, silently counting to ten. She'd been clean for a number of years now, but it was still a struggle, especially when surrounded by it on a regular basis. She had begged the council to give her a flat in a more reputable postcode, but it didn't look like that was going to happen. Once a month, she went to the council office to follow up and every time the advisor – Alan, his name was – told her the request was in the system and he would be in touch if anything became available. Every. Single. Time. She wondered if Alan was as bored by the interaction as she was. He didn't even pretend to check the file any more. Either way, she was pretty certain Alan didn't live on a rough council estate like Harrington.

Giving her neighbour's door one last thump with her foot, she felt only slightly mollified when some of the paintwork fell off. Back inside her flat, she went into the kitchen and decided that the only way to drown out the noise was with another shot of vodka.

2

Angela

Angela squeezed herself onto the Tube, trying not to breathe in the smell of sweat from the bodies pressed up against her. This wasn't where she wanted to be on the Friday night of the summer bank holiday weekend, but her parents had invited her specifically. In fact, she had been slightly intrigued as to what may have prompted the invitation for her to spend the long weekend with them. Angela tried not to think too much about the Astoria nightclub. It would have been a brilliant night out and her friends had been talking about it for weeks. Angela wasn't too bothered about the drugs, but she did like the music. When you worked in a stressful industry like law, you needed a release. Besides, she thought, she worked hard and she deserved a night out once every so often. Yet here she was, jammed on the Tube on the way to her parents' home in Tetbury. It was a good two-hour journey from her office in central London and she was getting the 4.15 p.m. from Paddington, which had meant leaving work early. She couldn't remember the last time she'd been outside her law firm during working hours other than to grab a sandwich to eat at her desk. Normally, she'd be ensconced in her cubicle working at least a sixty-hour week, often going in on weekends as well.

Escaping the stifling odour of the underground at Paddington, Angela got on the mainline train, happy to have found a seat, and took a few moments to straighten her new Jaeger suit. The eye-catching shade of green was perhaps a little too much for the corporate environment of Kings Solicitors, but it went fabulously with her dark hair and she knew she pulled it off by the number of admiring glances she received. The tailored trousers and fitted jacket with shoulder pads were so flattering. Besides, she didn't want to blend in with all the other associates in the office, and this was just one way to be remembered by clients and the senior partners. Satisfied with her appearance, Angela pulled out some papers from her bag and began to work.

Angela had her own key to her parents' house, a pretty bungalow built of traditional Cotswold stone, and as she let herself into her childhood home she inhaled the familiar aroma: a mixture of clean washing, fresh flowers, and the trailing scent of her mother's Estée Lauder perfume.

It was a few moments before she became aware of the stillness. She was used to the television being on or her mum talking animatedly on the phone about one of her various committees. Leaving her key and overnight bag in the hallway, Angela walked curiously through to the living room. Her mum and dad were sitting next to each other on the sofa, holding hands, and talking quietly.

'Hello, darling! We didn't hear you come in!' Her mum got up to embrace her and Angela gave her a perfunctory kiss on the cheek. Normally, she would drop down on the sofa, complaining about the journey, but there was something about her mum that evening that made her think twice. While Rosemary appeared as polished as ever, with her sleek silver bob and ever-present string of pearls, her face looked worried and drawn beneath her welcoming smile. Instead, Angela turned to her dad, who gave her a hug and, as she'd known he would, asked her about her journey. He didn't trust public transport and drove his beloved Jaguar wherever he needed to go, much to her mum's frustration.

'How are you?' Rosemary asked, already walking to the kitchen to put the kettle on, Angela following behind her. 'How's work going?'

'It's fine, Mum, thanks. Busy, as always.'

'Have they given you your promotion to senior associate yet?'

'Not yet, but I'm sure they will soon.'

While Rosemary understood very little about what Angela did all day, she was so proud that her daughter had grown up to be what she called *a career woman*. When Angela had graduated from university and got her place at one of London's top law firms, her mum had never tired of telling her how different it was from when she was growing up. *Back then*, the most common goal in life for women was to get married and have children, although Rosemary was one of the few women of her time who had been to university. Angela was part of the late baby boomer generation and, according to her mum, had opportunities that she herself had never had. Although Angela had only experienced middle-class life and all its privileges from her teenage years, she truly believed that success depended more on the drive of the individual rather than the current expectations of the day. How else could she explain her own success? She was confident, ambitious, and slightly entitled, as so many of her contemporaries were, and her work-hard, play-hard lifestyle had sustained her through her twenties. Now, at twenty-seven, she was in her element. She had a fantastic job, earned a good salary, was about to get promoted, and partied with her friends every other weekend.

Angela pushed away the twinge of anxiety she'd felt when she saw her parents whispering. She must have been imagining things. They just wanted to spend time with her over a bank holiday weekend – there was nothing more to it than that.

As they sat at the large dining table and relaxed after their evening meal, Angela could feel herself unwinding. A bottle of red wine and the roast lamb and mint-enhanced potatoes were a welcome change from the rushed meals she normally had during the week. Conversation had flowed easily, as it always did with her parents, and she enjoyed catching up with their lives and everything they had been doing. In his mid-fifties, her dad was in semi-retirement and came from a working-class family. Now, wealthy and self-made, he had his own business and owned multiple car dealerships across the country. While Angela had always had a strong work ethic, even as a young child, he was very much a living example of what could be achieved no matter what your background. Her mum, on the other hand, came from *old money* – or rather property – the recipient of inheritance passed down from generation to generation.

As the wine bottle emptied, conversation turned to the past.

'I found some of my old diaries while I was unpacking,' said Angela. 'I started reading some of the entries – so embarrassing when I look back on them now!'

Earlier, she had tried to slide her empty suitcase under the bed in the room she'd grown up in and, when it wouldn't fit, she saw a box of her old diaries was taking up the space. As Angela thumbed through a few of the ones on top, she was taken back to a very different time in her life.

'Oh, yes, I hope you don't mind,' replied Rosemary. 'I was clearing out some things and put them under your bed. I wasn't sure what you wanted to do with them.'

'Your mum's on a massive cleaning spree! I'm just hoping she doesn't turf me out as well!' joked James.

'Don't tempt me!' Rosemary smiled, giving him a kiss. 'Besides, I need to keep you, otherwise who will do all the DIY around the house?'

'Ah, yes, one of these days I will come back and find you with a hand drill,' said James, referring to his wife's aversion to a tool box.

'You never know,' laughed Rosemary. 'I might just surprise you!'

Angela smiled at her parents, before returning to the topic of the diaries. 'I'll have a think about the diaries,' she concluded. 'Most of them are rubbish.'

'But diaries are so important,' countered her mum. 'They remind you of things. Do you remember when you fell out of the tree in the back garden and we had to go to A&E? You were a teenager, but the look of pain on your face was heartbreaking. Your father still hasn't forgiven me to this day!'

'I remember,' said Angela, sharing a smile with her dad. She'd climbed the large oak after school most days when the weather was fine, her satchel swinging from her back, filled with books and an apple. She'd felt slightly childish, but she'd loved it up there, sitting quietly, hidden amongst the branches. Occasionally, she'd bookmark her page and glance down at the sprawl of green earth below. In those moments, she'd felt omniscient and powerful. That is, until one day when she'd slipped trying to get down and broken her wrist. James had come home, seen her lying on the sofa with her arm in a cast, and dramatically declared that the tree would be cut down so she couldn't be hurt climbing it again. It was a vivid memory because it was the first time she remembered someone being so protective over her. However, she still missed that tree and she suspected her mum had never really forgiven him for cutting it down either.

'And let's not even talk about the time you got your hair stuck in curlers,' recalled Rosemary. 'I had to cut them out. You were so distraught. I wonder if you wrote about that in your diary.'

Angela burst out laughing. She'd forgotten about that day. She'd been fifteen. They'd had to go to the hairdresser after school, but in the meantime she'd had to endure a whole day with an uneven hairstyle.

'What was I thinking?' grimaced Angela. 'All I wanted was to look like Elizabeth Taylor! You're right about the diaries, though. I'll take them home with me and read through them.'

'We had some fun times, didn't we, Angel?' said her dad, smiling at her, and she grinned at the use of her nickname. Standing, he gave her a kiss on the forehead before beginning to clear the plates away. As he turned towards the kitchen, Angela caught the glistening of a tear in the corner of his eye. As he quickly wiped it away, she glanced at her mother, who was looking at her husband in concern, before quickly hurrying to him to take the plates, chiding him into sitting down and resting.

In that moment, Angela knew that something was very, very wrong.

3

Wednesday, 5 February 1969

Dear Diary,

    I am so cold. It will be time for lights out soon – Nasty Nora says at St Matthew's Children's Home we always have to follow the rules. I stole this notebook, but I don't feel guilty. I'm writing in it under the covers in bed. It was in the cupboard under the stairs and I found it when Nasty Nora sent me to scrub the staircase again even though I did it already. I hate her. I'm going to write all my secrets in this diary. I don't have very many but I do have some. Like I know that Mary and Peter kissed. I had to keep watch. I hope Mary doesn't go to Hell. When I told her she might, she just looked at me and said it was all a load of rubbish. Mary's much older than me – she's thirteen! I can't wait to be thirteen.

    A.

Friday, 7 March 1969

Dear Diary,

Today Nasty Nora was ill. No one calls her Matron unless it's to her face. Fat Franny wasn't happy because she had to look after her as well as us, and stupid Baby Carole threw her food at the wall – what a waste. Everyone was shouting, and Carole was crying a lot. But she should be thankful she's a baby and will be adopted soon – all the babies are – they never stay long. In January, I was eight years old. Now I am eight years old and one month. Fat Franny told me it's unlikely I will be adopted, and I can leave when I'm a grown-up and have finished school, but that's a long way away. I asked her why my mummy would leave me at St Matthew's and then I asked her why I wasn't adopted when I was a baby. Fat Franny told me I asked too many questions, and if I asked any more she would give me another clip round the ear. Fat Franny isn't as quick as Nasty Nora, but she's been here a long time at the home. She said we all give her a headache. How? We're only allowed to speak when spoken to and never at mealtimes.

A.

Friday, 21 March 1969

Dear Diary,

Everybody is teasing me. Yesterday, stupid Peter told everyone I had nits and they all believed him, even Fat Franny, who dragged me into the bath and washed my hair with some disgusting shampoo while everyone watched and laughed. He told everyone at school about it. I hate him. I will get Peter back soon and he will be sorry.

A.

Sunday, 23 March 1969

Dear Diary,

Sundays are the worst. Even school is better than spending the whole day inside at the home. We have to be silent from morning to night – no talking, no playing. Just church. It's also bath day. When Nasty Nora is on duty, she scrubs really hard with the brush and it hurts. She said she has to wash all our sins away. When I asked what sins, I got a clip round the ear, so I stopped asking. It's also the worst day for food. Sometimes I save things up during the week, to stop me getting hungry on Sundays. This week I managed to save an apple – the dinner lady at school gave it to me. She told the other dinner lady that the poor mite looks half starved. I don't know what a mite is. I will ask Mary.

A.

Monday, 24 March 1969

Dear Diary,

I had to swap half of my apple with Mary to get her to answer my question and then when I handed it over she laughed and told me a mite was an insect. I asked her why the dinner lady would say I was an insect and Mary stopped laughing then. She grabbed me by the shoulders and told me that us orphans are worth less than insects. My shoulders hurt – I wish I hadn't given her half my apple now.

A.

Tuesday, 1 April 1969

Dear Diary,

The best day ever! I got Peter back for April Fool's and even made him cry! That will teach him to spread lies about me having nits. It was talking about insects with Mary that gave me the idea. I collected a lot of insects in a jar – flies, spiders, beetles, and I even stole a stick insect from school – and I woke him up by tipping all of them over his head! I got such a thrashing from Nasty Nora but seeing Peter cry like Baby Carole was worth it.

A.

Wednesday, 18 June 1969

Dear Diary,

When we got back from school today, a new girl had arrived. Fat Franny said her name was Nelly. She has red hair and a gap between her two front teeth. Fat Franny said I had to look after her and show her how we do the chores. Maureen said it wasn't fair that I got help with my chores from the new girl. Maureen is always whining. I told her to shut her face and then Fat Franny told us all to belt up otherwise there would be trouble. We knew what that meant so we all shut up and did our chores.

A.

Wednesday, 25 June 1969

Dear Diary,

While we cleaned the kitchen, Nelly told me that her last family let her play on a bicycle. I told her she was a liar – no one I know has a bicycle. She said I was just jealous and that they were the nicest foster family she had stayed with. Nelly said two families had fostered her before but they didn't have any bicycles. I asked her why she was in the home – why didn't she stay with the bicycle family? She told me that they were coming back to get her soon but she looked sad. To make her feel better, I told her that we didn't have bicycles, but I would show her the den in the back garden. We had a lot of fun playing hide-and-seek. It's much better than being indoors, and Fat Franny and Nasty Nora are just happy to have us out from under their feet.

A.

Thursday, 4 September 1969

Dear Diary,

The summer holidays are over. Nelly has stopped talking about her bicycle family. She has given up thinking they will come back and adopt her. Instead, Nelly will come to school with me. We are in Mrs Thistlethwaite's class but her nickname is Snapper because she has a ruler that she snaps on the desk to get everyone's attention. Fat Franny took us to lost property at school to get the leftover school uniforms. Nelly is bigger than me and she found a shirt while we both got ties. Fat Franny grumbled that she would have to buy us skirts. Only one each mind, so we mustn't get them dirty or get holes in them.

A.

Thursday, 4 December 1969

Dear Diary,

It's so cold in bed at night that we have pushed all the beds together in our dorm room and curl up to each other to keep warm. Even Fat Franny felt it because she brought us some more blankets. I sleep next to Nelly but I told Maureen to go and sleep somewhere else. She smells.

A.

4

Rosemary

Damn. Rosemary knew James wouldn't be able to contain himself when it came to Angela. But who could blame him, really? It had been a terrible shock. Still, this wasn't what they had agreed when they'd discussed it before Angela's visit. On the contrary, they'd decided to keep the news to themselves for as long as they could. But that was James all over. She knew he was an emotional man when she'd married him. He said what he thought and didn't give a fig for social convention or etiquette. Rosemary sat back with her sewing and reminded herself it was this that had attracted her to him in the first place. He was a charmer, a talker, and ultimately a salesman. It's how he'd done so well for himself. He was also highly intelligent. The more academic side had come later, of course, when she'd encouraged him to get his degree at university. While he was slightly older than the majority of other students, he'd done it – first class with honours, too.

Not that it had made any difference to her parents. In Selina and Jonathan Kershaw-Hughes' opinion, education was just a minor consideration and, anyway, anyone could get into university these days. It was social standing, the family name, and connections that counted. James had none of those – well, none worthwhile in her parents' eyes – and his East End accent didn't help either. But at the time Rosemary was so in love she didn't care.

She was still very much in love, although she couldn't help wishing things had turned out differently with her parents. If they were still alive today and saw how well her marriage had turned out, would they have accepted him eventually? She doubted it. Her parents had had serious plans for their only daughter and these didn't include cavorting with *someone completely unsuitable and unsavoury*. Rosemary remembered the conversation well because they'd actually used those words. But despite their best efforts to find her a suitable match, she'd had no interest. She didn't want to marry just anyone. Her mother would fret, constantly reminding her that she was running out of her best years, but Rosemary was far too focused on her work. She'd gone to university – a personal cause she'd battled for relentlessly until her parents finally agreed in the desperate hope that she would meet someone appropriate there. Yet, the quiet libraries and study halls of New Hall at Cambridge held far more appeal than any social engagement could. It was 1954 and she knew that, as soon as she got married and had children, she would have to stay at home. But for now, housekeeping and babies could wait. That was until she'd met James.

She had been working in the office of London Transport when she first saw him. She had nipped out for her lunch break and, as the weather had been pleasant, she'd decided to eat in a small park nearby. He had offered her a cigarette and that had been that. She didn't even smoke. But in that moment, she knew that nothing – not her parents, not her hard-earned degree, not her career – would prevent her from being with him. She'd expected love to be complex and muddled, but when it had arrived it had been simple and effortless. It was only later that it started to get messy.

5

Evelyn

Evelyn woke up late the next morning to a quiet flat. Looking around her, she saw the empty vodka bottle on its side – she had only meant to have a few nips, not finish off the bottle, for God's sake. She blamed Billy – the sight of him in his undies was enough to drive anyone to drink. But this was not the day for a hangover and a lie-in. She needed to be at the dole office in the next forty-five minutes to sign on.

Groaning at the throbbing in her head, she felt a light puff of the duvet as Charlie jumped on the bed, giving her cheek his usual morning lick before turning his attention to his nether regions. Urgh, thought Evelyn, disgusting animal. But despite his unsightly habits, she loved him more than anyone else in the world.

She'd found him when he was just a puppy, almost ten years ago. He'd been tied to a pole with a dirty rope on the edge of a construction site. She wouldn't have seen him if it weren't for the fact that she'd dropped some coins and was scrabbling around to pick them up. There was a gap between the pavement and the corrugated iron fence and Evelyn came face to face with the saddest eyes she had ever seen. He was almost in a worse state than she was. Too exhausted to move, he lay on his side, his body dotted with what Evelyn guessed were cigarette burns, and his breaths were coming in quick pants. Looking around her and seeing nobody, Evelyn untied the rope and gently scooped him up and took him home, stopping off only to buy a tin of dog food. She gave him some water and quickly spooned the food into an old bowl. She watched as the smell roused him and he tentatively investigated before finally tucking in.

Evelyn didn't like to think too much about the past. Forcing herself up, she put on yesterday's clothes and brushed her teeth before picking up her handbag. Then she put Charlie on the lead, and didn't even bother to look in the mirror before she left, firmly locking the door behind her.

Evelyn congratulated herself on making it to the dole office on time. She'd had a bit of banter with the other *dole-ies*, as they called themselves, and, to celebrate 'payday' Evelyn agreed to stop off at the pub with a few of them on her way home. A quick hair of the dog for medicinal purposes, she justified, and then she needed to go and get some shopping in.

It was another couple of hours before she made it to the supermarket and, as she shopped, she decided to pick up some milk for Doreen, who lived in the flat above her. While still active, Doreen was pushing seventy, and always appreciated the thought. Besides, her neighbour was more than generous with her drinks cabinet. Whistling to herself cheerfully, Evelyn popped in a pack of scones before starting the walk home. Her flat was part of a series of low-rise blocks that made up the grim Harrington council estate and, as she walked through the grey concrete buildings, she saw her various neighbours.

There was Dougie, a giant of a man at over six foot, strolling around with his vicious bulldog, Floyd, named after his owner's favourite rock band. He was bare-chested, his enormous stomach making the most of the August sunshine. It was always best to stay on Dougie's good side. He pretty much ruled over the estate and had a mob of sons who never hesitated to use their fists when something displeased a member of their family. Then there was Tara, with a fag hanging out of her mouth, pushing a pram endlessly around, trying to get her screaming baby to sleep. And, of course, the usual groups of lads who loitered around doing God-knows-what. Evelyn nodded to all of them. They had all lived on the estate for years and had a grudging respect for each other. Still, Evelyn didn't linger.

She pulled Charlie quickly up the stairs, going one floor above her own to the fourth floor to call on Doreen for a gossip and to hand over the scones and milk. While she was at it, she would ask her for a few ideas on how to deal with her noisy neighbours who had already started their bloody racket.

6

Angela

Angela could feel her heart beating faster. What on earth could be wrong that had her dad tearing up?

'Angela,' started Rosemary, 'your father and I have something we need to discuss with you. However, before we do that, the one thing I want you to remember during and after this conversation is that we love you unconditionally and have always loved you like our own. What we're about to say doesn't mean we love you any—'

'Oh, Rosemary, she knows all that,' interrupted Dad. Turning to Angela, he said, 'We think you should find your birth mother.'

The words fell over each other in his rush to get them out and Angela saw her mum give him a hard, disapproving look. The relief was instant though, and Angela released a long breath, the tension visibly leaving her body.

'Is that what you wanted to tell me?' asked Angela. 'I thought it was something serious!'

She had always known she had been adopted, although she rarely mentioned it to anyone. She had just turned fourteen when James and Rosemary Steele had visited the children's home. Initially, they had invited her to stay for a few weeks as a trial and then had gone on to adopt her. The Steeles had welcomed her so warmly and made her feel part of a real family. It had been the best thing ever to happen to her. They had given her everything a daughter could want or need, both emotionally and materially, and Angela had called them Mum and Dad pretty much from the very beginning. She thought back to evenings snuggled in front of the TV watching the nature programmes and exciting afternoons shopping for new clothes. She remembered when Dad had taught her how to ski and, after passing her driving test, how to change a wheel on the car. It hadn't all been smooth sailing and there had been some difficult times, but for the most part James and Rosemary had opened up a whole new world to her – one of class and privilege. No longer did she have to share a dorm with twenty other girls; she had her own room with its pretty lemon bedspread and matching curtains. Nor did she have to endure punishments for the smallest offences, Matron's slap echoing through the bleak hallways, the sting of her hand felt through young Angela's entire body. While life with the Steeles was easy, she never forgot her years at the home. If anything, they served as a useful reminder to push harder and be even more successful whenever she felt herself getting complacent.

Angela was suddenly struck by a thought.

'Why are you suggesting I try and find my birth mother now?' she asked her parents. Dad looked at Mum, as if to say *I told you so*. Mum started to speak but Dad held his hand up for silence.

'Angela, from the minute we adopted you, I promised myself that I would answer any questions as truthfully and as honestly as possible.' He paused, and Angela felt desperate to hear his next words. 'You're right, of course,' he acknowledged. 'There is a reason we are suggesting you get in touch with your birth mother now, but I was hoping it could wait until after…'

James's voice trailed off and, as she waited for him to continue, she looked at him closely – properly – for the first time since she'd got home. She hadn't noticed before, but his shirt was slightly too big and there were some small bruises on the backs of his hands.

'I've not been feeling the best lately, Angel,' he began tentatively. 'I've had some treatment and still have some more to come, but I didn't want to tell you until I was given the all clear…' He trailed off again and didn't get any further. Unexpectedly, Angela began to tremble. She didn't need her father to say the unspeakable out loud. Instinctively, she knew he was talking about cancer; she could barely say the word to herself. She felt her father's arms around her, holding her tightly, and as she sank into his embrace she was aware that it should be she giving the comfort, not the other way around. Still, she continued to shake as the two of them held onto each other waiting for the earthquake to pass.

Angela was too upset to ask too many questions. Instead, her dad gently led her to her bedroom, leaving her to get into bed while he went to the kitchen and made her hot chocolate. Angela was already under the covers when he returned, mug in hand, the aroma giving rise to adolescent memories. She felt fifteen again as he kissed her goodnight on the forehead and whispered it would all seem better in the morning. The reassurances worked just as well on her twenty-seven-year-old self as they did during her teenage years, and as the shock gave way to exhaustion, she slept.

Angela woke up late. She emerged from the haze of sleep, the reality of the night before only giving her a few moments before hitting her hard in the pit of her stomach. She sat up in bed and turned on the lamp. Her teenage bedroom appeared in a blaze of light, unchanged since she had left to study law nine years earlier. Her university scarf, which had 'Class of 1982' embroidered on it, still hung on the back of the door. She looked around her in disbelief and, for the first time since hearing the news, cried quietly into her pillow. Then she closed her eyes tightly, her mind frantically trying but failing to make sense of it all.

Eventually, resigned, Angela looked at the time and forced herself to get up. Catching sight of herself in the mirror, she saw that her eyes were puffy and red. Silently admonishing herself, she grabbed her toilet bag and went for a shower, fighting her tears. She was tougher than this – she had to be for her father's sake.

Angela thought back to when she'd first been introduced to James Steele all those years ago in Matron's office. Despite his well-dressed appearance, his large hands were calloused. She just remembered thinking how *capable* he looked: here was a man who could fix *anything*. There are those in life who can fill a room with their presence and he was one of them. As they began chatting, she had been startled to feel an immediate affinity, and this had only matured as they got to know each other better. While he had worked a lot during her years in Tetbury, when he was home he had an energy about him that was captivating and contagious. She knew Rosemary fed off it too by the way she would repeatedly look out of the window around the time he was due home from work. Angela also felt more interesting when he was around. He never tired of talking to her about school, her friends, her favourite books. He treated her like an adult, genuinely interested in her opinions. He liked to laugh and was forever telling his 'Dad' jokes. Rosemary was very kind but a lot more reserved and Angela had grown up understanding there would always be a part of her adoptive mother that was private.

Under the shower, Angela closed her eyes. Where did she go from here? Last night, her parents had reassured her that James would be fine and he was responding well to the chemotherapy, but she was pretty sure they were just trying to protect her.

'We just feel that now would be a good time to find your birth mother as we'll both be here to support you and answer any questions. It's a journey we really want to help you on… we just want to be prepared, just in case…'

Dad's reassurances from last night echoed in her mind. 'Just in case' what? Angela wondered. She knew, of course. Everyone did. The dreaded C-word was so often a death sentence, so why should her dad be any different?

As the water washed away some of the shock, questions attacked her accusingly. How long had he been ill? When was his next chemotherapy session? What else would the doctors suggest? Which hospital did he go to? How much time might he have left? The last one prompted a physical ache. It didn't make sense: they lived in the countryside with clean air; her father hadn't smoked for years; things like this didn't happen to people like them. Angela caught herself – she knew better than anyone how life was so often a game of chance. But they could fight this together – it was the only way – she decided as she dried herself. Her quick mind started to brainstorm ideas and, back in her room, her hand automatically reached for a pen to start jotting down lists and action plans in her diary. She wrote in it most days and often used it as a means of taking back control when she had a problem. The ink marks reassured her with their permanence: she would speak to the doctor herself; she would find every piece of information on cancer that she could – every case study of every person who was in remission – whatever was available, she would find it.

She kept writing until her ideas were spent, and as she closed the notebook she realised she felt better already. Finally dressed, she hurried through to the living room to find her parents, fired up to discuss a plan of action. But as she opened the door, her pace immediately slowed. Her dad was fast asleep in his armchair, his breathing slightly ragged, his bony wrists peeking out from his too-big shirt cuffs. It was eleven in the morning. As Mum tenderly covered him with a blanket, her face etched with anxiety, Angela looked on, her previous hopefulness once again replaced with despair.

The silence was unusual. It seemed inappropriate to talk about the mundane when her dad's health was at stake. Angela floundered as to how to start, but, surprisingly, her mum rescued her.

'I'm sure you have a lot of questions…'

It was late afternoon and Angela had almost anticipated Mum carrying on as normal, suggesting a walk or an early pub dinner. Rosemary, while loving, was not known for sharing her feelings and most upsets were brushed aside until they resolved themselves. But this was no minor upset and the fact that she was now broaching the subject showed just how concerned she and James were about Angela's reaction to the news.

'I'm sorry about last night,' started Angela. 'It must have been the shock.'

'There's no need to be sorry, darling. It was a shock to us as well,' said Rosemary. 'We're only sorry we had to tell you,' she added, shooting a pointed sideways glance at James.

'No, no, I'm glad you did. At least now I can help. I can come down every weekend and even during the week, if need be. I could even commute into London to help you both.' Angela had already planned her schedule, keen to be doing something – anything – to fight this horrible intrusion into their lives. James started to say something, but it was Rosemary who interrupted this time.

'You know you're more than welcome here any time, but we really don't want you to give up your life for this. We have lots of support from our friends, neighbours and the hospital. Betty still comes to clean a couple of times a week as well so there's not really a huge amount to do.'

'But…'

'How about we have some tea, and we can answer all your questions. There's no rush is there, though? We still have the whole weekend.'

Angela stared at her retreating back as she went to put the kettle on.

'Don't take it personally, love,' said James when his wife was out of earshot. 'You know what she's like. Your mum is coping really well – better than I expected, really. Of course, the news knocked her for six initially, but now we have a routine of sorts, we're trying to be optimistic. With all the medical advances, you just never know these days.'

Angela nodded. 'Yet you want me to find my birth mother now?' she asked. 'It just doesn't seem the right time somehow.'

'If there's one thing I've learnt from all of this, love, it's that there's never a right time. And you always said you wanted to get to know her. From the minute your adoption was finalised, I vowed that I would support and help you do that. I suppose this... this thing... has just speeded all that up a little bit.' He paused, giving Angela some much-needed time to think.

'You still do want to find her, don't you?' he asked when Angela was silent. 'I know you've been busy at work and everything... but you've always been so certain, even when you were younger, that you wanted to find her.'

Angela thought about it. He was right about that. She had always been vocal about it, if only to find out why anyone would leave their baby in a children's home. It was unimaginable yet it had happened. She'd had many years to come to terms with it, but it still hurt: her real mother hadn't wanted her enough and had left her – barely a few days old – to her fate. This had been in 1961, and as she grew from baby to toddler to child, the home was her only reality, until she had been adopted at fourteen. She knew how lucky she was. It was almost unheard of for older children to be adopted; couples normally wanted babies. Fate had been on her side, though. Apparently there had been a slight concern that James and Rosemary were too old to adopt a baby and they wouldn't be able to cope with the demands of a young child. As a result, Angela had been paraded out, told to be on her *best behaviour* and to go to Matron's office and meet some people *immediately*. At the time, Angela had wondered what all the fuss was about, but as soon as she met James and Rosemary she knew she wanted to live with them. They were kind, down-to-earth and educated. Angela had always done well in school without needing to try too hard. She found solace in her textbooks, escaping into a world so different from that of the children's home, with its constant screaming and crying, chores and punishment, hand-me-downs and lack of solitude. As James, Rosemary and Angela talked and got to know each other a little bit, she could feel herself relaxing. They were clearly impressed by her commitment and dedication to her education in what they later politely referred to as 'exceptional circumstances'. Although it was mainly James talking, Angela remembered how beautiful and elegant Rosemary was. Angela didn't think she'd seen anyone with such composure and grace. As the interview progressed, Angela realised that she wanted to be adopted by them – wanted it so badly she wasn't sure how she would cope with the disappointment if they didn't take her. After an hour, Matron whisked her out of the room, telling her to stop *prattling on*. But as she turned to say goodbye, James gave her a discreet wink. Hopeful, Angela had a feeling that life was about to present her with an incredible opportunity.

As she watched them leave, she knew she should find out more about them. Hearing Matron in the hallway seeing the visitors out, Angela crept back to the room and looked on the desk. On top, she could see a file marked 'Steele'. Flicking it open, she quickly scanned the contents, which revealed a sad story of lost babies and infertility. Hearing the front door shut and Matron's footsteps returning, she quickly closed the file and slipped out of the room. Hiding behind a nearby cupboard in the hallway, she listened as Matron and one of the day nurses went into the office.

'Well, that was unexpected!' announced Matron. 'Who would have thought they'd be interested in Angela? Asked for her especially!'

Bitch, thought Angela.

'Still, it will be great for her, won't it? Clearly from money, those two ...' replied the day nurse.

Angela struggled to remember the nurse's name. There were so many of them all coming in on different shifts and timings.

'Yes. Apparently, *she* can't bear to see babies – such a shame. I hear *he* is self-made, though. Originally from the East End and married above his station.'

'Can't be bad,' replied the day nurse wistfully. 'Anyway, I'd better get on.'

Angela breathed in slightly as she heard footsteps leaving the office and, when she was sure it was safe, she quietly left her hiding place.

Rosemary placed the tray on the coffee table. They were in the front reception room, Angela and James sitting together on the small two-seater sofa. A selection of biscuits lay on a plate decorated with pink roses, which matched the cup and saucer. As Rosemary poured, Angela was suddenly ravenous. She hadn't had anything to eat since last night. She sat back with the comfort of tea and biscuits as her mum began to talk.

'It was such a shock, really. You'd only gone for a check-up, hadn't you, James?' she said, turning towards him. 'The next thing we know, they called you back – just a couple of days later – to meet with a consultant as soon as possible. Well, you know how often that happens with the NHS – you're lucky if you can get an appointment within the week! Anyway, I went with him, of course, even though you didn't want me to, did you, darling? I remember everything about that day – one of the worst of my life. Prostate cancer, they said...'

As her mother faltered, Angela stiffened. She wasn't used to seeing her like this. Rosemary had always been so unruffled and in control. But what did Angela expect? The news of her father's illness had shaken her to her absolute core so what it must have done to Mum she could barely imagine. She was aware that her parents were older than those of her friends. She had never given it much thought until today, but now she could see those extra years in the worry on their faces.

Visibly pulling herself together, Rosemary interrupted her thoughts.

'The good news is, though, they caught it early and that's what we must focus on now. That, and the treatment. Your father has been so strong, you wouldn't believe...'

Angela struggled to take it in as Rosemary reached for the box of tissues on the small coffee table next to her chair.

'I didn't want to tell you,' she said, composing herself. 'But your father wanted to do it in person at some point and we know how busy you are...'

What an odd thing to say, thought Angela. Yet when she tried to remember when she had last visited her parents, she guiltily realised she couldn't. Had she declined their last invitation? Wasn't that the weekend of her friend's birthday? Angela sighed heavily.

'I'm sorry, Dad,' she said simply.

'Oh, love, it's not your fault. I'm just sorry that all of this has happened.' He waved his hand across the room as if trying to push away the bad news.

'Anyway, as I was saying...' Rosemary braced herself by sitting up straighter and taking a sip of tea. 'The good news is, there's a chance of recovery and that's what we need to remember. Isn't that right, James?'

'It is, my love,' he replied, getting up to give his wife's hand a quick squeeze.

'So, no need to worry too much,' joked James, turning to Angela. 'I'm not ready to go just yet!'

'That's true!' Rosemary agreed. 'He's still wandering around in the middle of the night, so that's a good sign!'

It was a running joke between them that James had a sweet tooth, which he especially liked to indulge during the night if he woke, like a child raiding the biscuit tin. The behaviour was so far removed from her dad's daytime persona that it made Angela smile. It was not uncommon to find a trail of biscuit crumbs and the latest novel he was reading face down on the kitchen table, the book's pages splayed like butterfly wings. Rosemary had long been used to his midnight wanderings, and each night before she went to bed she cleared the floors, making sure there were no stray shoes or magazines he might trip over.

'Anyway,' said James, 'enough about my health and all that palaver. Coming back to finding your birth mother – in hindsight, perhaps we should have talked about it earlier but there was always a reason not to. In the early years, you were too young, and then as you got older there were exams and your degree, and we didn't want to distract you from any of it. And then as time went on, it was almost like we forgot about it. Then, of course, something like this happens, and it makes you reassess everything.'

Angela nodded, thinking. 'I'm just wondering about the timing. I would rather spend the time with you – my real family,' she emphasised.

'Well, it's completely up to you, love,' replied James, 'but we know how important it's always been to you and we just want to make sure we're here to support you and help you with any questions.' He looked at the floor. Slowly raising his head, he went on, 'No one knows what the future holds or what will happen. The day you decided to call us Mum and Dad was one of the best days of my life.'

Angela felt a tightness at the back of her throat.

'But I don't want my illness to burden you,' he continued. 'You are destined for great things and we have tried our best to give you every possible opportunity. But sometimes you just need to know where you come from, and I have always sensed that need in you. I worry you won't settle until you do. Besides, it will take my mind off things, knowing that I'm doing something to help and you have additional support if... you know...'

Angela knew. He meant if he didn't make it. Squeezing her father's hand tightly, she closed her eyes. She took a few moments before opening them again. 'OK, Dad, I know you're right as usual. But just so you know, I'm planning to be here most weekends and I want you to call me at any time – even if it's in the middle of the night – if you need me. Promise?'

Her father nodded. 'That's my girl,' he whispered as he closed his eyes and leant back on the cushions.

As Angela sipped the rest of her hot drink, however, she couldn't shake the feeling that there was still something he wasn't telling her.

7

Monday, 19 January 1970

Dear Diary,

Today is my birthday – I am nine years old. Nelly gave me her favourite marble as a present. It's yellow like a daffodil and the only thing I own, apart from this diary. I need to hide it otherwise Peter might steal it. He has a huge collection, which he says he won in bets but everyone knows he steals. Apparently, he keeps his loot under his bed. We don't get birthday presents, but when I got back from school for tea Fat Franny gave me the biggest piece of chicken. When she's not clipping me round the ear, she's all right really. Better than Nasty Nora anyway – she didn't even say happy birthday.

A.

Saturday, 14 February 1970

Dear Diary,

Yesterday, we had to make Valentine's Day cards at school. When Snapper asked who I was going to give it to, I said Nelly and everyone laughed and Peter started chanting *lesbian! lesbian!* at the top of his voice and the whole class joined in. Mrs Thistlethwaite had to snap her ruler on the desk so hard it broke. Nelly said to ignore them. Peter is going to be so sorry.

A.

Friday, 27 February 1970

Dear Diary,

After school, me and Nelly went ice-skating on the lake in the park. We don't have skates, we just slide on our feet. I saw Peter and his mates skating as well. As soon as I got close to him I pushed him and he went flying head first onto the ice. It was so funny! I couldn't stop laughing but Nelly said I pushed him too hard and he could have really hurt himself. His friends had to pick him up off the ice and when he stood up he had blood on his forehead. Nelly said she doesn't want to be friends with a bully. I don't care – I bet he won't call me a lesbian in front of the whole class again.

A.

Monday, 2 March 1970

Dear Diary,

A horrid day – Nelly wasn't talking to me and Peter had to stay home. When I got back after school, Nasty Nora was waiting for me. I knew I was in trouble. Somehow she must have found out what I did to Peter. Maybe Nelly told her. As soon as I got through the door, Nasty Nora grabbed me by the hair and dragged me into her office. She didn't even ask me what had happened, just gave me the strap. I didn't cry but that seemed to make her even angrier as she gave me a few extra welts. Luckily, there was a knock on the door and Nelly told Nasty Nora she was needed immediately as there was a fire in the kitchen. Nasty Nora ran out and Nelly after her. I was in so much pain I had to force myself to walk to the kitchen. There was a small fire in the sink. Later, Nelly told me that she had stolen Peter's lighter from under his bed. I think Nelly's my friend again – it's not easy to get in the boys' dorm – she must have stolen the key from Fat Franny. My bum hurts so much I'm going to have to sleep on my front for a week.

A.

Monday, 30 March 1970

Dear Diary,

It's Easter Monday. Nasty Nora and Fat Franny let us join in the Easter egg hunt in the park. Nelly won a Cadbury's Easter egg and she shared it with me. After the hunt, we rolled down the hill – it was great fun. We are off school for one more week. In the morning, we have to do chores but in the afternoons me and Nelly sell lemonade. So far we've made five shillings. At the end of the week, we're going to go to Woolworths to buy sweets – I can't wait!

A.

Tuesday, 7 April 1970

Dear Diary,

I hate Nasty Nora – when she found out we were selling lemonade, she took all our money and told us it was her payment for looking after us all the time. Nelly said that we can make a plan to get it back but I told Nelly that she will know it's us if we take it. I had a better idea – I put itching powder in Nasty Nora's bed and when she woke up the next morning she was red and sore all over and scratching like a cat! And the best part? She has no idea who did it! Nelly was worried but I told her she deserved it. That'll teach Nasty Nora to steal!

A.

Tuesday, 5 May 1970

Dear Diary,

Nothing interesting to write about today. After morning inspection, we went to school, did our chores and then played in the den until dark. One good thing that happened was that we had potatoes, meat, vegetables AND custard for tea!

A.

Saturday, 6 June 1970

Dear Diary,

Baby Carole was adopted this morning. We all waved her off. A man and a lady came to collect her. The lady smelt sweet, like candy floss. I tried to talk to her to tell her that Baby Carole would need an older sister to help take care of her but Fat Franny told me to scoot quick smart. Candy floss lady was wearing a red coat. When I grow up, I'm going to have ten coats in all the colours of the rainbow. Me and Nelly watched them leave from the window. I wonder if Baby Carole will get a bicycle like Nelly did?

A.

Sunday, 14 June 1970

Dear Diary,

Yesterday was one of the best days. It was the Queen's birthday and, to celebrate, we had a street party. Fat Franny and Nasty Nora made jugs of juice and we had sandwiches, cake and scones. We put up banners and waved our flags. Afterwards, we played hopscotch and I won, even beating Maureen who always wins at hopscotch. Mary said she was sneaking off and if Fat Franny asked where she was we had to cover for her, but Fat Franny and Nasty Nora were asleep in their deck chairs. Nasty Nora snores like a pig. I thought about drawing a moustache on her but Nelly told me not to otherwise I would get the strap again.

A.

Friday, 21 August 1970

Dear Diary,

Fat Franny and Nasty Nora are whispering in the common room with a policeman. A group of boys have been throwing rubbish at us over the fence and calling us nasty names. Peter slipped through the fence and started fighting with them. He ended up with a black eye. I thought he would get the strap but Nasty Nora just gave him some ice for the swelling. Mary said he was a hero. Fat Franny says she's had enough of all this riot nonsense. After the police moved them on, Nasty Nora told everyone to start picking up the rubbish. It wasn't fair – why did we have to pick it up?

A.

Monday, 7 September 1970

Dear Diary,

Today was the first day at school. Nasty Nora says I can only leave school when I'm fifteen, which is ages away. Nelly wants to stay on until she's eighteen – school is much more fun with her so maybe I will too. Our teacher this year is Mr Wright. He doesn't have a ruler but he has a quick backhand. Everyone talks about how Martin – a boy from last year – ended up with a burst lip because he gave backchat to Mr Wright. Apparently, there was blood everywhere and he even had to clean it up himself. We had assembly in the morning and then we got brand-new schoolbooks! I love writing on the first page.

A.

Wednesday, 14 October 1970

Dear Diary,

Today after school there was a big fight in the den. Maureen said Jennifer had rabies because she played with a dog. Jennifer pulled Maureen's plaits and pushed her, and Maureen fell over on her knees. Maureen then pushed Jennifer and they started fighting. Peter had to stand guard to make sure Nasty Nora and Fat Franny didn't come while Mary broke up the fight. I think Jennifer won as Maureen now has a big scratch down her face.

A.

Sunday, 1 November 1970

Dear Diary,

Fat Franny says we're old enough now to go to Bonfire Night in the park by ourselves as long as we stay close to Peter and Mary and we're back home by 9 p.m. Any later and the door will be locked and we'll have to sleep outside. Nelly says she doesn't believe they would do that really. I didn't tell her that two years ago they did it to Carl and Jacob and we had to let them in through the window, and then they had to sneak back outside again in the early morning to pretend they had been there all night.

A.

Thursday, 5 November 1970

Dear Diary,

Bonfire Night was the best night ever! The park is a fifteen-minute walk away. Mary and Peter disappeared as soon as we got there, but it's better without them. Me and Nelly had one piece of toffee each and we even got to hold sparklers! The bonfire was so big and warm – I didn't want to leave, as I knew it would be cold when we got back but, we couldn't risk being locked out.

A.

Thursday, 24 December 1970

Dear Diary,

Next month, I will be ten years old! I can't wait! Nelly has promised to get me a new marble for my birthday present. Tonight is Christmas Eve. We all had to go to church and then Fat Franny made everyone hot chocolate – it was really nice. We even have a tree, although there are no presents under it. Fat Franny says there might be some when we wake up in the morning. I really hope so! Even though it's a sin, I will pray for a television! Fat Franny told Nasty Nora that Nelly is a *good influence* on me. I don't know what that means but Nelly is my best friend and we're going to live together forever and when we grow up we will have a big tree with lots of presents under it and a television in every room.

A.

8

Rosemary

Rosemary couldn't sleep. Not for the first time did she wonder why James was so insistent that Angela initiate the search for her birth mother. It was true that Angela had always said she would want to find her at some point, and of course his cancer was a worry, but was now really the right time? Didn't they have enough on as a family without digging into the past? After all, it was Rosemary who had been the real mother to the girl. *She* had raised Angela and, while that hadn't been from birth, everyone knew that the teenage years were some of the most difficult. And look at the job she'd done! She silently congratulated herself on her daughter: a graduate, working in one of the top solicitor firms in the City, and no doubt with a great career ahead of her. And beautiful as well, although Rosemary couldn't take credit for that. She did, however, take credit for style, grace, and manners, of which Angela had plenty.

Rosemary had given up work to make sure that she would be there when Angela woke up, came back from school, and went to bed. She was available to drive Angela to the various parties, study sessions and netball practices. She'd developed a predictable routine to ensure Angela always knew what to expect. Rosemary didn't talk about Angela's life at the children's home, nor did the girl bring it up. *Least said, soonest mended* had been Rosemary's philosophy on that one. There was a little bit of gossip in the village at the beginning but, like most things, the adoption was, if not forgotten, then certainly not an issue, and Angela became very much the child Rosemary and James had never had.

And yet…

Rosemary thought back to the day James had brought Angela home. It had been a Monday and James had taken the day off work to go and pick her up. Rosemary remembered hearing the car in the driveway and opening the front door to greet them. Angela got out of the car and looked around her, a small smile on her lips. She was taller than Rosemary remembered, her clothes too small for her gangly, growing frame. James came up behind with her small suitcase.

'Hello, Angela. How was your journey?' asked Rosemary.

'Great! I like your car,' replied Angela.

'Thank you – James loves it, too.'

'Come through – I've got the kettle on – or would you prefer some orange juice?'

'Can I see my bedroom? James told me all about it on the way over.'

'Yes, of course,' replied Rosemary, slightly thrown. Leading her down the hallway, she opened the bedroom door.

'Here it is. I hope you like it.'

She'd spent the last few weeks decorating it, choosing lemon and white striped wallpaper with matching bedding and grey furniture, including a dresser that could double up as a desk. She hadn't put up any pictures or posters as she thought Angela might like to choose them herself. She had, however, hung a frame that had space for six photos. She'd already placed a photo of herself and James, leaving the remaining ones empty. Angela stood silently in the doorway, looking into the room, before walking in and examining the bookshelf, one finger running along the spines. She then sat on the bed, testing the mattress, before getting up again and working her way around the rest of the room. Rosemary looked at James, unsure what to do. He winked and put his arm round his wife.

'I think she likes it,' he whispered before putting the case in the room and going back outside to park the car in the garage.

Seeing Angela looking at the photo of her and James, Rosemary inched her way into the bedroom, trying not to feel like an intruder in her own home.

'I thought we might take a few photos of the three of us over the next few weeks and get them developed so we can fill the frame,' suggested Rosemary. 'What do you think?'

Angela simply nodded, continuing to look at the photo, and Rosemary turned away from the strange intensity of her stare.

Over the years, Rosemary had always wondered when the 'mother's bond' might reveal itself. She wasn't delusional – she knew there was no substitute for giving birth – but she had hoped for... for what? Rosemary struggled to find the right word and eventually settled for *something more*. It wouldn't have been so obvious if it weren't for the fact that James and Angela had appeared to bond instantly. Shouldn't *she* be the one closer to Angela after spending so much time with her? Rosemary mentally chided herself. It didn't do any good to go down that path, but she had worried she was doing something wrong. Despite James being out at work most of the day, even friends and neighbours commented on what a sheer delight it was to see Angela and James together. When she'd tentatively brought it up with him, he had just laughed, told her she was doing a great job and it was all in her imagination. At the time, she'd felt he was missing the point, but perhaps it was all in her head? She'd been through a lot, after all.

Rosemary remembered the day James had told her that the children's homes considered them too old to adopt a baby. She had been devastated. It was only second to the feeling of loss when the doctor told her she was unable to bear children. On both occasions, James had held her as she'd cried but not even he could ease the sense of loss. As her last chance to hold an infant in her arms evaporated, Rosemary couldn't help but wonder if this was a sort of punishment for going against her parents' wishes and marrying James.

It had taken some persuasion on James's part to convince her to consider adopting an older child. Initially, she had resisted the idea, mainly because she felt so emotionally drained and she had no one to blame but herself. She'd taken it for granted that pregnancy would come naturally. Then her second mistake had been to assume that a children's home would jump at the chance to offer them a baby: they had plenty of money, their own home, and lots of love to give. She'd never for one moment thought that their age would be an issue. Yes, they'd been almost forty but still, she was hardly over the hill. She'd been foolish and there was a part of her that was just ready to accept her fate as a childless wife. She still had James and that was the most important thing.

But at the back of her mind was the fear that if she couldn't give James a child, even an adopted one, he might leave her. She didn't know where such irrationality had come from as he'd never given her cause to believe such a thing. So while Rosemary was reluctant to adopt an older child, James had convinced her and had suggested a girl, thinking that his wife would have more in common with the child. And for the most part he was right. They'd had a lot of fun together shopping and experimenting with make-up, and doing the various things mothers and daughters do.

And yet.

9

Angela

Angela entered the large offices of Kings Solicitors at six in the morning. She had come back from Tetbury late the night before and was hoping to be one of the first in so she could get some work done before the demands of the partners began. As an associate in a big City law firm, she'd spent the first few years 'gofering', but while many in that position had complained, she had just been happy to be there. The long hours, constant demands and tough deadlines had not put her off; on the contrary she had thrived, and it wasn't long before her work ethic and positive attitude had been noticed. It helped that she had a natural talent for the work. She loved research and writing, and had always had a good memory, retaining and retrieving information easily. Her job consisted of working with corporate and commercial clients, but she had chosen criminal law as her speciality, despite it being fiercely competitive. It was the contentious nature of criminal law that attracted her to it. She'd met some dangerous characters and was more intrigued by them than anything else, helping her develop the clinical approach that was required. She had learnt early on that you had to set aside any prejudices or judgement, and for the most part she was successful. It had certainly led to the best outcomes for her clients.

Sitting down at her desk, Angela went through her in-tray before heading to the kitchen to put the kettle on. As she walked back through the cubicles, she saw that she wasn't the first in the office. In fact, she was fairly certain that the majority of the younger associates hadn't taken any time off for the bank holiday weekend at all, simply treating the day off as another working day. There was a reason many of the chairs in the associates' lounge were reclining and you were encouraged to keep a spare suit and a toothbrush in the office. Sitting back down at her desk, Angela felt drained despite having taken the time off. The visit to her parents' weighed on her mind but, pushing it aside, she got down to work.

Angela's stomach rumbled. It was 1.30 p.m. and she hadn't eaten anything since breakfast. Tempted to simply open her snack drawer and work through lunch, Angela made a conscious decision to take a fifteen-minute break and go and pick up a sandwich from the deli next door. It was going to be a long afternoon, and it was unlikely she would get the chance again due to the number of meetings in her diary that day.

Standing in the queue, Angela browsed the day's newspaper, which someone had left on a nearby table. As she turned to the classifieds, a small ad caught her attention.

ADOPTED?

Looking for support? Trying to find your birth parents? As an adult adoptee, you have the right to know your background. We can support you on this journey. For more information, call Family First Adoption Support Group, London, or visit St Bride's Church, EC4Y 8AU, every Tuesday at 8 p.m.

Before she could think, Angela quickly slipped the newspaper into her bag while placing her sandwich order. She'd intended to eat at her desk, but as she collected her food and stepped into the sunshine she paused and thought of her dad. When was the last time she'd made the most of the good weather? Sitting down on a nearby bench, she felt the warmth on her face coupled with a light breeze. It was a beautiful day. She wondered if Dad was enjoying it as well.

'Hello, Angela!'

Angela started at the sound of her name. Dismayed, she saw one of the partners – a hulk of a man called Clive Mooring – hovering over her.

'Enjoying a break, are we, sweetheart?'

He was her least favourite partner, mainly because he assumed all the women in the office were secretaries. Despite Angela's constant reminders that she was an associate, his blatant lack of respect and overt sexism always left a bitter taste in her mouth. Unfortunately, he was also one of the most successful partners, thanks to his extensive network, which he cultivated on an almost daily basis through his entertainment account.

'Just catching up on the news, Mr Mooring,' Angela replied without missing a beat, yet silently furious about being seen taking a break.

'I can see that,' Mooring replied sardonically. 'Well, don't take too long. I've just come back from a weekend of golf with the Sedgwick board. There might be an opportunity to get their business and we need to start today.'

'Yes, Mr Mooring,' replied Angela automatically, her mind frantically trying to see how she could turn this chance encounter to her advantage. Quickly packing up the rest of her sandwich, she stood up, falling into step with him as he marched to the office.

Angela's thoughts were on rapid fire as she pulled up the name 'Sedgwick'.

'Are we going to pitch for their new alcohol business venture?'

Clive Mooring paused in his stride and looked at her. 'How do you know about that?'

'A good contact of mine mentioned it in passing,' replied Angela vaguely.

'Hmm. Not just a pretty face, are you? Yes, that's the plan. And being as you know so much about it, you can prepare the contracts. I was planning to ask Raymond but he's still in recovery mode after last night's client dinner. Stupid idiot can't handle his drink.'

Angela silently thanked fate. Raymond Montgomery had started at the firm the same day she had. Privileged, entitled, and used to getting by on his family's wealth and name, Raymond was one of the most arrogant people she had ever met. Like had attracted like with Clive, though, and the senior partner had immediately taken him under his wing, which meant Raymond got to work on some of the best cases the firm had.

'Absolutely, Mr Mooring. I'll start right away.'

'Good girl, be sure that you do. And no more breaks, eh? We don't want to encourage the other associates now,' he winked.

Walking away, Angela silently congratulated herself for taking the Sedgwick account away from Raymond. It was about time Clive saw her as more than *just a pretty face*. Forgetting all about the adoption ad, Angela hurried to her office in anticipation of a long night.

'Well, well, well, missy... Raymond might have some serious competition!' guffawed Mooring.

The rest of the partners laughed, and Angela forced herself to give a polite smile. She had just finished her presentation to management about how they could win the Sedgwick business. Not only had she prepared the contracts for the client's new business venture, she had also put a complete strategy together to secure the remaining legal work that the conglomerate might require. If the Sedgwick board agreed, it would be a huge coup for the firm, and indeed for Angela herself. It had been a long week. Doing the contracts was reasonably straightforward but the strategy planning had taken a lot more time and effort, and she'd had to do it in addition to her already heavy workload. She'd also had to persuade Mr Mooring to let her present to management herself. She didn't just want to impress Clive, she wanted to wipe the self-satisfied smirk off his face. As a result, she had done sixteen hours a day that week with very little downtime. But as she stood in front of the partners on a late Friday afternoon, quickly and easily answering their questions and objections, the thrill of success ran through her. The presentation had gone well. If they won Sedgwick, it would be the perfect opportunity to finalise her senior associate promotion, which had been on the table for a while now but never confirmed. This deal could provide the final momentum to make it official. Of course, Clive would execute and claim the fame, but this meeting was proof that she was leading the charge.

'Good work, Angela, we will take a vote on this tonight,' said Steve, the managing director. 'That's all for now.'

Dismissed, she left the room. Adrenalin had been coursing through her for the last few days and now she felt the pleasure of mental exhaustion, knowing she had given it her all.

Sitting back down at her desk, Angela checked her watch. It was almost seven. Feeling the satisfaction of a successful week, she tidied up her papers and made a quick call home to check on her parents before leaving the office. Her dad's voice came cheerfully down the phone and Angela felt relieved to hear him sound like his normal self.

As she left the office, she decided to stop at Archie's, a pub just a few doors down, which had become the local for everyone at Kings. She would have a drink with her colleagues before heading home. It was the last thing she felt like doing but she knew how important it was to be seen socialising with the team.

Threading her way through the crowd, Angela approached the bar to order a drink.

'So,' a plummy voice behind her said, 'I heard you managed to impress the powers that be.'

Not needing to turn round to know who it was, Angela kept her eye on the barman. 'Yep, they're probably voting on it now.'

'Well, congratulations then...' Raymond's slurred words suggested he'd been at the pub for a while.

'Thanks, but it's not confirmed yet,' she replied, trying to put him off any further conversation with her. She was tired and the last thing she wanted was a difficult time from

Raymond, especially when he'd been drinking. He was bad enough when he was sober.

'Oh, I'm sure it will be. Goody-two-shoes Angela always achieves what she sets out to do – even if it means stealing business from other associates.'

'That's not what I heard,' she retorted. 'I heard someone was too hungover to do the job.'

'Yeah, yeah, I'm sure you did – whatever helps you sleep at night. Anyway, enjoy it because it will be the first and last time you get the opportunity to work with *my* clients.'

'I'll see you later, Raymond,' said Angela, finally getting her drink from the barman. 'Don't get too drunk now,' she added, unable to resist a smirk.

She weaved her way through the crowd, joining some of her other colleagues to talk shop. Many of them had already heard about her successful meeting with the partners and she enjoyed being the centre of attention so much that she lost track of time. It was several drinks later when she decided to head home. Stepping into the darkness, Angela started walking in the direction of the Tube station, thinking about nothing but her bed.

IO

Tuesday, 19 January 1971

Dear Diary,

Today I'm ten years old! At school, the class sang 'Happy Birthday', and everyone gave me the birthday bumps. At lunchtime, Nelly gave me a red marble. It's beautiful. I'll keep it with the yellow one she gave me, under my pillow at night. Even Maureen let me play with her doll this afternoon, although we had to stay inside as it was so cold. I hope it snows. That would make this the best birthday ever! Fat Franny says I'm in *double digits* now and it's a special age. I wanted to ask her what was special about it, but the younger kids started crying and she had to go and *sort them bloody littlies out*.

A.

Saturday, 27 February 1971

Dear Diary,

Today, me and Nelly had to go to the market with Nasty Nora. She says it's because she needs help with the shopping bags but we know the real reason! It's because she can't work out the new money. Nasty Nora has to keep asking the shopkeepers, *what's that in old money?* Sometimes even the shopkeepers struggle and they complain about having to buy and use new tills. Me and Nelly are really quick at working it out because Mr Wright has been drilling us for ages so we have to convert the cost for her from shillings and pence. We know she wants to keep our help a secret because she gave us an apple each to eat on the way home. Nelly and I decided to keep her secret, although it was cold and wet and very drizzly on our way back home.

A.

Saturday, 27 March 1971

Dear Diary,

Today we went to the shops with Nasty Nora and again she gave us an apple each. She's getting better at working the new money out as she's started to get the correct amounts now. I told Nelly that I'm going to tell her it's wrong even if she gets it right, otherwise she might not need us to go shopping with her any more and we won't get the apple. Nelly said I shouldn't do that because it's wrong and she said she will tell on me if I do it. I didn't speak to her for the rest of the day. Best friends aren't supposed to tattle-tale.

A.

Monday, 29 March 1971

Dear Diary,
I am still not speaking to Nelly and she's not speaking to me.

A.

Tuesday, 30 March 1971

Dear Diary,
Nelly finally talked to me. She said she wouldn't tell on me but that she wouldn't go to the shops with me either. I don't want to go to the shops with Nasty Nora by myself so I said we could be friends again. Anyway, the last two days weren't as much fun without Nelly.

A.

Friday, 16 April 1971

Dear Diary,
When we got home from school today, there was a man with a bald head and a clipboard poking his nose in my cupboard under the stairs. Fat Franny said he was the *Homes Inspector*. When I asked what he was doing here, she said he was checking on how everything is run

and then he would write a report for the government. Nasty Nora and Fat Franny were very polite to him and I even saw Nasty Nora smile, which has never happened before.

A.

Wednesday, 26 May 1971

Dear Diary,

Nasty Nora dragged me out of bed this morning because I overslept. I was up whispering with Nelly until late and I just couldn't get up. Even Nelly tried to wake me but I was so tired. Nasty Nora said if I wasn't ready in two minutes I wouldn't get any breakfast. I didn't get up so Nasty Nora dragged me and shoved me down the stairs two at a time, and threw my shoes after me even though I didn't have my socks or my tie on. Luckily, Nelly had saved me a piece of bread, but I had to go the whole day at school with no socks and everyone called me a scrubber.

A.

Friday, 4 June 1971

Dear Diary,

After all the chores, I played outside. I was happy because I won at jacks, but Maureen beat me at skipping. She thinks she's so good at everything. She says that Mr Wright told her that she might get moved up to big school a year early because she's good at remembering things. I don't believe her because she's a liar, like when she lied about her mother coming back for her, telling everyone she was only here for a few weeks, but she's still here. I'm worried Peter will discover my secret hiding place for my diary and tell on me. If Fat Franny finds out, I will be in big trouble. Peter is always trying to annoy me. Maureen thinks it's because he likes me but she doesn't know that I know that he and Mary like each other. They're planning to run away together. Fat Franny told me I still have a few years to go until I'm grown up and then me and Nelly can leave and I won't need to see Maureen's face any more.

A.

Tuesday, 27 July 1971

Dear Diary,

We have been begging Fat Franny and Nasty Nora to take us to the seaside all summer and today it finally happened. We all took the train to Brighton and went to the beach. It's the first time I saw the sea and it was freezing cold. Me and Nelly were screaming every time our toes touched it. The littlies had to stay with Nasty Nora and Fat Franny but us older ones were allowed to wander along the pier. The boys went to the fair while we bought some popcorn. Peter won his shooting game and gave his prize to Mary. Afterwards, we all had a picnic on the beach and threw pebbles into the water. When we got on the train back to London we all fell asleep. It was one of the best days of my life.

A.

Wednesday, 18 August 1971

Dear Diary,

Nelly has received a letter from her old foster parents. She read it out to me under the covers last night in bed. It says that they miss her very much. She asked me if I thought they would come back for her. I said no because no one our age gets adopted. She said she thought they might and I said but what about our plan to live together? Then Fat Franny did the rounds and told us to be quiet.

A.

Monday, 6 September 1971

Dear Diary,

Today was the first day of term and we are the oldest in the whole school! Me and Nelly sit next to each other and we pass notes to each other all the time, although sometimes she shushes me when she's trying to listen to the lesson. She's such a swot! Our teacher is still Mr Wright but he's better than Snapper as long as you stay out of his way. He said this is a very important year for everyone, especially those looking to attend grammar school. We have to work very hard if we want to pass the 11+.

A.

Tuesday, 14 September 1971

Dear Diary,

Nelly has received four letters from her old foster parents so far. It's very annoying because she always writes back immediately even if we're in the middle of skipping. I asked her to wait until we've finished but she says it's too important.

A.

Wednesday, 22 September 1971

Dear Diary,

Today I was off school, as I wasn't feeling very well. Fat Franny says I have a fever and should stay in bed. It was boring, though, so after everyone left for school I went downstairs. The postman had been, and I saw a letter for Nelly. I picked it up and put it in my pocket. I will give it to her later when she gets home from school.

A.

Thursday, 23 September 1971

Dear Diary,

Yesterday, I forgot to give the letter to Nelly and it was still in my pocket this morning. I was off school again and when Nelly came home I wanted her to play jacks with me, so I didn't give her the letter again as I knew that she would leave the game to write back.

A.

Friday, 24 September 1971

Dear Diary,

Fat Franny says I have been off school long enough. I told her my throat still hurts but she made me get dressed and leave with the others. I gave Nelly her letter on the way to school. I told her I had forgotten to give it to her. I thought she would be cross but she just looked at the letter and put it in her satchel.

A.

Tuesday, 12 October 1971

Dear Diary,

When we got home after school today, the bald man was in the kitchen with his clipboard again. He was having a cup of tea with Fat Franny and Nasty Nora and sat at the table like he lived here. We all came into the kitchen and started asking questions but Fat Franny shooed us away to play outside.

A.

Saturday, 6 November 1971

Dear Diary,

It's really cold, especially at night, so we pushed all the beds together again to keep warm. Fat Franny brought us some extra blankets but there was only a small bowl of porridge for breakfast this morning. Nasty Nora grumbled about *tough times ahead* as she ladled it out while Fat Franny gave her one of her *warning looks*. After breakfast, we had inspection and then Fat Franny told us all to line up in the common room. Nasty Nora then announced that St Matthew's would be taken over by someone else in January. No one said anything but Fat Franny had her hanky out. We were all then dismissed to do our Saturday morning chores, but in the afternoon everyone was talking about the news. Mary said she heard that Nasty Nora and Fat Franny got sacked because they didn't pass the inspection. Martin said that was stupid and that he heard the government was taking over the running of the homes. When I asked Nelly she just shrugged and said it didn't make any difference to her as she most likely wouldn't be here anyway. She still believes that she's going to be adopted and when I told her she wasn't, she stormed off and told me I was just jealous because no one was writing to me.

A.

Friday, 31 December 1971

Dear Diary,

Today was Fat Franny and Nasty Nora's last day at the home. Fat Franny was blowing into her handkerchief all day until Nasty Nora told her to pull herself together. They let the older kids stay up till midnight and we sang songs until the clock struck twelve and then we sang 'Auld Lang Syne'. We had all written thank you notes and knitted scarves for them, and when we gave them they both started crying and then everyone was crying.

Fat Franny hugged me and even Nasty Nora patted me on the arm and told me I would be fine as long as I stayed out of trouble. It will be strange without them – they are all I've ever known. I wonder what the new people will be like.

A.

I I

Angela

Angela discreetly glanced at her watch: it had just gone
8 p.m. She had been here only ten minutes, but it felt like
an hour already. What the hell was she doing here? Tempted
to leave but mindful of her promise to her dad, she looked
around her. The church hall was old, its decay emphasised
by the naked glaring bulbs hanging from the ceiling. A circle
of chairs was placed in the middle of the room, not unlike
how she imagined they'd be at an Alcoholics Anonymous
meeting. It unnerved her – like her adoption was a problem.
Several people were milling around the coffee and tea
station, chatting quietly, and she felt reluctant to join
them.

It had been several weeks since she had seen the advert in
the newspaper regarding the adoption support group. Visiting
her mum and dad most weekends, and with so much to do at
work, she hadn't been in touch with them sooner, but finding
herself with a free ten minutes due to a client running late, she
had made the phone call and had been invited to join the next
meeting the following Tuesday evening. Luckily, it was just a

twenty-minute walk from her office, and she planned to go back to work afterwards.

'You must be Angela?' The brisk voice came from a confident-looking woman who appeared to be in her late fifties. Her tie-dyed scarf and black gypsy skirt were at odds with her competent, efficient approach. 'I'm Susan.'

'Yes,' replied Angela. 'I called a few days ago.'

'Welcome to Family First,' said Susan, holding out her hand and giving Angela's hand a firm shake. 'I hope you find tonight's session useful. Why don't you help yourself to a tea or coffee and then take a seat?' She indicated to the circle of chairs.

While Susan had explained on the phone that the meeting focused on support and counselling as opposed to just tracing birth parents, it was still a shock for Angela to see so many others in the same situation as herself. She had expected only a handful of people to turn up, but by the end of the session there were twenty of them in the room.

Susan started the meeting with introductions, welcoming the new members and then inviting people to share their stories and updates. As Angela listened, she realised not everyone was as comfortable with being adopted as she was. A young girl called Katie, probably no more than eighteen or nineteen years old, sat with a sleeping baby in her arms.

'I've been in regular contact with my birth mother over the last few years,' began Katie quietly. 'We've sent cards and gifts for birthdays and Christmas, and speak on the phone occasionally, but since having my own daughter, my feelings are all over the place. One minute I'm fine and the next I feel sick at the thought of seeing my birth mother – like I'd just want to bash her head in, you know?'

Angela didn't know. She tried and failed to imagine what it would be like to have a child. Katie was just a child herself!

What on earth was she thinking, getting pregnant? She was too young for such responsibility and what could she do with her life now? She was trapped. Angela looked around the group, as if seeking confirmation at the idiocy of Katie's actions, but instead she was met with a sea of sympathetic faces.

'Having a baby has changed everything,' announced Katie. 'Before, I was more open to understanding and forgiveness but now I look at my birth mother and think: how could you give away your child? I just feel so angry!'

Sympathy turned to agreement, as various group members nodded. Angela struggled to comprehend it. She tried to keep her face neutral but inside she was irritated. Of course having a baby would change everything – what did she think would happen?

'I don't want to be in touch any more but how can I tell her without hurting her feelings?' concluded Katie.

'Thank you for sharing,' said Susan quietly. 'That can't have been easy.' Turning towards the group, she asked, 'Does anyone have any advice?'

Katie tended to her baby, who had begun to mewl quietly, and Angela saw a tiny arm fight its way out of the blanket.

'I think you have to just bite the bullet and tell her directly,' said a voice to Angela's right. Turning to see who had spoken, Angela saw a dark-haired, clean-shaven man. He stood out because he was the only one, apart from herself, dressed in a suit.

'As young adoptees, we never had a choice, and our futures were determined by others. But now you do have a choice,' he emphasised, 'and I think you should do what feels right for you.'

'But what if Katie's feelings are temporary?' countered an older lady, who wore her glasses perched on the end of her nose. 'Perhaps a result of post-pregnancy hormones? I had only a few years with my birth mother before she died, and although I went through the whole range of emotions, I was patient and worked through it. Staying in contact is not for everyone but I think, for me, it helped.'

'Thank you, Linda,' replied Susan. 'I agree that it's important to be patient.' Turning to Katie, she continued, 'Don't make any rash decisions. These things take time. One piece of advice is to write down your emotions, perhaps in a diary. It may help you process them and come to a decision. Katie, perhaps we can have a chat in our next one-to-one session and discuss it in a little more depth,' said Susan, her tone more of a statement than a question, skilfully bringing the debate to a close.

Angela wanted to leave. She didn't want anyone's advice or sympathy. All she wanted to do was find her birth mother and she was completely emotionally equipped to deal with that. She didn't need to be at these meetings. She would call Susan tomorrow and pass on the details for her to start the search for her birth mother but would politely decline the attendance at the support group. Before she could get up from her seat, though, Susan had invited her to speak. Not wanting to appear rude, Angela decided she would give the basic information and then discreetly leave the meeting to get back to work. But as all eyes swung towards her, patiently waiting, Angela felt a moment's hesitation as she quelled an unexpected rush of nervousness. Sensing her unease, Susan tried to reassure her. 'This is a safe space for you to share as much or as little as you like, or you simply may have questions and that's fine, too. There are no rules here except that we all respect each other.'

I'm a solicitor, not a child, thought Angela crossly. She just needed a minute, that was all.

'OK, well, I...' Angela faltered, surprised. Clearing her throat, she tried again. 'I grew up in a children's home here in London before I was lucky enough to be adopted by an amazing couple – James and Rosemary. I was a little older than most kids who got adopted, but they took such good care of me and I think of them as Mum and Dad. I wouldn't be where I am today without them. While I have always been curious about my birth mother and knew I wanted to find her, it's only recently that I have decided to do something about it. My dad's not well, you see, so...'

She hadn't planned on talking about her dad's cancer. What was she doing? Angela quickly wrapped up. 'They want me to have as much support as possible and to be there to help me... during the process... if I find her.'

'Thank you, Angela,' said Susan. 'It's not easy sharing your story with the group for the first time. Your parents sound incredibly supportive.'

Angela swallowed hard. 'Yes, they are,' she managed.

Relieved that she could now finally escape, Angela sat back in her seat. She hadn't expected this at all. She'd lived with the knowledge of her adoption all her life but she wasn't used to talking about it. In fact, very few people knew, and she only disclosed it when absolutely necessary such as for medical reasons. While she told herself she wasn't ashamed, she knew that people would see her differently if they knew the truth about her background. But this meeting had made her feel like she had an issue to overcome. She'd never seen it that way before. Angela's take on it was that life with the Steeles was every adoptee's dream – she had no reason to complain. Did it hurt that her mother had given her away? Of course, but it didn't help anyone going over and over it. It was best to simply get on with life. But as the rest of the members continued speaking, sometimes tentatively, sometimes angrily, and occasionally with tears, each story picked at Angela's subconscious like a seam ripper. It was only when Susan called the meeting to a close that she realised she had forgotten her plan to slip away early.

As the various group members stood up and started to leave, Angela briefly closed her eyes. She felt drained. She told herself that the long working weeks were having more of an impact on her than they used to. In her early twenties, she could easily do twelve-hour days and then socialise in the evenings and at weekends for months on end. All she wanted to do now was go home but she needed to get back to the office. Angela thought wistfully of her tiny but beautiful flat in South Kensington. Maybe she would stop off at the pharmacy and see if she could pick up a supplement to help her energy levels.

As she was about to walk towards the door, Susan gently took her to one side. 'Thank you for coming today. I do hope it wasn't too daunting. As you can see, people have had so many different experiences with adoption and, as a result, have different emotions and opinions.'

'Thanks for having me,' replied Angela politely. 'It was an interesting session.'

'Have you got very far with your search yet?' enquired Susan.

The search. Angela had almost forgotten that that was the reason she was here.

'Not very far, no. To be honest, I haven't really done much about it apart from get the details from my parents and get in touch with you.'

'I see. Well, as I mentioned on the phone, we have a rule that new members should attend a few meetings first,' advised Susan, before adding, 'We've found it just helps to prepare adoptees a little better for any possible outcome. I'm sure you understand.'

'Yes, of course,' agreed Angela, vaguely recalling that particular part of the conversation but wondering how she could get out of it. 'However, I'm really keen to start looking as soon as possible.' She paused. 'You know, with my dad and everything,' she added persuasively. Leveraging James's illness wasn't her finest moment, but did she really want to be spending her Tuesday evenings exploring her feelings? Not really. Susan looked Angela directly in the eye as she contemplated the request. She would make a good barrister, thought Angela as she waited to see what the older woman would say.

'OK,' agreed Susan eventually. 'These searches can take a while anyway. If you give me the details, I'll run them through our records to see what we can find.'

'Thank you,' said Angela.

'Is it best to contact you at your office if I need to get in touch with you about anything?' asked Susan.

'Yes, that would be fine.' Angela was now itching to leave but Susan wasn't prepared to let her go just yet.

'Great. In the meantime, I'll look forward to seeing you each week at the meeting and then I can also update you in person as well.'

'Of course!' replied Angela, her smile hiding her frustration that she would still have to attend.

Her schedule was busy enough with work and visits to Tetbury. She had been making the journey most weekends, arriving late in the evening on Fridays and either leaving late on Sundays or early on Monday mornings. It was a huge change to her routine, and while she would never say it, she missed her weekends, especially her nights out.

She had a circle of female friends from university, most of whom lived in or around London, and they met about once or twice a month on a Saturday night in a noisy bar before going on to a club. She'd noticed over the last couple of years, though, that the group was shrinking as the silent yet ever-present call to arms of marriage and motherhood beckoned. Sunday hangovers and young children did not go together well, apparently, something Lucy, her closest friend, had explained in great detail to her several times. Angela always changed the subject. It was to be expected really that they would have different priorities but still, it was a shame because she wasn't as close to the other girls. In fact, even Lucy had accused her of being a closed door on occasion, which Angela had felt slightly unfair. She was a private person – what was wrong with that?

However, it was Lucy she had called when she'd first learnt of her dad's illness and, despite Lucy shouting at her kids every five minutes during the conversation, Angela had been glad she could share her worrying news with someone.

Friends aside, though, the majority of the time recently Angela had found herself busy, and not just with work. For all her mum's insistence that everything was in order, there was always something to be done to help her parents in Tetbury – medication to be understood, odd jobs around the house, the garden to see to, neighbours to be visited – and with a hectic work schedule as well, Angela was beginning to feel the impact of having no downtime. But it was nothing compared to what her dad was going through, she reminded herself, and so she carried on: home, office, railway station, Tetbury, home, office again, and now the adoption meeting – her life on a loop, and she couldn't help but wonder how and when it would all end.

As Angela finally left the church hall and stepped out into the crisp autumn air, she bumped into the clean-shaven suited man who had spoken during the meeting.

'Hello,' he said, simply.

'Hello.'

'First time?'

'Yes. Not yours, I'm guessing,' she added, trying not to notice how good-looking he was.

'How could you tell?' He grinned. 'Mitchell – pleased to meet you.'

'Angela.'

'Cab?' he asked, flagging one down.

'No, thank you, I'm heading back to the office and it's quicker to walk.'

'OK, well, see you next week!' he said over his shoulder as he jumped into the car.

Maybe attending the meetings wouldn't be such a chore after all, she thought as she started walking towards the office.

Angela wasn't unaware of her own beauty and, as such, recognised and appreciated it in others. She hadn't had many long-term relationships, convinced that her dedication to her career eventually scared them off.

It had been two years since Carl, her last boyfriend, and she'd ended it the minute he started whining that he didn't see her enough. She remembered how stunned he'd been, almost in disbelief at her abrupt decision, but she wouldn't put up with any distraction from her career and she'd been clear with him about that from the beginning. Carl had called her for weeks after, an uncomfortable and annoying period for Angela, her ex-lover's pleas ricocheting from undying love and everlasting affection to enraged and impassioned insults. Calling a woman an ice-queen bitch was hardly going to make her change her mind now, was it? Eventually, she'd unplugged her answer machine. When he had then come round to her house, she hadn't hesitated and immediately called the police, her only concern at the time being what the neighbours would think. As it happened, there were no flashing lights and loud sirens and Carl had gone quietly. The last she'd heard was that he'd married some girl just six months later and they'd had a baby. She wasn't bitter about it – in fact she was relieved. Some people just couldn't function well on their own. Luckily, she wasn't one of them.

12

Monday, 3 January 1972

Dear Diary,

The new people are wonderful! We can talk as much as
we like on Sundays! And… they even bought a television!
Every Saturday, we're allowed to watch *The Two Ronnies*
before we go to bed. It's very funny. The new people are
called Raymond and Kathleen, but we can call them Ray
and Kath. I think they are married because they sleep
in the same room. Ray has a pointy nose and is always
smoking and Kath looks a bit like Twiggy, with short
blonde hair.

A.

Wednesday, 5 January 1972

Dear Diary,

Today was the first day back at school. It was freezing

cold and raining. Kath says there will be no snow in London this winter. When we did the inspection after breakfast, Ray said we looked like a bunch of ragamuffins and we needed new clothes. Peter's trousers are so short his ankles are showing. We told him we don't get new clothes, only old ones from the charity shops or from the school lost and found. Kath and Ray looked at each other. I told them it's true – we don't buy new clothes. Ray said he would see what he could do. He left the room shaking his head.

A.

Saturday, 8 January 1972

Dear Diary,

I still can't believe it happened. It was like a dream. This morning, Kath took me, Nelly, Mary, Jennifer and Maureen into town to buy new clothes. Before we were allowed to leave the house, we had to wash thoroughly and comb our hair and put on our *best* old clothes. Kath told us we were ladies now and warned us to be on our *best behaviour*. We went on the Tube and Kath took us to C&A. The shop was so big. They had a whole area for school uniforms and Kath told us to choose three shirts and two skirts and take them to the dressing room to try them on. A woman helped us in the dressing room while Kath went to get us tights, shoes and coats. When we had everything on, we all looked in the mirror and started laughing. We looked so shiny – just like new coins!

A.

Sunday, 9 January 1972

Dear Diary,

I can't WAIT to wear my new school uniform tomorrow.
A.

Thursday, 13 January 1972

Dear Diary,

Kath is a good cook. She makes nice roast chicken with lots of gravy. She said Ray likes to have a *man's meal* every day. I don't know what a man's meal is but I like all the food she cooks. Since Kath came, we have meat three times a week. The babies are getting fatter. Kath said she would teach me how to cook if I wanted to. She showed me all her wooden baking spoons. She told me they were a wedding gift and the first thing she unpacked. I counted eight in total of all different sizes. They hung in a row on the wall. I asked her if she knew how to make a birthday cake and she laughed.
A.

Saturday, 22 January 1972

Dear Diary,

For my birthday, they gave me a party! I've never had a birthday party before. They made me a chocolate cake with eleven candles and gave me a present wrapped in birthday paper. It was a *Mandy* annual book – I've always wanted one of my own. I only let Nelly read it, though,

as the others might tear it. It was the best birthday
ever.
   A.

Saturday, 19 February 1972

Dear Diary,
   Every Saturday morning, Ray takes the littlies to the
park. He says they are too young to play our rowdy
games in the den. They must get very tired because they
stay out all morning even when it's cold.
   A.

Tuesday, 21 March 1972

Dear Diary,
   Me and Nelly played outside after school today. Our
favourite game is Pat-a-Cake where we have to bounce
the ball against the wall, clap, and catch it again. We also
played skipping and One Potato, Two Potato. Mary says
she's too old for our games. When I asked what she did
instead of playing, she said none of my business. I bet she
steals cigarettes and smokes them.
   A.

Friday, 7 April 1972

Dear Diary,
   Today, Nelly received another letter from her old

foster parents. She has a whole collection in a shoebox, but she doesn't let me read them any more although I let her read my *Mandy* annual. It made me cross. She says they're private, but I told her that friends are supposed to share everything. Nelly said not this, and she wouldn't change her mind even when I asked nicely.

A.

Saturday, 8 April 1972

Dear Diary,

Kath asked Nelly to help her prepare the vegetables. While she was gone, I sneaked into the dorm and read one of her letters. I was very careful when I opened it and put it back exactly where I found it. I don't know what's so private – the letter was boring.

A.

Wednesday, 17 May 1972

Dear Diary,

Everyone except Mary is working really hard at school and we are revising for the exam. Me and Nelly test each other for the answers and sometimes we let Maureen join in. Nelly told me I shouldn't be so mean to her. When I told her she deserved it, Nelly went off and revised with Maureen.

A.

Friday, 14 July 1972

Dear Diary,

Today was the last day of school. The teachers let us play games and sing songs and then we could read books. I'm looking forward to the summer holidays more now that Kath and Ray are here. I told Kath about the time Fat Franny and Nasty Nora took us to Brighton and she said we could do that again. They are so much fun, and they have started giving lollipops to the littlies as a reward when they do as they're told.

A.

Tuesday, 1 August 1972

Dear Diary,

Yesterday, Nelly received another letter from her foster parents. This time she showed it to me. It said that they were talking to Ray and Kath about adopting her by the end of summer. Nelly said she would write back and ask them if they could adopt me too and then we would be able to stay together. Maybe they still have the bicycle? Maybe they will buy a new bicycle for me!!

A.

Monday, 21 August 1972

Dear Diary,

Me and Nelly have been waiting every day for the postman to bring a letter from her foster parents. While we wait Nelly tells me about them. They seem nice but their house is very far away – not even in London but in a place called Surrey. They have a big garden and a shed where the bicycle lives.

A.

Tuesday, 22 August 1972

Dear Diary,

The letter came. We were so excited to open it. But when Nelly was reading it, I could tell by her face that they had said no. When I asked why, she said they can only afford to adopt one child and that they would come and collect her on Friday. Why don't they want me? I ran to the den because I didn't want Nelly to see me cry. Nelly must have told Ray I was upset because he came into the den and hugged me for a long time.

A.

Sunday, 27 August 1972

Dear Diary,

It's been two days since Nelly left. I can't believe she's gone. Why would she leave me? I hate her for leaving.

A.

Sunday, 3 September 1972

Dear Diary,

Ray found me crying in the den again. He gave me lots of hugs and offered me a cigarette. He told me it would make me feel better. I tried it, but I coughed everywhere. Ray started laughing and then I started laughing. He told me not to worry, I would find a new friend soon. He told me he had a secret but if he told me, I had to promise not to tell anyone. I crossed my heart and hoped to die. He said that a new girl might be coming soon and she was the same age as me and she liked playing skipping and ball games as well. Perhaps she could be my new friend? I said I would think about it. That made him laugh and then he offered me the cigarette again – the second time I didn't cough as much and Ray told me I did very well. Fat Franny and Nasty Nora never told me I did well, even when I got full marks on my spelling test.

A.

Sunday, 10 September 1972

Dear Diary,

Ray and Kath said they had a surprise for us last night. They had placed a cloth over the TV and Ray whisked it away like a magician. When he switched it on, it was in colour!! Ray and Kath told us all to say thank you and afterwards we all watched TV, except Mary who sat in the corner without speaking to anyone. Ray said she had *a face on her* and to leave her alone. After TV, we all went to bed, but we couldn't stop talking about the new colour TV. When would we be able to watch it again? Mary told us to shut up and stop going on about Kath and Ray. Maureen said they were wonderful – we had new clothes, birthday parties, and a colour TV. Mary told her she was stupid and blind. She's so moody these days.

A.

Monday, 2 October 1972

Dear Diary,

Ray showed me a new den! It's hidden, and you have to go through the trees at the bottom of the garden to see it. Ray said it was our secret and he built it just for me as I was so sad about Nelly leaving. I told him that Nelly hadn't even bothered to write to me. He said that's why I needed my own den. It's better than the old one. It has blue plastic material pulled over poles of wood, like a tepee. Ray said it's even waterproof so I can come here when it's raining. He said to meet him here every day after school before chores and he will give me a cigarette. I told him that I might not always have time as we have homework now as well. He said to try my best.

A.

Friday, 6 October 1972

Dear Diary,

I love my new den! Ray has made it nice and cosy with an old blanket and some pillows. He shares his cigarette with me. I don't really like it but I'm getting used to the taste. Ray made me promise not to tell anyone about the den. I asked when the new girl would be coming and he said very soon. I asked him if I could tell her about it when she comes and he said best to just keep it between us for now.

A.

Sunday, 19 November 1972

Dear Diary,

I still haven't received a letter from Nelly. She must be very busy with her new family. This morning, I went to my secret den with my *Mandy* annual. One of the littlies must have discovered my den by accident as I found a lollipop wrapper in the corner under the blanket. I bet it was Julia – she's eating those lollipops every week. I told her her teeth will fall out if she keeps eating so many.

A.

Tuesday, 5 December 1972

Dear Diary,

I am writing this under the covers. The lights were supposed to be turned off ages ago but we can hear Ray and Kath arguing upstairs. Everyone is quiet, pretending to sleep, but we're all listening to them. It's very loud. Kath was saying she's not going to get involved this time. Involved in what? Then there was a big smash and now everything has gone quiet. Julia is crying herself to sleep. She's been doing that for the last few nights. These littlies need to toughen up – at least they have a chance of being adopted.

A.

Wednesday, 13 December 1972

Dear Diary,

This is our last week at school before the Christmas holidays. Today, we made Christmas cards and we have to post them. I wrote five – one for Ray, one for Kath, one for Maureen, one for Mary, and one for Nelly, even though she hasn't written to me once. But Mr Wright said it's the season for *forgiveness and reaching out*.

A.

Thursday, 21 December 1972

Dear Diary,

Kath is turning into Nasty Nora. She's always in a bad mood these days. She doesn't just use those baking spoons for baking but to give us a good hiding. She even gave Michael, one of the younger boys, a crack round the head with one for telling a rude joke. Normally, she would find it funny. When we asked if there would be any Christmas presents, she said we've had more than enough already this year.

A.

13

Rosemary

Rosemary glanced at the red display on the digital clock by her bed and sighed: 5.45 a.m. It used to be her favourite time of the day after they adopted Angela, mainly because it was just the two of them. For much of their married life, James had been an early riser. He liked to be up and showered with a good breakfast inside him and out to work. He would wake, go downstairs and make some coffee and bring her a cup to sip in bed while he then took his shower. While he got dressed, Rosemary would prepare breakfast and they'd eat it together while reading the newspaper and chatting over their various plans for the day. He'd always been ambitious, but he used to say she'd given him a purpose. Years ago, Rosemary had hoped it had nothing to do with proving himself to her parents, because if so, she knew it to be futile. James was working class and it didn't matter how successful he became, he would never be good enough for Selina and Jonathan Kershaw-Hughes.

After James had left for work, Rosemary would get herself ready. When Angela had come to live with them, she had seamlessly slipped into the routine as well. But since James had become ill, there were days when he stayed in bed until ten or eleven in the morning. Sometimes, he was up and dressed, and Rosemary could well imagine that his diagnosis had just been a horrible nightmare. She would suggest a picnic or a trip to an antiques market and he would agree, but an hour later she would find him napping in his armchair, Rosemary all dressed up with nowhere to go. She'd learnt to get on with things – there was always something to do – but inside she was frustrated. She had looked forward to James's retirement for so long, had spent countless hours planning what they would do and the holidays they would go on. And best of all, it would just be the two of them. But it wasn't meant to be. These days she spent most of her time caring for him. Not that she minded – she would do anything for him – but she couldn't help feeling thwarted.

From the moment he had slipped a ring on her finger, Rosemary had always worried that she would lose James, a fear she had managed to keep hidden for the most part. Over the years, she'd begged him to be careful driving his beloved car, certain that she would receive a phone call from the hospital saying he'd been in an accident. Or perhaps she would find him strewn across the garden, having fallen from the stepladder while trimming the hedges. Or bent over his workbench in the shed, face down, after suffering a heart attack. Or splayed across the hallway after tripping on the rug.

In her superstitious effort to prevent the unspeakable, there were very few scenarios Rosemary hadn't envisaged, but cancer had given her imagination the slip and the silent but deadly disease had crept up on them both. Now that the worst had happened, she couldn't deny there was an element of relief – the fear of the unknown was always worse than the reality of the specific – but as the weeks went on, not even Rosemary could have visualised the sheer horror of watching a loved one succumb to cancer. The disease toyed with them, retreating and advancing depending on the stage of chemotherapy, but always poised ready to wage war again. And with every battle fought, James was left a little more defenceless and Rosemary realised her greatest fear would eventually come true.

14

Evelyn

Evelyn stumbled through to the kitchen, eyes unseeing. She managed to pick up an empty glass from the sink and fill it with water. She leant down to Charlie's water bowl, her hand shaking as she poured some of it in, before finishing the rest herself in massive gulps. The smell of dog food made her feel queasy and she left Charlie to it, going into the living room and flopping on the sofa, face down. She closed her eyes and tried to block out the voice on the phone, barely noticing when the music from next door started up.

It had been just after lunch on a Tuesday afternoon. Evelyn didn't usually answer the phone during the weekdays because it was frequently the utilities companies following up on their bills, but when it rang for the second time in thirty minutes, Evelyn wondered if it was Doreen from upstairs. Picking it up, she heard a woman's voice on the end of the line introducing herself as Susan from the Family First Adoption Support Group. Instantly, Evelyn wished she'd left it to ring and she found herself holding onto the curls of the phone cord as if they could stop her falling.

'Is that Evelyn Harris?'

For a moment, she considered lying. *No, I'm afraid you've got the wrong number.* But then what?

'It is,' replied Evelyn warily.

'Good afternoon, Evelyn. How are you?'

'Fine, thank you.' She did not return the question.

'That's good to hear. Would you have an idea why I might be calling today?'

After so many years of dousing the memories, her mind betrayed her: St Anne's Mother & Baby Home for unmarried women in South London, her changing body, the shame and anger at Jimmy, and ultimately the determination to give her baby a better chance in life. She didn't remember anything of the birth – just the horrific pain of the contractions and her screams as they echoed through the maternity unit.

St Anne's was run by the Church of England and was overseen by an unsympathetic, pious woman called Joan. Evelyn hated her on sight. Her hooded eyelids were unable to conceal her judgement and her thin lips never smiled. When she was particularly irritated, which was frequently, they pressed together as if she were trying to stop her thoughts from escaping. Although it was her sharp tone instructing the midwife to '*knock her out and keep her quiet*' that Evelyn last remembered before giving birth. Later, she learnt that it was common practice to put mothers in a drugged state so their screams didn't scare the other girls.

Evelyn's own mother had arranged the confinement as soon as she found out about the pregnancy and it was several months before Evelyn was allowed to leave the hidden grounds of St Anne's. To passers-by, it looked like a normal family home – a driveway with a sloping front garden leading to a large detached house – but the iron gates were always locked and the large English oak trees surrounding the house camouflaged a world of hidden pregnancies, forced adoptions and quiet reprimands.

'Hello? Evelyn? Are you still there?'

'Yes, I'm here,' she replied, dragging herself back into the present.

'I'm sorry. I'm sure this must be difficult. Would it be easier if I came to see you?'

Evelyn couldn't speak. She'd worked too hard to forget. She didn't deserve the indulgence of wondering, remembering. Without replying, she quietly replaced the receiver in its cradle and went into the kitchen to pour herself a large double.

Evelyn opened her eyes and closed them again, reluctant to face reality. Somewhere in the back of her mind, she knew the vodka wasn't working, but she'd been down this path before. It never obliterated the memories completely. But now, they came in full force and she didn't have the strength to refuse them. She'd never seen her child. The midwife had whisked the small bundle away before she woke up. It wasn't a surprise, of course. With no wedding proposal forthcoming, Evelyn had had to give up her baby – the social stigma of being a single mother would have ostracised her for life – but still Evelyn had been shocked by the depth of desire to shield her new-born from the world, and even more so by the need to hold her baby in her arms. It was an ache that would never be pacified, and as it became more unbearable, Evelyn found her own way of forgetting through a mix of drink and drugs. It worked for a while; it was the swinging sixties, after all, and there were all types of hedonistic pleasures available. But while the sorrow would go away for a time, it would always come back stronger and Evelyn had to take more and more drugs to make it disappear.

It was years later, when she woke up on a park bench, covered in vomit and with half of her clothes missing, that she realised she would die this way if she didn't get help. And while she'd been clean for several years now, at least from drugs – she wasn't prepared to give up her vodka – she still fought the addiction.

Evelyn could feel the tingle of desire race through her body. *Just one hit,* a voice whispered, *and all of this will go away.* Evelyn sat up on the couch. It would be so easy: some cash and a quick word with one of the lads on the estate. No, Evelyn thought. No, no, no...

As if sensing her need for a distraction, Charlie barked and went to the front door, eager to go out for his walk. She quickly picked up his lead, deliberately leaving her purse behind.

Evelyn walked Charlie down Hornsey Lane to the park on the corner of Highgate Hill and Dartmouth Park Hill, focusing on nothing but putting one foot in front of the other. She counted 839 steps before she felt somewhat in control. The numbering was a trick her counsellor had taught her to use whenever she felt her addiction start to take over. Still, she didn't stop counting, even when she got to the park and followed Charlie as he explored his surroundings.

Her daughter would be twenty-seven years old now, almost twenty-eight. What was she like? Was she happy? Evelyn hoped with all her heart that she was. She wrapped her arms around her skinny waist, remembering how big her belly had been. At six months, she wasn't sure her stomach would stretch any further, but it had. Perhaps if Jimmy had stuck around things might have been different. Evelyn let herself imagine a different life, one where Jimmy had married her and they'd raised their daughter together, perhaps even giving her a brother or sister. But it was too late for all of that now. Back then, Jimmy had left and she'd had no choice. But now she *did* have a choice and an opportunity to make the right one. She just had to find the courage.

When the phone rang two days later, as she knew it would at some point, Evelyn counted six rings before picking up the receiver and agreeing to meet Susan that afternoon. She had offered to come to her flat and Evelyn guessed it was part of an assessment to see how she lived.

Putting the phone down, Evelyn looked at the clock. It was late morning and she was thankful that she only had a few hours to wait. By some miracle, next door was quiet, and Evelyn hoped it would stay that way until after Susan's visit. She was coming at two o'clock and Evelyn wondered what she would say. Would she ask about her past? Would she know about her drug addiction? Would she ask about Jimmy? How, after giving birth, she had gone to his parents' house asking for him. She'd gone to his dad's garage as well, but he'd said Jimmy didn't work there any more and was off somewhere in the city. It must have been on her sixth visit when it became clear that he'd told his family not to tell her where he was.

'Go on, clear off,' his mum had finally shouted from the front gate of their house. If only you knew what kind of son you have, thought Evelyn bitterly as she had walked away, humiliated.

She'd tried living at home with her mum, but it was unbearable, her mistake the final brick in the wall that had grown even higher between them since her father's death. In the end, she'd found a live-in cleaning job for one of the big hotels in Park Lane but struggled to hold down anything permanent.

Evelyn didn't like to think too much about what happened after that: the squatting, the drugs, complete days of oblivion where she'd wake up not knowing where she was or who she was with. But at least they didn't know about her illicit pregnancy and her time in St Anne's. To them, she was just Evie – a free spirit looking for the next hit. Her body never betrayed her secret either. Her breasts stopped leaking, her stomach became flat, and on some days it was like she'd never even given birth. But while her body complied, her mind rebelled, and she never managed to escape the shame and guilt, no matter how many drugs she took.

Closing the door behind Susan, Evelyn heaved a sigh of relief that the meeting was over. She couldn't remember when she'd last been so nervous and, pulling the bottle of vodka from the cupboard where she'd hidden it, she took a long guzzle.

Her daughter's name was Angela and she had been searching for her. Susan couldn't give any more information – not even her second name – but Evelyn had been surprised by just how sympathetic Susan had been to her situation. By the end of the hour, for the first time ever, Evelyn felt someone was on her side. And so, after all these years, there was a chance to finally meet her birth daughter. She took another swig and wondered what she was like.

15

Angela

The call had come one Monday morning while Angela was sitting at her desk preparing for another presentation to management. She'd come back late the previous night from another weekend in Tetbury and once again was playing catch-up at work. She was so engrossed that when the phone's shrill tone pierced her concentration it made her jump. Absent-mindedly, she picked up the receiver.

'Angela Steele speaking.'

'Hello, Angela, this is Susan. How are you?'

'Susan…?' It took Angela a moment to realise it wasn't a client or colleague. 'Susan, yes, of course! So sorry, I'm knee-deep in paperwork!'

'No problem,' responded Susan. 'I'll get straight to it as I know you're busy, but I wanted to let you know as soon as possible.'

Angela swallowed, the presentation forgotten. Surely they couldn't have located her birth mother already?

'We've found her,' announced Susan almost triumphantly, leaving no room for doubt.

As Susan's words sunk in, Angela was reminded of the time she had almost fallen off a horse. She'd just turned sixteen and her parents had given her a riding lesson as a birthday present. She'd never ridden before, but it seemed easy enough: pull the reins to stop and press gently with your heels to go. She'd been assigned a gentle horse, but when a large green bin bag had blown past during their slow trek the animal had panicked and bolted, metal-shod hoofs scraping and sliding across the asphalt as he leapt into a gallop. Angela held on as tightly as she could, but her terror intensified as she saw the main road ahead of them, cars darting past, oblivious to the oncoming danger. Even if she didn't fall off, she was now certain they were going to be hit by a car, or even worse, a lorry. By some miracle, just moments before the horse could cross the main road, she felt a tug on the reins and saw one of the instructors riding alongside her, pulling them both to a stop. She'd survived but she'd never ridden a horse again. She experienced similar feelings of panic and helplessness now and she floundered.

'I'll be honest,' continued Susan when Angela didn't respond, 'we were surprised that we managed to find her so quickly, but she's right here in London, living in Archway.'

'London?' All this time, her birth mother hadn't been more than a few Tube stops away. Angela felt a prick of resentment puncture her pride.

'Yes,' replied Susan. 'Look, I know it's a lot to take in – especially when you're at work. Why don't we meet after the adoption group session tomorrow and we can talk it through?'

Angela forced herself to sound normal. 'Yes, that sounds good. OK, I'll see you then.'

Slowly replacing the receiver, Angela sat back in her chair, trying to absorb the news. What would happen now? Would they meet? Would they like each other? What did she look like? Perhaps she was a free spirit, wearing flowing skirts and stacks of exotic gold bracelets. She would have long, silky hair in a plait and spend her days in writing classes and doing pottery. She would live in a pretty detached house, full of eclectic knick-knacks and paintings, which she had gathered from her travels all over the world. She would open the door to Angela and gather her in a hug laced with incense and—

'Angela!'

Startled, she opened her eyes. Clive Mooring was leaning over her cubicle, his face red and bulbous. From other desks, she could see heads bobbing up, like meerkats, eager for gossip to be used as currency.

'What the hell are you doing?' he bellowed. 'We're waiting for you in the boardroom. Get in there now – we're late.'

Glancing at the clock, Angela saw that he was right. Quickly gathering her things, she hurried after him, the romantic daydream getting further away with every step.

Later that day, Angela went to put the kettle on in the staff kitchen. She felt in need of a large coffee. She'd had to work even harder in the meeting to make up for her lateness, but she had succeeded. Her plan that she had presented to the senior partners was solid. By the end of the three hours, Clive was crowing over Angela like a proud mother hen, telling everyone how he was grooming her for stardom. Raymond had glowered in the corner.

'Not bad for a girl, eh, Raymond!' Clive had said at the end of the meeting to the chuckles of the other partners. It was hardly a secret that they liked to goad associates in order to make them more competitive, so while Angela had seethed she had ignored the backhanded compliment as best she could. However, she knew Raymond would be planning his next move. He wouldn't let this go lightly.

With the meeting over, Angela's thoughts turned back to the call with Susan. She was anxious to talk it through with her tomorrow. So far, Angela had attended four adoption support meetings and as she talked with various members and listened to their stories, she had to admit that she could identify with some of their feelings. During her life, she sometimes had moments of what she called 'blind anger' – a fury that gripped her at the oddest of times. For example, she could be relaxing in bed, reading a book or watching TV, and unexpectedly a rage would course through her body, making her clench her fists. It was only for a few moments and she had learnt to breathe and let them pass – and so far, that's all they had been: moments that occurred sporadically and infrequently. But the anger had always been there. Growing up in the children's home, she had channelled her fury into books and it had propelled her, giving her a surge of energy to overcome her *challenging circumstances*. During the adoption support group meetings, she had discovered how some members also experienced this rage but they had struggled to control it or it had increased over time so that it was a constant companion, driving them to create trouble wherever they went. She also saw how some adoptees were reluctant to have children, or if they did, they experienced depression. In some cases, it was the opposite effect, such as with Katie, who openly admitted she wanted a baby so she would have someone to love and someone to love her in return. One woman, Tracey, had adopted several children and wanted to adopt more but her husband had refused. It had got to the point where her marriage was on the line. Fascinated, Angela had watched as Susan gently probed and prodded, eventually leading Tracey to what everyone in the room knew but Tracey herself: that she wanted to 'save' children from the fate she herself had encountered – a horrifying tale of maltreatment and neglect. Of course, Angela had read about the current investigations into the abuse that had swept a plethora of children's homes across the country since 1960. In fact, Mitchell, clearly frustrated, had brought it up at the last meeting.

'The government needs to do more,' he urged. 'These are heinous crimes that have been going on for the last twenty years and will continue to go on unless someone does something.'

Angela admired his passion. While she herself had always tried to look after and protect the other children, she never hesitated to put herself first. Life in a children's home was an ongoing battle and you learnt to be street-smart from an early age. If you weren't quick enough, you missed out on everything, from food and toys to getting the most comfortable bed.

'I understand why you feel this way, Mitchell,' replied Susan. 'What can we all do to help?'

'Well, for starters, we can get a petition going,' responded Mitchell. 'I'm also happy to talk to the newspapers to see if anyone is interested to investigate further and put pressure on the local government.'

'I wouldn't bother. You know it's all going to be a waste of time,' said Katie emphatically, her small hands holding her sleeping baby to her closely. 'Why should they do anything? Why should they care?'

'Because it was wrong,' said Simon quietly, a shy boy just out of his teenage years. He continued looking at his shoes.

Angela had never heard him speak before and she wondered about his story.

'So?' said Katie, turning to him with scorn. 'When has that ever meant anything?'

'We should at least try,' urged Mitchell.

Katie ignored him and went back to rocking her baby.

'I agree,' said Susan. 'Is anyone else willing to help?'

The members nodded, some more enthusiastically than others. Only Katie didn't respond, lost in the world of motherhood as she breathed in the sweet scent of her baby.

'What about you, Angela?' asked Mitchell. 'You work in law – is there anything you can do?'

Caught off guard, she hadn't known how to respond. 'I'll give it some thought,' she promised him. And she had. She had also reached out to some people of influence, but so far she hadn't accomplished very much – she had been too busy with all her other work. She reminded herself to follow up but she actually agreed with Katie. Who would care?

'Well, as you may have gathered, it wasn't too difficult to locate your mother,' said Susan, as they sat down after the adoption meeting. Everyone else had left and it was just the two of them. Susan had led her into a small office at the back of the church hall. It had no windows but someone had tried to make it cosy with two armchairs, a desk and a lamp. The desk was piled high with paperwork and Angela was reminded of her own cubicle, each file meticulously organised and numbered. Susan had no personal memorabilia – no special photos or trinkets.

Angela approved. She frowned upon her colleagues who plastered their cubicles with pictures of their latest night out or, even worse, those small posters from Athena with trite sayings, such as 'Girls Just Wanna Have Fun'. Angela knew how important first impressions were and thought them incredibly unprofessional. Instead, she had treated herself to a luxurious black cashmere wrap, which she kept handy on the back of her chair. Each evening before she left, she would carefully fold it back in its tissue paper and place it in her office drawer for safekeeping. It was the first thing Angela had bought for herself with her first salary from Kings and she loved the feel of it. She had a low-maintenance palm plant (she'd read that plants purify the air and sharpen concentration), a list of phone extensions pinned to the cubicle partition and two small drawers where she kept stationery and healthy snacks. She idly wondered what Susan kept in her desk drawers – a few crystals, probably.

Susan indicated for her to sit down and Angela noticed the box of tissues on the small coffee table in front of her. She wondered how many times Susan had had a meeting such as this one. Who had sat in the armchair before her? Katie? Mitchell? Tracey? How had they taken the news that their birth parents had been traced? Shocked? Angry? Relieved? Curious? Guilty? Nervous? Angela examined her own feelings and found herself to be undecided. She'd worked so hard to build up her life to where she was today, and she wasn't sure she wanted to be reminded of where she came from.

'So, just to recap,' started Susan. 'Your birth mother lives in a flat in Archway. Here, with her permission, I've written down her address and phone number for you.'

The news became tangible as Angela took the yellow, square piece of paper, astounded that a mere Post-it note held the details to her past.

'Of course, you already know her name – Evelyn Harris – thanks to your adopted parents. I only wish all parents were as helpful.'

'Thank you,' said Angela distractedly, her gaze still on the slip of paper. Questions competed for attention. Had she been there all this time? Had they bumped into each other on the street? Waited at the same Tube station, perhaps?

'We take adoptee privacy very seriously,' continued Susan, 'and our top priority is always to protect our members. The only thing Evelyn knows about you is your first name and it will remain as such until you decide to share any personal information. You have various options now, but I would suggest as a first step that I get in contact with Evelyn to set up a meeting. Are you happy for me to do that?' Susan's modulated tone filtered through to Angela.

'Yes, of course,' replied Angela.

'All being well, you can then meet with Evelyn yourself or we can act as an intermediary to facilitate contact. Or…'

Angela looked up at the pause.

'Or,' Susan continued, 'there is one more option and that is that you do nothing with this information and simply go about your business. It's entirely your choice.' Knowing that she now had Angela's full attention, Susan let her words sink in before resuming.

'Reunions can be wonderful, but they can also bring a lot of disappointment. Expectations often run high on both sides, and they aren't always met,' she cautioned. 'On the other hand, meeting your birth mother can also bring a lot of joy and for many people, it really is a gift.'

Angela wondered which category her reunion would fall into. She hoped the latter although she didn't see how. There were too many questions with unsatisfactory answers. Still, she thought of her dad and she knew how important this was to him. He was right in that she'd always said she wanted to find her birth mother, but as she was slowly beginning to realise, there was a huge difference in saying it and actually doing it.

'I understand,' replied Angela. 'No, do set up the meeting.'

'OK. I'm so pleased for you. It breaks my heart when someone decides they want to meet a birth parent and we're unable to locate them or they've passed on.'

Changing the subject, Susan asked, 'How are you finding the meetings?'

Time-consuming was Angela's first thought, but she instinctively knew she should say what Susan wanted to hear.

'Good, thanks – really helpful. I have to admit, at first I was a bit sceptical, but hearing everyone's stories has really helped me sort out some of my own feelings. I'm luckier than most, that's for sure.'

'I'm so glad to hear that,' replied Susan. 'You've been attending for almost two months now. Believe it or not, some of our members have attended for years. It's an invaluable support system for them.'

'I can well believe it,' complimented Angela, secretly shuddering at the thought.

'How's your dad doing?'

Angela nodded non-committedly. 'OK. He's tired a lot of the time but that's to be expected. Hopefully, we'll have some good news soon.'

'I'll keep everything crossed for you.'

'Thank you. Well, I'd best get off,' said Angela, keen to have some time alone to get her thoughts in order. 'Thanks again.'

'You're welcome, and if you need anything else, I'm just a phone call away.'

Leaving the church hall, she paused in the doorway before stepping out into the evening to walk back to her office. After just a few minutes she heard panting and footsteps behind her. Heart pounding, she turned, ready to lash out.

'Angela!'

It took a moment for her to realise it was Mitchell's voice.

'Mitchell – you scared me! What are you doing?'

'Sorry,' he said, catching his breath. 'I decided to wait for you after the meeting, but when you didn't come out I guessed you might be with Susan. I thought you might be in need of a chat after it,' he said sheepishly.

Regretting her snappiness, Angela smiled back at him.

'Thank you – that's so thoughtful. Sorry, I was a bit on edge!'

'No worries. Do you fancy a chat before you go home?'

'Thanks, but I'm going back to the office. I won't be going home for a while yet.'

'To the office – whatever for? It's almost half past nine!'

'I know but—'

Mitchell cut her off. 'That's not healthy. Come on, let's go for a drink instead – much more enjoyable.' He grinned at her and for the first time in a long time, Angela was tempted to leave the work until the next day.

'I really shouldn't; I have so much to do,' she protested.

'Look, there's a pub right round the corner. Just one drink and then you can go back to the office. Deal?'

'OK,' she relented. 'One drink, and then I have to go.'

★

Angela looked at her watch. There was no point going back to the office now.

'I'll walk you to the Tube station,' said Mitchell. 'Will you be all right getting home from there?'

Angela nodded happily. She had enjoyed her evening. As one glass of wine had turned into two and then they'd decided to order a bottle, she had forgotten all about work. Mitchell was funny and interesting, and they had a lot in common. As well as both being adopted, she quickly discovered he was as much of a go-getter as she was.

'Mrs Pattison took me under her wing,' he reminisced. 'She ran the home with her husband. She really was a good 'un – all the kids loved her. It also helped that I was wickedly charming,' he added.

Angela laughed. 'I can just imagine! So, you were adopted when you were five?'

'Yep, Mrs Pattison came in one day to tell me I had some visitors, and would I like to meet them? She put me in my best clothes, smoothed down my hair, and that's when I met Max and Laura. It was love at first sight,' he joked, although Angela heard a touch of irony in his voice.

'Being adopted at five was strange as I was really sad to leave Mrs Pattison. She was all I had really known but I have a lot of respect for Max and Laura. I gave them some tough times, but they always stood by me.'

Angela thought about her own parents and how they had done the same. It was such an incredible act of love for people to give so much of themselves to children who weren't their own.

'Well, I'm sorry you didn't make it back to the office,' said Mitchell as they arrived at the Tube platform.

Angela laughed. 'Really?'

'Nope! You got me. I enjoyed getting to know you,' he replied with a smile. 'Life's too short to spend so much of it working!'

'Pot. Kettle. Black,' teased Angela.

She looked up at him. He really was very handsome, so when he asked for her phone number she didn't hesitate.

'There's no need to wait with me – the train will be here in a minute.'

'Always trying to get rid of me, aren't you?' he joked. As the train hurtled noisily into the station, he leant down and gave her a kiss on the forehead. It was strangely intimate.

'I'll call you. See you next week,' he said, before turning and walking quickly up the stairs. Angela smiled after him. Gratefully stepping on board, she found herself grinning like a teenager. She knew she would pay for it tomorrow, but she'd had a much better time than she'd expected. It was good to talk about something other than work. As she looked for a seat, she briefly saw her reflection looking back at her in the window. I even look like I've had far too much wine, she thought, smiling as she grabbed the last remaining seat.

16

Dear Diary,

I'm glad Christmas is over. Ray and Kath are still arguing most nights. I wish they would stop. Kath is always grumpy these days and she doesn't cook as much for us any more. I think she forgot that she was going to teach me because when I reminded her she just looked at me as if she felt sorry for me. On Christmas Eve, she did make us hot chocolate, though, and the next morning we all got one present each. The littlies got sweets and an orange, some of us got a book, and the boys got a ball or marbles. I was hoping for a matching eye shadow and lipstick set from Woolworths. When Mary opened hers, she got a nightie. It wasn't like our normal cotton ones but bright red, and it slithered through your fingers when you tried to hold it. It was very beautiful. I thought Mary would be happy but she quickly hid it away.

A.

Wednesday, 17 January 1973

Dear Diary,

Ray said he has a big surprise for me for my birthday. He says as I will be twelve years old, I will be a woman and all grown up! He told me after school on Friday to come to the den and he will give it to me. I don't think I'm going to be able to sleep! I wonder what it is.

A.

Friday, 19 January 1973

Dear Diary,

I can't believe I'm twelve and a woman! When I went to the den, Ray had the present waiting for me and I could tell from the size that it was the eye shadow and lipstick set!!!! I ripped it open and Ray started laughing. He told me a lady would open it slowly, but I was desperate to try the colours. There are four eye shadows and one lipstick and they are in a compact in the shape of a butterfly. I put the coral colour on my eyes and the pink lipstick on – Ray had even brought the hand mirror so I could see how I looked. He told me I looked beautiful and I agreed it made me look older – even as old as fourteen or fifteen! Ray asked me if I was going to thank him and I said thank you and he said, no, you have to thank me like a lady thanks a man, with a kiss. I got a funny feeling in my stomach, but I leant over quickly and kissed him on the cheek, like I had seen Mary do with Peter, but at the last moment he turned his face and he ended up with lipstick all over his lips. I could smell his cigarettes, so I brushed my teeth extra hard afterwards.

A.

Thursday, 15 February 1973

Dear Diary,

Last night after tea, Ray gave me and Mary a *special job*. We had to babysit the littlies and put them to bed and make sure all the lights were out by 8 p.m. Ray said Mary was *in charge* of everyone and I was *second in charge*. I told him Mary wasn't the boss of me. He said it was for one night only as he was taking Kath out for Valentine's for a romantic meal. Mary said she would do it but only for two cigarettes. He handed them over and gave two to me as well, even though I still don't like them. When Kath came down the stairs she looked like a film star. Ray said isn't my wife the most beautiful woman on earth and she looked really happy then. After they left, we all went wild, putting the TV and radio on, eating from the snack cupboard and running around jumping on furniture. Me and Mary did funny impressions of Kath and Ray bossing everyone around and everyone was laughing. We had a great time. Then we told everyone to go to bed and they all did except Julia, who started crying. The boys went to their room as well. I held Julia until she eventually fell asleep and then me and Mary sat on the doorstep and smoked our cigarettes even though it was freezing cold. I think we both liked being in charge.

A.

Monday, 12 March 1973

Dear Diary,

Last night something strange happened. We were all in bed – Julia has started sleeping next to me, probably because I hug her to stop her crying – it's the only way to get some rest. Anyway, I fell asleep, but in the middle of the night, the door opened to our room and someone came in. Nasty Nora always used to lock the door at night. Sometimes Fat Franny would come in after lights out with extra blankets or to check on us, but we always knew it was her. Anyway, I was so scared I couldn't move and then eventually the person must have left. But why would someone come in the room and just stand there watching?

A.

Friday, 20 April 1973

Dear Diary,

Every week Ray has been asking me to go to my den and meet him. I have been telling him we have homework to do but he said just for twenty minutes. We smoke and talk and sometimes he asks me to thank him for looking after us so well. Afterwards, he gives me a long hug, and he said if I need anything I should always come to him first. He doesn't talk about a new girl arriving any more. Today was Good Friday. We don't have to go to church, but Ray has promised to take us all to the Easter egg hunt in the park.

A.

Tuesday, 15 May 1973

Dear Diary,

   Mr Wright has given me a warning at school. He said if I don't start concentrating, he's going to report me to Mr Biggs for not doing the homework. Mr Biggs is the headmaster. I've only been in his office once before – it smelt funny like an old musty library. He's so old-fashioned he still wears a bow tie. Mr Wright asked me why I was struggling with the work. I told him I wasn't struggling, just that I don't always have time to do the homework. He then asked me what I was doing instead and I told him being a lady. He told me not to be cheeky, that I had a bright future if I concentrated, and he would leave it at that for now. But he said if I missed homework again I'd be in trouble.

   A.

Thursday, 28 June 1973

Dear Diary,

   I am so tired and I haven't written my diary for a few weeks. I REALLY don't want to see Mr Biggs so I've started doing my homework at night in bed after going to the den and doing my chores. My eyes hurt but at least I've finished it all. We only have two more weeks of school left and then I won't have to do this any more.

   A.

Friday, 13 July 1973

Dear Diary,

Today was the last day of school. I am so happy it's over. Ray said while school is OK, it's more important to learn about being a lady. He said it will be an easier life for me. I asked if it meant I could leave the home soon, and he said yes, in a few years. Ray told Kath to give me cooking lessons as well. I still have to go to the den in the afternoons before chores, but only on weekdays. He tells me to sit on his lap and talk to him. Sometimes, he has a small present for me, which he gives me for doing so well at being a lady. I wish we could go back to just talking.

  A.

Wednesday, 29 August 1973

Dear Diary,

It's been over a year since Nelly left. She promised she would write to me but I've never received any letters. Maybe they won't let her send any? But she said her new mummy and daddy were really nice so I think she just forgot about me. I wish they could have picked both of us, then we could have lived together and shared a room! It would be pink and we would each have our own dresser filled with make-up. Mine would be pink and hers would be peach and they would have mirrors with lights around them. We would also have our own bikes with baskets on the front. Ray and Kath are arguing again. Kath is screaming at him. Sometimes Ray calls her an old fishwife. This time we know what they are arguing about, though – Mary has run away.

A.

Sunday, 2 September 1973

Dear Diary,

Ray found Mary and brought her home. She looked awful – her hair was wild and she had a cut on her lip. When she saw Peter she started shouting and swearing at him, calling him a dobber. Ray held her by the arm but she escaped and started hitting Peter. Ray grabbed her and pulled her arms back until she begged him to stop. Then they took her to the kitchen and they closed the door. We could hear Kath using her wooden spoons on her and Mary was screaming. Then they took her upstairs to their bedroom and after a few minutes she was quiet. When I looked at Peter, he had tears on his face even though he's fifteen. When he saw me looking at him, he said, it's not my fault – they made me tell them where she was. Dobber.

A.

Saturday, 13 October 1973

Dear Diary,

When the littlies came back from the park this morning, Julia wouldn't stop crying. Ray said she had fallen over in the playground. Kath told me to get the little brat to shut up or she would get the wooden spoons out. I quickly took Julia to the common room. Julia said it hurt but she wouldn't tell me where. I found her teddy and gave it to her and put the television on for her, and she seemed quieter.

A.

Thursday, 1 November 1973

Dear Diary,

Mary doesn't come downstairs very much any more. As she's the oldest, Ray and Kath said they have given her her own room with posters of David Bowie and she stays in there most of the time smoking. Ray says she's a very disturbed girl and she needs medication to keep her calm. When we do see her, Mary doesn't hit Peter any more but sometimes her eyes are a bit funny – like she just woke up from a bad dream.

A.

Tuesday, 4 December 1973

Dear Diary,

One of the boys, Stuart, has a broken arm. Ray was outside playing with him and said he broke it while playing out in the den and slipped on some ice. Stuart was crying a lot. Ray took him to the hospital and now he has a cast on. Stuart let me write GET WELL SOON on it when he came back. Ray and Kath took him to another room upstairs, so he could rest without us bothering him.

A.

Wednesday, 5 December 1973

Dear Diary,

Maureen says we have to do something about Mary. We haven't seen her for ages. Maureen says she's being held a prisoner. I told her that was silly and that she has her own room with David Bowie posters as she's the oldest. Mary can come down if she wants to, but she needs medication to keep her calm. Maureen looked at me and asked, is that what Ray told you? Why does she always want to make me feel stupid? I said yes, but I would ask him again when I go to my den. Your den? she said. So I told her – all about the special den Ray had built just for me. I can't be that stupid if Ray built it just for me. Show me, demanded Maureen. I should have said no, but it was too late anyway – the secret was out. So I took her. And that's when we saw Ray in my den with Julia. She was sitting on his lap and sobbing quietly. I ran away and was sick in the bushes. I got it on my shoes.

A.

17

Rosemary

The trouble with having a successful career woman as a daughter, thought Rosemary crossly, was the difficulty in getting in touch with her. That was the second message she'd left with the receptionist that morning. What was her name? Melanie? She'd left the first message with Nina. They were like triage nurses assessing the seriousness and importance of the caller. Apparently, *mother* fell into the non-urgent category. If Angela had got back to her two weeks ago when she'd first mentioned it, she wouldn't be having to chase her now. Rosemary looked forward to her monthly day out in London and tried to coincide it with her daughter's diary, so they could have a coffee or lunch together. It was several hours later when Angela called her back, sounding panicked.

'Mum, is everything OK with Dad?'

'Yes, yes, everything is fine with your father. Sorry to bother you at work but I just wanted to see if you had time for lunch or even a coffee? I can come any day this week, whenever suits you best. I know how busy you are.'

'Oh, right, well, that's a relief,' replied Angela.

'It would just be nice to get out of the house for a bit,' added Rosemary, hoping she didn't sound desperate.

'Lunch, er, let me see…'

Rosemary could hear pages of a diary flicking.

'Wednesday could be a possibility, but I'll need to confirm with you the day before as I'm waiting to hear back from a client. Hmm, let me check Thursday. No, that's out.'

Rosemary heard Angela sigh. 'Sorry, Friday, I'm booked up solid the whole day.'

Rosemary held back her disappointment.

'Of course, darling. I was thinking Wednesday anyway, so I'll plan for that and you can let me know when you're ready.'

'Sounds good, Mum, thanks. You wouldn't believe how busy it is at the moment. We have a new client…'

Rosemary listened to her daughter for the next fifteen minutes, eventually interrupting.

'Well, darling, it seems like you have a lot on, as usual. Let me know if you're free for an hour on Wednesday, otherwise I will see you when you next come home.'

Hanging up the phone, Rosemary knew that it was unlikely she would hear back. With a sigh, she picked up the phone and made a lunch reservation for one.

18
Evelyn

Evelyn woke up and grunted. She had been dreaming about Mother. It was bad enough that she had to go and visit her every week, but to have to put up with her in her dreams as well was too much.

Forcing herself up, she pulled on her dressing gown and looked in the mirror. She took in her gaunt face, ravaged by years of drug use, her greying hair that had once been a rich chocolate brown, and her turkey-neck. She looked old and tired, and she cursed her neighbours for continuing their incessant music and disturbing her sleep. At this rate, she may have to break her golden rule and at least threaten to call the police. Deciding it was too much effort to take a shower, Evelyn crawled back into bed and closed her eyes.

It didn't take a genius to work out why she was dreaming about Mother. She captured remnants of the dream and turned them over in her mind. Ellen Harris's prim and proper ways had made her strict and overbearing rather than loving, but from her early childhood years Evelyn had known her future – Mother had mapped it all out. Work hard at school, say 'please' and 'thank you', get a typing job and then marry a nice boy and raise children. She didn't blame her – it was, after all, how Mother herself had been raised – but the unexpected arrival of Jimmy in Evelyn's life had changed everything.

Evelyn was attractive enough as a teenager but even she knew Jimmy was out of her league, which was perhaps why he had been able to persuade her so easily. When Ellen had discovered their relationship, she had beaten Evelyn with a hairbrush and banned her from ever seeing Jimmy again. But forbidden love is always the most irresistible and Evelyn couldn't believe her lucky stars. Jimmy was everything she had ever dreamt about and represented a life far away from her overbearing mother.

Even today, Ellen wouldn't let her forget her disobedience all those years ago, but Evelyn had never been able to bring herself to cut Mother off completely. Instead, she endured the weekly chiding and berating, and told herself that it was understandable Mother was so grumpy: Ellen was housebound, overweight, and could do nothing but sit in her chair and watch the world go by as she drew closer and closer to leaving it. Evelyn normally visited on a Sunday afternoon and it was her secret habit, as she made her way there, to imagine the various things she would love to say to her mother. *You ruined my life, you miserable cow.* Oh, how she would love to see the shock on Mother's face as she gave her what for! But it was never going to happen; it simply wasn't how she'd been brought up. Evelyn guiltily considered how long she would have to continue the weekly visits and pushed the thought aside immediately. Ellen had survived two world wars – she wasn't going anywhere any time soon. There was nothing to be done; she just had to get through the visits as best she could.

Mother lived up in Finchley, in a small bedsit, and Evelyn usually took a week's worth of shopping. After putting the food away and making tea, they sat together with the television blaring (Mother was slightly deaf) to disguise the fact that they had nothing to say to each other. After an hour, Evelyn would ask if there was anything she could do around the house and Mother would grumble that there was but she wouldn't do it properly so what was the point, and then Evelyn would sit for a few minutes more, before dutifully kissing Ellen on the cheek and telling her she'd see her next week. On her way back home, she often continued her imaginary outburst of rage towards her, the hurtful words buzzing around her brain, frantically trying to escape.

19

Angela

'So, how are you feeling, Dad?' asked Angela on one of her weekend visits home. It had been two weeks since she'd last seen her parents, unable to come the weekend before as she had to prepare for an important client meeting. Arriving last night, she had tried to hide her shock at the change in her father's appearance in such a short period of time. His face was practically hollow and he seemed to have aged several years. He had lost even more weight and his trousers hung off him. She made a mental note to check with her mum about buying him some new clothes.

'I'm fine, thanks,' he replied, smiling weakly. 'Better today. Yesterday was difficult. Sometimes the chemo just floors me. The doctor did say I would have bad days, so I can't say I haven't been warned.'

'Can I get you anything else?' Angela asked, worriedly.

'No, no need. I might just close my eyes for a bit, though.' She had come to her parents' bedroom to collect his breakfast tray, which Rosemary had taken up earlier that morning. It was just past ten and Angela quietly left the room with the untouched food. Going into the kitchen, she found her mother browsing her recipe book at the dining table while a pot of tea brewed.

'Do you prefer lasagne or roast chicken?' she asked her daughter absent-mindedly. 'I'd ask your father, but he doesn't seem to eat much of anything I make these days,' she added sadly, glancing at the leftover food on the tray in her hands. Dumping the tray near the kitchen sink, Angela took a chair opposite her and poured a cup of tea for each of them.

'I know the doctor said the chemo would be hard on him,' continued Rosemary, 'but I thought it was supposed to make him better. After every session, he just seems to deteriorate more and more.'

Angela silently agreed, but as Rosemary pulled out a tissue, she knew it was optimism and encouragement that was needed now.

'I know, Mum, but we are going to beat this. There will be good days and bad days, but ultimately, the treatment will help, I'm sure of it.'

'Do you really think so? I've been trying so hard to be positive but when I see him like this… it just feels so hopeless.'

'I really do, Mum,' replied Angela firmly, pushing her own doubts aside.

'The doctor is such a lovely man, but it's hard to get a definitive answer, if you know what I mean,' Rosemary explained. 'I know there are no guarantees – he was very clear about that from the beginning – but I so just want to be told everything will be all right.' Rosemary looked Angela in the eye. 'Does that sound ridiculous?'

'Of course not. We all have days like that. But, everything *is* going to be all right. By Christmas, Dad will be in a different place completely.'

'Yes, you're right, of course you are. Thank you, darling. Sometimes I just get bogged down in it all.'

Glad to have been able to help, Angela asked about coming to the next doctor's appointment.

'It's a lovely idea but I would check with your dad,' Rosemary said. 'You know what he's like. He didn't even want me to be there really, but I insisted. "For better or worse," I reminded him.

'Of course,' replied Angela. She was pretty certain her dad wouldn't mind, and once again she wondered if her mum was trying to put her off. 'I'll ask him when he wakes up.'

Rosemary suddenly stood up, severing the proximity between them. 'What about work?' she asked, turning her back to Angela as she started to do the washing up.

'Don't worry, Mum, I'll sort it.'

'OK, well, see what your dad says. You have a lot on yourself. How is the adoption support group going?'

Angela had told her parents about the meetings over the phone and James had sounded particularly pleased she'd taken the initiative so quickly.

'Actually, I have a little bit of news on that,' said Angela tentatively, wondering if this was the right time to bring it up.

'Oh?' Rosemary's concentration was still very much on the soapy bowl in front of her.

'Yes, Susan – you remember I mentioned her – she's the organiser and founder of this particular group.' Angela took a quick breath. 'Well, she's found my birth mother.'

Rosemary swivelled then, clearly taken aback, the submerged dishes forgotten. Angela immediately backtracked. 'Sorry, Mum, perhaps this wasn't the best time to tell you.'

'Of course it was, darling! Sorry, I hadn't expected it to happen so quickly. I'm just surprised, that's all.'

Relieved, Angela continued, 'Me too. When Susan called to tell me, it was a bit of a shock.'

'I can imagine!' Rosemary replied, quickly turning back to the dishes.

'Well, it's thanks to you and Dad really. Susan said all the information you provided made it one of the easiest searches she'd done.'

'I'm sure. Your dad was adamant about getting all your background information. He even had a solicitor involved to cross-check everything. It seemed excessive to me, but he wanted to make sure you would have the option to find your birth mother,' she replied, as she carefully placed each plate on the drying rack. 'So, what's next?'

Angela noticed the singular use in her mum's speech: *He wanted to make sure.* Had her mum not wanted her to find her birth mother? She mentally filed the question away to think about later.

'Well,' replied Angela, 'Susan said the organisation can act as an intermediary or I can meet her myself. Either way, Susan has already contacted her to make sure she's open to meeting.'

'And is she?'

'What?'

'Open to meeting you?'

'Yes, according to Susan she is.'

'I see.'

Angela tried to interpret her mother's tone. She was beginning to regret sharing the news. What was her problem? She should have waited for her dad to be there so she could tell them together.

'So, what will you do?' asked Rosemary.

'I'm not sure yet. What do you think?'

'How is your relationship with Susan?'

'Good – she's very supportive and very experienced. She's been doing this a long time.'

'Well, it's up to you, of course, but if Susan can help make the process a little easier it would seem like the right choice to me.'

'Yes, you could be right. Susan would basically come to the meeting, make introductions and then let us talk. That's how it was explained to me, anyway.'

'Sounds like a good approach. No one likes surprises, and this way they can prepare you for what to expect.'

'What do you mean?' asked Angela.

'Well, just that you don't know what she's like, do you? It could be a shock for you meeting her for the first time.'

Angela didn't respond.

'Don't listen to me, darling. It will all be fine, I'm sure,' Rosemary said. 'Just remember that your dad and I are both here if you need us, OK?'

Slipping off her chair, Angela made her excuses and went to her bedroom. Lying down on her bed, she was surprised to feel drowsy. It was a late Saturday morning and usually she'd be on her way to the office by now to put in a few extra hours. She'd just close her eyes for a few minutes. As she drifted off, Angela wondered why her mum wasn't as keen as Dad on finding her birth mother. While she had assumed they were both in agreement when they had first mentioned it, it seemed to her that Mum might not be quite so in favour.

It was a good two hours later when Angela woke with a start. She didn't know where she was at first. She had been dreaming, the impressions still vivid in her mind. Her dad was in a hospital bed but instead of being surrounded by wires and tubes, he was sitting up, animated, and talking loudly. He seemed happy. A woman was sitting on the bed next to him, holding his hand and laughing with him. Angela thought it was her mum, but as she approached, the woman turned to look at her before swivelling back to her father and ignoring her. It was then Angela saw it wasn't her mum at all but an older version of herself. Agitated, she called out.

'Dad?'

He also ignored her and continued talking, the woman grasping onto him. Angela didn't know who she was, but she knew she had to find out.

'Dad!' she tried to call again.

She was struggling with her voice – the more she tried to speak, the harder it became. She could feel the panic rising in her chest. Suddenly, the conversation stopped, and the woman got up from the bed. She walked slowly towards Angela, her face passive, her suit crisp, her walk robotic. She was no longer smiling.

Shaking off the last remnants of the dream, Angela could smell what she guessed was the lasagne cooking in the oven. How could she have slept so long? She was supposed to be here to help. Quickly rinsing her face, she headed to the kitchen.

'Just in time for lunch,' said James, as she sat down at the table. 'I thought I was the only one who napped around here,' he joked.

Angela kissed him on the cheek. 'I honestly don't know what happened. One minute I was awake and the next...' Angela shook her head in disbelief. She never napped.

'Here you go,' said Rosemary, placing the lasagne in front of her. 'Those long hours have to catch up with you at some point.'

'Thanks, Mum,' Angela replied, digging in, suddenly starving. 'It smells great!'

A few minutes passed as they enjoyed their lunch.

'So,' started James, 'Mum says you might have something to tell me?'

'I thought you might want to tell him yourself,' said Rosemary.

Still fuzzy from the sleep, it took Angela a second to work out she was talking about the discovery of Evelyn. Angela took a deep breath before telling him the news. How would he respond? She needn't have worried. He was thrilled.

'Oh, Angel, that really has made my day. I'm so happy for you. And she wants to meet you, too!' James exclaimed. "Well of course she does! She'd be a fool not to!"

'We haven't had the first meeting yet, but I think Susan will act as an intermediary.'

'Of course, of course,' replied James. 'But the main thing is she's here and well in London. It's a good first step, Angel. Well done!'

Angela warmed at the praise. To see her dad so cheerful had made all the time spent at the meetings worthwhile.

'What do you think, Rosie?' he asked. 'Great news, eh?'

'Indeed.'

Angela took a discreet sideways glance. Rosemary's expression was neutral, her efforts concentrated solely on the food in front of her.

'So, when is the meeting set for?' asked James, seemingly oblivious to his wife's silence.

'Next week. Susan's offered to come with me and facilitate.'

'Good idea. I don't like the idea of you going to her flat alone.'

'Her flat?' said Rosemary.

'Flat, house, whatever,' he responded, turning to Angela again. 'This Susan sounds like a really good woman.'

'Yes, she's been really helpful so far,' agreed Angela.

'Perhaps you want to take a few pictures of yourself from when you grew up here?' James suggested. 'What do you say, Rosie, love? Would that be a nice thing to do, or rubbing her nose in it, do you think?'

'Oh, James, I'm not sure about that. Why don't you let them get the first meeting out of the way first?'

'Yes, you're probably right,' he replied. 'But still, one photo wouldn't hurt, would it?'

Angela watched her dad. He seemed animated, excited almost. It was a stark contrast to her mum's reserved demeanour. As they continued their almost one-sided conversation, Angela listened. She could almost feel sympathy for her mum. It couldn't be easy seeing the daughter you raised go off and meet her birth mother. What if she were planning to meet her birth father? She wondered if her dad would be as enthusiastic.

20

Wednesday, 16 January 1974

Dear Diary,

Me and Maureen are planning our escape. We're going to take Julia with us. We just need to try and get Mary to come too. But Kath won't let us upstairs to see her. I wrote to Nelly for help and stole the money from Kath's purse for a stamp. I posted it myself on the way to school instead of giving it to Ray. Ray doesn't buy me gifts any more and Kath always gives me the smallest portion of meat, if any. They ignore me as long as I do my chores. I don't think they will be throwing me a birthday party this year.

A.

Saturday, 19 January 1974

Dear Diary,

Kath found out that I stole money from her purse. I

don't know how she knew. She came storming through to where we were doing our homework and demanded to know who had done it. When she saw it was me, she yanked me into the kitchen and used every wooden spoon she had on me. One cracked me on my temple, splitting the skin. She sat down at the kitchen table then, and put her head in her hands, telling me to get out. Maureen had to help me clean up all the blood. Some birthday that was.

A.

Wednesday, 13 February 1974

Dear Diary,

Maureen thinks we should leave in April when it's warmer. I think we should tell Mr Wright. Maureen says if we tell anyone Ray will break someone else's arm. I asked her what she meant. She told me that Stuart didn't fall over. Stuart had told a teacher that Ray and Kath weren't good people. Ray found out. When Stuart tried to run, Ray caught him and punished him.

A.

Friday, 15 February 1974

Dear Diary,

Ray and Kath have grounded all of us for two weeks. We're not allowed to play outside any more and the TV has been taken upstairs. Peter tried to sneak upstairs to see Mary, but he got caught and Ray said he was going to get the thrashing of his life. We could hear his screams all the way through the house. Ray said that because of Peter, we will all be punished, and we should consider ourselves lucky it's just for two weeks. Everyone is quiet in the house – even the littlies. Peter has had to stay off school as his face is so purple and covered in bruises.

A.

Thursday, 21 March 1974

Dear Diary,

The bald Home Inspector is coming! This could be our chance. Last time he came, he replaced Nasty Nora and Fat Franny so maybe he can do the same again and get Nasty Nora and Fat Franny back? Me, Maureen and Peter discussed it at school. Peter said if we tried to escape we would starve as we're not old enough to earn any money. I said we could go to Nelly's. Peter told me not to be stupid – we don't have money to get there. We decided that we would slip a note into the Inspector's bag and tell him about Kath and Ray and how they're bad people. Then the Inspector would have to get rid of them. Maureen wrote the note because she has the best handwriting.

A.

Sunday, 24 March 1974

Dear Diary,

We have spent the whole weekend cleaning for the Inspector and we weren't allowed to play outside even though it wasn't raining. On Sunday afternoon, though, Ray told Kath we all looked pale and that we could play outside for an hour before bath-time. He said we have to look our best for the Inspector. We played skipping with the littlies but I couldn't concentrate – what if the Inspector doesn't come with a bag? How will we pass him the note without Ray and Kath seeing?

A.

Monday, 25 March 1974

Dear Diary,

Our plan worked! The Inspector brought a black leather briefcase with a side pocket. He put it on the chair next to him while he was having his cup of tea with Kath and Ray. They were very friendly to him and Kath had even made him a cake. When they took him on a tour, Maureen slipped the note into his bag and gave me a secret smile.

A.

Tuesday, 26 March 1974

Dear Diary,

Peter thinks nothing will happen for at least a month. I bet him my yellow marble that Kath and Ray would be asked to leave within the week. I imagine them being handcuffed and led away into a police car. The Inspector then introduces two nice old ladies to look after us and they bring bikes for everyone to make up for the nastiness of Kath and Ray. One lady can cook and the other is really good at making clothes.

A.

Wednesday, 27 March 1974

Dear Diary,

Nothing has happened. When I'm in the den with Ray, I listen for the Inspector's footsteps.

A.

Wednesday, 3 April 1974

Dear Diary,

It's been over a week. I had to give Peter my yellow marble. I wanted to throw it at him.

A.

Friday, 5 April 1974

Dear Diary,

The Inspector finally came at four o'clock today. But there was no police car. He sat and drank tea as usual while me and Peter listened behind the kitchen door. We couldn't hear very much but as soon as we heard the chairs scraping back we scarpered. Ray and Kath both saw him out. After he left, Ray locked and bolted the door and drew all the curtains. Ray had a face like thunder. I think we all knew it was bad. One of the littlies wet themselves.

We were asked to line up for inspection. But there wasn't an inspection. In Ray's hand was the note me, Maureen and Peter had written, which he held up and demanded to know who was responsible for it. We were all quiet. All of a sudden, he grabbed Julia and made her kneel down and began taking off his belt. He wouldn't, I thought, but he had cracked it on the soles of her feet before I could even blink. She screamed – a shriek like a cat when it's in a fight. Peter and I jumped forward. I grabbed Julia and hugged her hard, trying to squeeze the pain out of her. *I did it,* said me and Peter at the same time. Maureen said nothing, the coward. Ray looked at us both and I felt sick. He made me and Peter step forward. Everyone had to watch while he lashed us with his belt. But that wasn't the worst part. He then forced us to remove our clothes so we were completely naked in front of everyone and made us bend over on our hands and knees. By now, the littlies were beside themselves. He shouted at them to shut it before telling everyone that this is what happens when you lie. He made them all watch as he beat us on our bare backsides, over and over again, until I eventually must have passed out.

A.

Friday, 19 April 1974

Dear Diary,

I now know where Mary is. She's not in her own bedroom, smoking and looking at her David Bowie posters. She's locked up in the basement with just a thin mattress to sleep on and a bucket to do her business. I know because I was locked up with her for almost two weeks. She slept a lot. Every morning, Kath came down, gave her a pill and some food and water and she went back to sleep. My skin is not my own any more. It burned a lot, especially when Kath put the cream on it. Kath said I should be thankful I'm getting cream to help it heal. I don't feel thankful. I wish I'd died down there in the basement. I was kept off school and I thought about my mother a lot – why would she leave me in a place like this?

A.

Monday, 20 May 1974

Dear Diary,

I didn't go to school today. My feet just carried on walking past the school gates. I just wanted to be alone for a long time. I went to the park and sat on the bench. I was only going to stay for a few minutes and then go straight to school. But it was so nice in the park – no crying, no Ray, no Kath, no punishments. I lay on the grass and looked at the sky. I will have to forge a sick note tomorrow.

A.

Sunday, 23 June 1974

Dear Diary,

We had scrubbed the place from top to bottom a couple of weeks ago. My knees were sore from cleaning the floors. I was dusting the old desk when I found them. They were in a bundle held by an elastic band all addressed to me in Nelly's wobbly handwriting. I stared at them for ages. A nice strange feeling, like eating fish and chips on the beach, went through me. Nelly hadn't forgotten me after all. I was so busy looking at the letters, getting excited at the thought of reading them, that I didn't see Kath come up behind me. She grabbed the letters from my hand and dragged me by the arm so hard I thought it would come out of its socket. I knew I was going to get a beating, but I didn't care. Nelly had written to me! But as Kath dragged me to the kitchen, still holding the letters, she lit a match and I knew it was going to be much worse than a beating. Shall I tell you what happens to snoops? she said. They burn in hell, just like these letters. I didn't realise I was screaming or thrashing at Kath. I didn't feel it when Ray thundered into the kitchen demanding to know what was going on or when he carried me down to the basement still shouting – I wasn't aware of anything. All I knew was that those letters were the only good thing in the horrible world I was living in, and like everything else, Ray and Kath had destroyed them.

A.

Wednesday, 17 July 1974

Dear Diary,

A new boy has arrived at the home. His name is Mark and he's fifteen. He is big but not fat. He would win in a fight. He looks older than fifteen. He doesn't talk – not even to Peter.

A.

Saturday, 17 August 1974

Dear Diary,

Ray sent me and Mark to do the shopping. Ray tries to joke with Mark. He told him he's strong enough to carry the shopping. It's a thirty-minute walk to the market and Mark didn't talk at all. About ten minutes into it, he says he has to make a stop. I tell him we can't – Ray told us to go and come straight back. I think Mark noticed my panic because he said it would only take a minute. We slipped down a street with terraced houses. When we reached number 32, Mark rang the bell and the door opened a bit. Within a minute we were inside. The man living there had piercings all over his face. I wonder if they hurt. He asked Mark who I was and if anyone saw us come in. Mark said no, told him I was no one, and handed over a small package. The man with piercings handed over some ten-pound notes. I've never seen so much money in my life. Then Mark said let's go. He was right – it was only a minute but if Ray found out, we would be dead. I asked Mark what was in the package. He said nothing and to keep my mouth shut. I looked at Mark and decided he could probably give a good thrashing too.

A.

Monday, 2 September 1974

Dear Diary,

It's the first day back at school – it was terrible. I'm in the same clothes as last year, which are too small. Kath didn't even bother to check the lost and found for us. My shoes pinch my toes and I tripped walking to PE class. I'll have to go to lost and found myself.

A.

Tuesday, 8 October 1974

Dear Diary,

School is better than being with Ray and Kath but sometimes I skip school and go to the park instead. Today, I saw Mark there and he was sitting on the grass near the trees. I went up to him and told him he was in my place. He laughed but in a nice way. He told me to sit next to him and offered me a cigarette. I took a long drag and Mark told me to go easy. It wasn't a cigarette like Ray's, though. When I asked him what it was, he told me it was a roll-up – something that would make all the pain go away. It felt like I was floating. It was a really nice feeling.

A.

Wednesday, 6 November 1974

Dear Diary,

Last night was Guy Fawkes Night. A few of us went to the sports club to see the firework display. There was a huge bonfire and everyone was standing around it. Someone had put on top of it an effigy of Guy Fawkes – I imagined it was my mother burning up there instead.

A.

Friday, 29 November 1974

Dear Diary,

Ray has started buying me presents again. When I went to the den, he told me I'd been such a good, quiet girl lately that I deserved a special treat. He gave me a wrapped box and inside was a bracelet-making set. He said I could make them for all my friends at school. I didn't tell him that I don't really have any friends at school. Instead, I said thank you and tried to leave but he said aren't you going to thank me? I gave him a kiss but it wasn't enough and he grabbed me and pulled me down next to him. I wanted to scream but I knew if I did, it would make it all so much worse. Eventually, he let me go back inside. Later, I asked Mark if he had any more roll-ups. He told me to meet him tomorrow at the park. I couldn't sleep for thinking about it. I just want to float away from this hell.

A.

Monday, 16 December 1974

Dear Diary,

It's the week before Christmas and the Inspector came today after school. Yesterday, Ray told us that if there's any trouble this time, we will ALL pay for it. The Inspector came and drank his tea. When he was leaving he shook hands with Kath and Ray and told them they were doing a great job. I don't know who I hate more – the Inspector, Kath and Ray, or my mother for leaving me here. I hope they all die.

A.

21

Rosemary

Rosemary took pride in the fact that she always managed to stay level-headed. The art of composure was a necessary skill growing up in her family. Even as a child, she instinctively knew that any sort of display of excessive emotion, such as a tantrum, would not be tolerated. Yet, not for the first time, Rosemary felt her patience thinning with Angela. What was she thinking, telling her the news about meeting her birth mother? There Rosemary was, clearly in pieces about James, and Angela was insensitive enough to think it appropriate to make such an announcement.

Rosemary sighed. Young people were so self-involved these days. But Angela had always been like that. She was polite, but she *never* hesitated to put herself first in any situation. Was that fair? pondered Rosemary, or was it more that Angela always had to be the centre of attention?

She thought back to a wedding anniversary, years ago now. She and James were all dressed up ready to go out for dinner and she'd been looking forward to it for weeks. Mrs Henderson from down the road was coming to sit in with

Angela just in case she needed anything and was already settling herself comfortably with a cup of tea in the living room. But just as they were about to leave, Angela had complained of a temperature and not feeling well. Standing there, wrapped up in her pyjamas and dressing gown, she'd turned her beseeching dark eyes to James and said in a low voice that she didn't want to be alone. Before Rosemary even had a chance to respond, James had cancelled their plans, telling Angela to get into bed and he would bring hot lemon and honey. Was she sleepy? If not, he could bring the television up to her room and they could sit together and watch it for half an hour.

Biting her tongue, Rosemary had told herself what a wonderful father James was, so caring, but later that night when Angela was sleeping, she pressed her hand against Angela's forehead. She wasn't in the slightest bit warm. And as such instances happened over the years – not many, but enough for Rosemary to know that she was being manipulated – a tiny fragment of mistrust lodged itself like shrapnel under the skin.

22

Evelyn

There was nothing else for it – Evelyn would have to call the police. It was the last week in October and she'd tried to get Dougie and his sons involved but he was having none of it. Apparently, her neighbours were renowned drug dealers – not just a bit of weed either – and far too unpredictable to go messing around with when there was nothing in it for them. Half the lads on the estate were already losing business to them and in Dougie's opinion the whole situation was a firecracker waiting to go off. Piss them off, he said, and God knows what they're likely to do, especially if they're high. Nope, reiterated Dougie with certainty, if you asked him (which Evelyn was beginning to regret doing), his advice would be to stay out of it and put up with it. They would move on soon enough.

While Dougie's words made sense, Evelyn was sick and tired of not being able to sleep properly. It was making her even crankier than usual. Doreen hadn't come up with the goods either. Her only recommendation was to ask Dougie, and look how that had turned out. It was when the music had been playing for ten nights in a row until the early hours of the morning that Evelyn knew she would have to do something drastic. One evening when the music was so loud she could barely hear her own TV, she found the courage to call the police. The phone was picked up immediately.

'What's your emergency?'

Startled, Evelyn was unsure how to begin.

'What's your emergency please?'

'Er, the police, but I just want to check—'

Before she could continue, the call was transferred. How rude, thought Evelyn. This time, there was at least a dial tone, but it didn't last long before another voice – female, this time – was ordering her to state her emergency. This time Evelyn was ready.

'I have a noise issue – from the flat opposite. It's so loud I can't sleep at night.'

'I see – and have you asked your neighbours to turn it down?'

'Of course I have!' replied Evelyn indignantly. 'Not that it's made the slightest bit of difference. This is my last resort – calling you. But I want it to remain anonymous – can that be done?'

'Of course. This information won't be shared with anyone. Now if I can just take a few details, Mrs... er?'

Evelyn hesitated. 'Mrs Harris,' she replied tentatively.

'My name is Constable Farrows. Can I have your address, please?'

As Evelyn provided all the details, she started to feel reassured by the friendly-sounding constable and her guilt at involving the police began to recede. It helped that the music was so loud that Constable Farrows could hear it down the receiver and she agreed that Evelyn was well within her rights to report it. But within minutes of hanging up, doubt crept in. What the hell was she thinking? Having made the complaint, a new solution came to her. She could have paid another visit to Alan at the council and urged them to find her a new flat. She could easily get the forged paperwork together to state she had medical issues. The police had said on the phone that they would look into the matter, but what did that mean exactly? Would they come over? And if they did, would her neighbours know it was her who had called them? Of course they would: they weren't stupid. There were only two flats per floor – hers and theirs – and they must have heard her banging on their door and complaining. Should she call them back and withdraw the complaint? But then how would she sleep?

All that evening, Evelyn felt agitated and not even her TV shows could distract her from the worry of the potential backlash of getting the police involved. But as the hours turned to days and the police didn't even bother to visit and check, she eventually forgot about it.

23

Angela

'Hello.'

The voice came from behind as Angela was getting a cup of tea. Involuntarily, she shivered in anticipation and then told herself to pull it together – she wasn't some damsel in distress, for goodness' sake.

'Hello,' she said turning around to face Mitchell. He was a good few inches taller than her and his dark blue suit exuded quality and taste. With his dark hair and piercing eyes, both softened by a lazy grin, Angela was glad she had left the office and attended the meeting tonight, and not just to talk more about her birth mother.

'I enjoyed our drink last week,' said Mitchell, a smile playing on his lips. Looking up at him, she was just about to respond when Susan interrupted them.

'Come on, you two. Are you ready to sit down?'

Tearing her eyes away from his, Angela sat and looked around the rest of the group. Out of the corner of her eye she could see Mitchell trying to catch her attention. Sneaking a peak at him, he wiggled his eyebrows at her. Stifling a laugh, Angela attempted to concentrate on what Susan was saying.

'So, the good news is we've had a couple of breakthroughs this week locating birth parents, which is definitely one of the most rewarding parts of my job! I'd also like to welcome a few new members to the group.' As Susan did a round of introductions, the rest of the members politely murmured a series of greetings.

'Right,' continued Susan briskly, 'who would like to start? Angela, how about you?'

Susan had already checked with Angela that she would be happy to share her story, so she was prepared.

'Yes, absolutely,' replied Angela. 'Well, I am one of those breakthroughs you mentioned earlier in terms of finding my birth mother, and I would like to thank you, Susan, for the amazing opportunity you've given me.' Angela had rightly guessed that Susan would enjoy the public praise.

'It's what I'm here for,' murmured Susan.

'I'm really looking forward to meeting my birth mother in person.'

Unexpectedly, a round of applause rose from around the room.

'Well done, Angela, we're all so proud of you,' said Susan over the din. Angela, feeling slightly overwhelmed and surprisingly emotional, nodded her thanks.

Turning to the rest of the group, Susan said, 'As some of you may remember, it can often be a very difficult decision to make to meet a birth parent. Suddenly, it all becomes very real, and we have to accept that what we have in our imagination may not be the same as reality. Ken, you recently met your birth mother, didn't you, and had a very positive experience? Are you happy to share that with the group?'

Ken cleared his throat as if preparing for an important speech. He was clearly thrilled to be called upon. 'Yes, thank you, Susan. Well, I was nervous, of course. I remember the day well – it was a Saturday morning – and Susan had arranged for us to meet in a coffee shop. Susan had shown me a photo, so I knew what she looked like. I remember everything about that day. We met at ten o'clock, and for about the first half hour we just hugged and she just kept saying how sorry she was, over and over again. We ended up staying in the coffee shop for about five hours, we had so much to talk about. She cried; I tried not to cry,' he grinned, 'but it was very emotional. I had a lot of questions and she tried her best to answer them, although I could see that some memories were very painful for her. Before I left, she asked if I would be willing to meet her again.'

'And did you?' asked Angela, her curiosity getting the better of her.

'Yes, of course,' replied Ken. 'I think the apology also helped me. Susan had warned me not to expect it, but it was good to hear. I've spent many years wondering about her and I wanted to know more – *needed* to know more,' he emphasised.

Murmurs of, 'Well done, Ken' and 'I agree' floated across the room as Ken sat back down in his chair.

'Thank you, Ken,' praised Susan. 'For some people, that *need* to know is a very important part of the healing process, and I know you're on the right track. Right, who would like to go next? Leo?'

Angela looked across at a man slumped in his chair. He was a new member who was currently staring intently at Katie and her baby. His jeans cuffs were caked with mud and his trainers, once white, were now a dull grey. His red hooded jumper covered his head, despite the warmth inside the church hall.

'Leo?' repeated Susan.

Tearing his eyes away from Katie, he looked Susan straight in the eye.

'I'm not ready.' It was a simple statement, but Angela detected a slight hostility in his tone.

'No problem, Leo, take your time. Maybe try again next week.'

Leo didn't respond – just turned his attention back to the tiny baby cradled in its mother's arms.

Angela sat across from Susan in the little office behind the hall, tense with anticipation.

'OK, Angela, I've already spoken to your birth mother and set up the meeting for Thursday evening. I will be there with you, of course.'

Angela nodded, still trying to process that she would soon come face to face with the woman who gave her up when she was just a few days old. What would she say to her? What would she want to know? How would she feel when she met her? As Angela signed her acceptance on the documents Susan placed in front of her, she hoped her experience would be as heart-warming as Ken's.

24

Wednesday, 1 January 1975

Dear Diary,

Well, 1975, I hope you're going to treat me better than 1974. What a joke in this hellhole. I don't know how I'm going to survive the next two years. Maureen and Peter have completely given up trying to escape. But I haven't. I'm just going to bide my time for a while. In a couple of weeks, I will be fourteen. I can easily pass for sixteen if I do myself up. Mark says he can get me a part-time job that pays better than shop work. I just need to get a bit of money together and then I can get out of here.

A.

Sunday, 19 January 1975

Dear Diary,

I spent my birthday today smoking pot in the park

with Mark. I did chores this morning and then sneaked out after lunch. I'll probably get punished when I get back but who cares? It's my birthday. Mark said I should take some pot back for Ray. I laughed and told him why would I waste the good stuff on him? Mark said it might soften him up a bit. I told him anything's worth a try.

A.

Tuesday, 25 February 1975

Dear Diary,

Mark has got me a job interview! It's on Friday at 9 p.m. It's at the White Hart pub about ten minutes' walk from here – luckily not Ray's local. Mark says I have to dress really nice. The owner, Keith, likes to employ pretty girls. Does that mean Mark thinks I'm pretty? I told him I don't have any pretty clothes. He told me he would sort it for me.

A.

Wednesday, 26 February 1975

Dear Diary,

After school, I went to C&A. It reminded me of the time Kath took us on our 'girls' shopping trip'. But unlike last time, I didn't have Kath's purse strings to pull at. Rifling through the clothes, I saw a mustard-coloured zip-up top, which I slipped into my school bag. It would be perfect for the interview.

A.

Thursday, 27 February 1975

Dear Diary,

Mark told me to meet him in the park tonight. It was really dark when I got there, and he made me jump when he called my name. I told him not to go sneaking up on me like that. He just laughed. We sat near a lamppost, the glow of its light shining on Mark's open rucksack. Our breath showed up as clouds in the cold air. Inside was a pair of hot pants, some white platform boots, and a short-sleeved, V-necked top. I showed him my mustard top with the tags still on and he grinned at me, not needing to ask how I got it. He told me Keith was just going to ask me a few questions. He told me to say I was a quick learner. He also gave me a fake ID. I asked Mark what would happen if I got the job – what would I tell Ray and Kath? He said not to worry about it and just get the job first. Afterwards, despite the cold, we sat back and smoked before sneaking back. It was so bloody cold, I had to cuddle up to Julia to keep warm.

A.

Saturday, 22 March 1975

Dear Diary,

My life is made up of school, Ray, homework, and working at the pub. It's tiring but every time I feel the weight of my purse, I feel hopeful. This is my ticket to freedom. I work four nights a week at the pub and Ray and Kath are fine with it, but I have to give them a percentage of my wage. However, it does mean I get a bit more freedom and Mark is teaching me to think 'long term'. He also reminded me about my tips. Keith is all right – a bit of a gobby flirt, but as long as he keeps his hands off me he can say what he likes. The punters can be a bit rowdy, especially if the football's on, but it doesn't take much to get a decent tip from them – a wink, a smile, and those drunken idiots are putty.

-A.

25

Rosemary

Rosemary carefully pulled the cover up over James. After gently kissing his forehead, she looked into his face. What was once chiselled was now gaunt, his smile no match for the puppet lines that pulled his mouth downwards.

'I love you, Rosie,' he said now, cupping her face with his left hand.

'I love you, too,' she replied, stifling a sob.

'Hey,' he said gently, 'everything's going to be fine, OK?'

She nodded, determined not to cry. Turning away, she left the room to let him sleep. They'd been to the hospital that morning for chemotherapy, and while James rarely said as much, she knew it took everything out of him.

Rosemary went into the kitchen to put the kettle on. She wasn't going to think about what would happen if the treatment didn't work. Instead, she was going to do what she had always done in a crisis: keep busy.

Pouring hot water over the tea leaves, she went over her to-do list. The main thing was the paperwork. Normally, James would see to it, but with everything going on over the last few months it had piled up and it needed to be sorted and filed. Rosemary also wanted to sort through the never-ending boxes of photos. She would do the paperwork first and she hoped by the time that was finished James would be awake and they could go through the photos together.

Rosemary sat back in her chair, satisfied. It had taken a couple of hours but she'd worked without a break sorting the correspondence into the manila files in the cabinet. It was mainly bills but there were also letters and circulars that needed dealing with.

As she put the key to the cabinet back in the desk drawer, she decided to check on James. Stepping into their bedroom, she saw the bed was empty. That was a good sign: he must be in the bathroom, she thought.

Going back to the office, she brought two boxes of photos into the living room so that they could sit on the sofa and sort through them together. She also made some tea, put two scones with cream and jam on plates, and placed everything on a tray to take through. James was already in the living room looking through their wedding album when she came in.

'Hello, darling. How are you feeling?'

'Much better, thanks. What have you been up to? Are those scones?' he asked in surprise.

Rosemary smiled. 'Well, I thought you might need a treat in return for helping me sort out all these photos.'

She sat down next to him and he put his arm around her while they flicked through the heavy pages together.

'It was a marvellous day, our wedding, wasn't it, Rosie? The best day of my life!'

Rosemary agreed. While James's family had turned up in droves, she'd only had a few friends from her side. Despite that, she'd never had any regrets.

'Look at the size of my kipper tie. And my flares! I loved those trousers. I wonder where they are now,' reminisced James.

'I have no idea. Probably in the loft somewhere,' replied Rosemary, 'which I also need to sort out at some point. What about the size of my beehive? I can't believe I managed to get the veil over it!'

'You were so beautiful,' said James. 'I remember it like it was yesterday.'

Rosemary leant her head on his shoulder, each of them lost in their wedding day. Kissing her on the forehead, James placed the album to one side and picked up an envelope with a handwritten label that said 'Angela 1977'.

'Angela was sixteen then,' said James, as he browsed through the images. 'Oh, but those were great days, too, weren't they? You, me, and our lovely Angel.'

Rosemary looked at the photos and remembered. A family holiday to the Spanish islands where they'd spent their days sunbathing and swimming. The trips to London where they would have lunch at Brown's Hotel and shop for new clothes. The relaxed evenings barbecuing in the garden when James got home from work. They were great days, as James said, but Rosemary wouldn't want to go back to them.

'Sorry, love, nature calls,' said James.

Rosemary took the photos from him, so he could make his way to the bathroom. As she placed them back in the envelope, a picture fell out that she didn't remember seeing before. Rosemary smiled as she saw the close-up shot of James and Angela hugging, grinning at the camera, their cheeks pressed together. Just then the doorbell rang and, with the photo still in hand, Rosemary went to answer it. She was expecting some clothes she'd ordered from a catalogue.

'All right, Mrs Steele. How are you?'

'Hello, Simon.' She'd met the delivery man on several occasions and he was always friendly.

'Sign here, please.'

She leant over to print and sign her name, the photo of Angela and James still in her hand.

'Is that your husband and daughter? Don't they look alike then! Two peas in a pod, I'd say.'

Taking the form and pen from her, he turned to leave.

'See you next time, Mrs Steele.'

But Rosemary didn't hear him. She was too engrossed staring at the photo.

26

Angela

The crackling fizz of walkie-talkies bounced off the walls as Angela climbed the stairwell.

'One unidentified body, female with multiple stab wounds to the stomach and chest. Over.'

'Received and confirmed. Awaiting ID. Over.'

Curious rather than alarmed, as she approached the third floor, Angela could see several people on the landing outside a flat. The door was open forty-five degrees and she glimpsed streaks of blood on the walls in the hallway.

'You live here?' asked a policeman, his uniform a smart contrast to the squalor of his surroundings.

'No, we're just visiting someone in this block,' replied Angela as Susan came up behind her, slightly out of breath.

'What happened?' asked Susan, more to Angela than the constable.

'Can't disclose that at the moment, madam,' he responded. 'Which flat are you visiting?'

'Flat 3B – this one here, just opposite.'

'OK, well on you go then, nothing to see here.'

Susan was already ringing the doorbell but Angela had the sudden urge to bolt. A dog had started yapping and, after a few seconds, she heard footsteps. Susan had prepared her for this very moment so why did she have a bad feeling? Was it the scene in the flat opposite giving her jitters? Either way, she didn't feel ready. Her life was clean, organised and busy. When she'd first seen the council estate where her birth mother lived, she tried to hide her dismay at the flashes of graffiti, overflowing rubbish bins and blaring music. This area of London was a far cry from her own home. Susan had walked confidently past the groups of teenagers, some just loitering, some messing around on skateboards. As the sharpness of a wolf-whistle rang out across the open area of grey concrete, Angela wished she'd worn something a little subtler. She'd dressed carefully that morning, choosing a royal-blue skirt suit that hung off her slender frame and emphasised her height. She had told herself it was because she had an important client conference that day, but she wondered now if she'd wanted to convey a message to Evelyn: *Look at how well I'm doing – I didn't need you then and I don't need you now.*

'Charlie, shut it,' came a voice behind the door. The dog continued barking, but as the door swung open, Angela finally came eye to eye with the woman who had given her away.

When she looked back, she was ashamed to say that her immediate thought was that Susan had made a mistake. How could this person be related to her? Evelyn was forty-five but looked at least a decade older, her greying hair had been combed from a side parting. Her wide-set eyes – the dark shadows underneath like bruises – scanned Angela from head to toe. A cigarette hung loosely from her thin lips, the crevices around her mouth confessing a lifetime of habit. Large, gold-hooped earrings sliced through her hair on either side of her pockmarked face, while a large, heart-shaped silver pendant hung around her neck. She was dressed in a lime-green, fuzzy jumper over black leggings, her cork slippers revealing flaked gold nail polish. As they stared at each other, Angela saw something in her eyes. Fear? Disdain? Envy? Excitement? It was a flare of emotion before a hardness returned.

'Hello, Evelyn, nice to see you again. Can we come in?' said Susan warmly.

Without responding, Evelyn snapped her eyes away from Angela's to look over her shoulder at the commotion in the flat opposite.

'What the hell is going on over there?' she shouted.

The police officer turned. 'There's been an incident, madam.'

'I can bloody see that – that's not what I asked. Is that blood?'

'Unfortunately, I'm not at liberty to say.'

'Of course not. Typical,' muttered Evelyn, before turning her attention to her visitors.

'Come in, come in,' she said. She went back into the flat, leaving the door open. Angela looked at Susan questioningly. There wasn't going to be any hugging today. Nodding her head indicating for Angela to enter, Susan stepped inside the flat and they both followed Evelyn and her dog down the hallway.

'Bloody bobbies,' said Evelyn. 'I told them, I did,' she said to Susan as if to convince her. 'Even though I didn't want to.

But no one ever listens to me, do they?' She continued talking about the issues she'd been having with the neighbours as if Angela weren't even there. Susan had explained Evelyn had had a difficult past with drugs and had lived on benefits for much of her life. She'd also warned her that Evelyn could come across as slightly defensive and to tread gently, but, still, Angela found it difficult to hide her surprise.

As the sounds of her birth mother's complaints continued to drift over her, Angela looked around the flat. She guessed it had been recently cleaned as she could see a smear of furniture polish across the coffee table, yet the smell of cigarette smoke lay heavy in the air and Angela spotted a heavy glass ashtray overflowing with cigarette butts on the arm of Evelyn's chair. The dog was now sitting at his owner's feet, cleaning himself, one leg cocked in the air. Angela felt a strong desire to open a window.

'So,' started Susan, gently interrupting Evelyn, 'having spoken to you both, I'm here to help facilitate this first meeting between the two of you. Evelyn, I know Angela has a few questions. Do you think you might be up to answering—'

'Look, before you even start,' interrupted Evelyn, 'it wasn't my fault. Back in those days, we had no idea.'

Angela, too stunned to respond, was taken aback.

'Anyway, it looks like you've turned out all right, doesn't it?' continued Evelyn, nodding at Angela, before drawing on what must have been her second cigarette in a matter of minutes. 'I doubt you'd have turned out so well if you'd stayed wi' me.'

She laughed, a cackle that sounded hollow to Angela's ears, and Angela knew then that Evelyn was nervous.

'So, a solicitor, eh? That's what Susan said you do. Bet you get paid lots of money an' all.'

'I work in the City,' acknowledged Angela, ignoring the reference to her salary.

'Fancy,' smirked Evelyn. 'Anyway, so what do you want to know? I'm not sure how much I can tell you because I was out of it for most of the time.'

Angela looked at Evelyn questioningly.

'Giving birth,' clarified Evelyn impatiently. 'I presume that's one of the things you want to know. It's not like it is today with all these new-fangled ideas.'

Curiosity piqued, Angela waited for her to continue.

Sensing her interest, Evelyn seemed to straighten up a little. Angela realised that despite her abruptness, Evelyn liked being the centre of attention.

'Well, like I said,' she began, 'I was eighteen back then and quite frankly I had no idea about anything. It was the early sixties and free love was all the rage – anything went. Things like AIDS didn't even exist, and pregnancy was something that only happened to bad girls.' Evelyn rolled her eyes.

'It was only one morning when I struggled to fit into my clothes that I thought something might be up,' she continued. 'I mentioned it to Jackie – we were close – I had grown up with her and we went around together, although Mother didn't approve. Not that she approved much of anything, mind. We used to sneak out at night and go to nightclubs. I'd been seeing Jimmy then for almost a year and most people thought of us as a couple. He gave me this pendant – vintage, it is now,' smiled Evelyn, fingering the heavy silver between her fingers. 'Probably worth a bob or two, an' all. Anyway, I didn't really believe Jackie when she said I might be pregnant but as I got bigger and bigger, I knew she was right. I was terrified. Mother never forgave me but she dealt with it like she deals with everything – only thinking about herself.

Stone-cold, that woman is. Mother made up some cock-and-bull story about me being offered a live-in service job and then sent me to St Anne's Mother & Baby Home. It's not there any more but they used to take women in and arrange for the babies to go to children's homes. It was hell, but what alternative did I have? I managed to get a message to Jimmy through Jackie. She told me he'd said he would sneak in to come and see me but whether he got caught I don't know, as I never saw him again.'

Jimmy. Her parents had not said much about her birth father – mainly because they had had very little information themselves – only that he hadn't been present at the birth.

At his name, Angela was assailed by a memory from her time at the children's home. Going to bed, she would imagine that Marlon Brando were her real father. In her fantasy, he would find and rescue her, all the while apologising over and over for leaving her. It was a technique she used to help her fall asleep, her mind able to conjure up all sorts of pleasurable possibilities that were a world away from her current reality. As she remembered, she wondered why she held her birth mother solely accountable for giving her up while romanticising the role of her birth father. Was it unfair? Perhaps, but this woman who sat before her, smoking her cigarettes, complaining, and generally playing victim, had carried her for nine months. Evelyn knew her before she even arrived into the world; knew when she liked to sleep and when she liked to kick and play. Evelyn would have put her hands on her belly, feeling life grow within, the roar of motherhood – promising to protect – already coursing through her body. So why hadn't her birth mother listened? Did Evelyn even feel an inkling of remorse? She didn't appear to.

Angela saw Evelyn look out of the window as if lost in her past. For a brief moment, Evelyn's face softened, and Angela saw the woman that Evelyn perhaps once was – young, vibrant and in love.

'Can you tell me a bit more about Jimmy?' asked Angela, still unsure if she wanted to shatter her childhood celebrity illusion.

'Not really,' replied Evelyn unhelpfully. 'He was a bit of a cad, if truth be known. He was good-looking, that's for sure. All the girls wanted him, so I was feeling rather pleased with myself that he'd chosen me. He'd grand ideas about his future. Ha! Can you imagine! He worked in his dad's family business, but he never took it seriously. The last I heard of him was that he'd managed to wangle his way into a sales job. That was Jimmy: could talk his way into – and out of – anything,' she added ruefully.

Angela wondered if she looked like him. Although she didn't see any similarity between herself and Evelyn, she had the sudden urge to ask her if she had a photo from when she was younger before the drugs got her.

'But Jimmy never did the right thing, did he?' continued Evelyn, her face hardening. 'Never asked me to marry 'im, did he?' she said, looking at Angela as if it were all her fault. 'No. Obviously off with someone else and I never heard from him again.'

The room went silent.

'That must have been very difficult for you,' said Susan softly, her over-used response an annoying catchphrase to Angela's ears.

'Well, what could I do?' said Evelyn, turning to Susan. 'Life isn't rainbows and unicorns. I had to get on with it and do the best I could.

'Anyway,' said Evelyn, recovering, 'typical fella, if you ask me: got away with murder. He was a handsome chap in those days – probably still is. Men – they don't need to deal with anything really, do they? And childbirth! Well, don't even get me started on that. Back then, it was brutal. I don't remember much of it, thank God, as they drugged me up to keep me quiet. It didn't do any good for the other girls, you see, to hear us shouting our heads off in agony.'

For one brief moment, all three women were quiet.

'They didn't even let me hold you,' continued Evelyn quietly, staring off into the distance. 'Just whisked you off while I was passed out. Apparently, I didn't wake up until the next morning. I took a few days to recover and then I left that place as fast as I could.'

As Angela entered her own home, the all-white décor a soothing welcome, she felt exhausted. She'd imagined that after meeting Evelyn she would feel an element of closure or at least some relief. She'd concentrated so hard on finding Evelyn that she'd not given as much thought as to what would happen next. Instead, she felt like Lucy entering Narnia in *The Lion, the Witch and the Wardrobe*. When she was growing up in a children's home, her birth mother was someone very far away, almost mystical. While the home was tough, there was a sense of camaraderie amongst the children, a bond that had united them in their situation almost as tightly as an umbilical cord. Meeting Evelyn had also made her hyperaware that her adoptive parents had not brought her into the world, even though she loved them, called them Mum and Dad, and had her milestones documented in family albums.

As Angela sat at her mirrored dresser, applying night cream, she knew that Evelyn was nothing like her. She had expected to see some sort of similarity – a gesture or perhaps similar features, the curve of a jawline, or an eye colour – but there was nothing. Nothing that Angela could see, anyway. She had gone into this hoping she could build some sort of relationship with Evelyn, but she was just a stranger. Angela couldn't see how they could be a part of each other's worlds; the gap just seemed too big. They were like two jigsaw pieces that didn't fit together even though they were part of the same puzzle. Getting into bed, Angela felt disappointed, but not surprised, at the absence of connection, and as she closed her eyes she tried to ignore the sliver of resentment that sat in its place.

27

Dear Diary,

I woke up last night to a huge commotion. It sounded like someone was breaking in. The littlies in the dorm were scared. I told them to keep quiet while I tiptoed to the top of the stairs. Peter had the same idea. We could see the top of Ray's balding head as he stumbled around the hallway. He'd probably just come in from the pub and had too many. Maureen had followed me out and I whispered to her to go and settle the others and reassure them it was just Ray, drunk from a night out. As I turned to follow her, I tripped on my nightie and almost fell down the stairs. Peter managed to catch my arm, but not before Ray glanced up. He had a nasty grin on his face when he saw us. 'Oi,' he shouted. 'What're the pair of you up to? Doing things you're not supposed to? Get down here NOW.' His words slurred together and he was already removing his belt. I was terrified. I had seen what he was capable of sober – what would he do when drunk?

Slowly, I started to walk down the stairs, but I felt Peter's hand on my arm stopping me. Not this time, he seemed to be saying. Before I could stop him, he rushed down the stairs towards Ray, knocking him to the floor. Peter had grown a lot as a teenager but he was still no match for Ray and, despite being drunk, Ray turned on him and was on top of Peter in moments. I couldn't just stand there, so I ran down the stairs and tried to drag him off. Ray was punching him over and over again and I was afraid he was going to kill him. I looked around and saw the telephone book. I grabbed it, and I hit Ray across the side of his head as hard as I could. It didn't do very much but it did stop the beating. Peter was covered in blood – he wouldn't be able to take much more. He was groaning on the floor while Ray stumbled around holding his head. Rushing over to Peter, I tried to think, but there was so much blood everywhere. Where was Mark? Why didn't he come downstairs? Maybe he was out. I started to clean Peter's face with my nightie. Behind me, I could hear Ray swearing. He was furious. I turned to look at him and his face was contorted into pure evil. Forcing Peter to sit upright, he dragged him to a chair. There was a skipping rope that one of the littlies had left by the door and he used it to tie Peter up. Not that he was going anywhere – he was a mess. Ray used the back of his hand to knock me to the floor and it was a few moments before I realised what he was going to do. As he undid his trousers, I felt sick. It was my first time. He was heavy and I struggled to breathe. I was fighting him, twisting to try and get out from under him, and as

I turned my head towards the stairs, I saw Kath at the top watching. She saw me looking at her and she quickly hurried away. I swore then that even if it took me a lifetime, I would find and destroy everyone who had hurt me – including my so-called mother who had left me in this hellhole.

A.

Sunday, 24 August 1975

Dear Diary,

I haven't written for months. There doesn't seem to be much point. I don't remember very much after that night – the fight between Ray and Peter and what followed. Ray told Kath to take Peter to hospital and say he got into a fight in town. I prayed that Peter would find the strength to tell the doctors what had happened but I was doubtful. We had tried it with the Inspector and it had backfired on all of us. All I feel is hate.

A.

Monday, 25 August 1975

Dear Diary,

It was a bank holiday today and Keith wanted me to come into work. He said the bar was going to be busy and to get my sexiest outfit on if I wanted lots of tips. I was just happy to be out of the house. Ray and Kath only speak to me to give instructions. The newspapers are still full of the murder and kidnap of Lesley Whittle. I hope they catch the man who did it and kill him on sight. People like that don't deserve to live.

A.

Sunday, 14 December 1975

Dear Diary,

I am writing less and less in this diary but I don't care. I haven't really had any good things to write about. But over the last few weeks, two things happened. 1. The police caught the murderer of Lesley Whittle. They call him the Black Panther in the press. I hope he rots in Hell. 2. Mark sneaked me out to my first concert to see the Sex Pistols. It was amazing, and for the first time in my life I felt free. Mark gave me a pill, which he called LSD. He told me it was like weed but better and he was right! Mark said when I turn fifteen next month he will take me clubbing for my birthday.

A.

28

Evelyn

Evelyn shut the front door with a sigh of relief. She knew she hadn't handled meeting Angela as well as she'd have liked, but the scene behind Angela and Susan when she had opened her front door had shaken her to the core. The police were literally everywhere. How had it come to this? She'd only wanted to make the noise stop and now she had the boys in blue all over the estate. Her neighbours would never forgive her if they found out she had called them. It wouldn't be long before they were at her door asking questions. And then when she saw the bloodied streaks down the walls, she felt panicked. Murder? It looked like something out of a scene from one of her TV shows.

Evelyn had fought the instinct to flee and instead had forced her attention on the young woman on her doorstep. This couldn't possibly be her daughter. She looked completely out of place, a peacock against the dank grey stairwell. As she took in Angela's immaculate blow-dried hair and her undoubtedly expensive outfit, Evelyn scrabbled in vain for even a whisper of maternal love for the child she had given up all those years ago. Instead, she tasted the sourness of spite that this woman who stood in front of her today had clearly succeeded in life. Evelyn felt meaningless, as if her life had been for nothing, which she supposed in a way it had. She took no joy or pleasure at the sight of her daughter. While she had given birth to Angela, it was somebody else who had raised her and only they could feel that wonderful sense of parental pride at having done the hardest job in the world – raising a child to become a successful, confident adult. All at once, Evelyn felt a jealousy so intense towards the woman who had clearly succeeded in the gamble of motherhood that she'd had to walk away, leaving Angela and Susan to follow her.

She had attempted to relax during the meeting but the more she tried, the stiffer she became. As a result, she feared her words came across as defensive, stilted and brittle. Ironically, she was annoyed to realise that she sounded just like Mother. Well, they say it happened to every woman at some point in their lives. It was hardly likely to happen to Angela, though: the woman was like an ice queen in her composure.

As her daughter sat down on the sofa, her long, slim legs elegantly placed to one side, for the first time in her life Evelyn suddenly saw her home as an outsider might see it: messy and disorganised. She'd given it a once-over with the duster and the Hoover but Angela's presence seemed to highlight every speck of dirt.

Nervously, Evelyn had drawn another cigarette out of the packet that sat on the arm of her chair and inhaled deeply. She had been talking too quickly and she could sense Susan looking at her, but Evelyn's only thought was to prove to Angela how different times had been back then. She knew she was coming across in a factual, practical manner, but she just didn't have the words to express her true feelings during the birth and the aftermath. They had been buried for so long and she had had years of practice at suppressing them. And what had made her go on so much about Jimmy? Probably the necklace. She hadn't worn it in years but it seemed appropriate to wear it that day being as he'd gifted it to her all those years ago. She'd planned to give it to Angela, a sentimental offering that seemed ridiculous in hindsight. She had been glad that she'd held onto it. It was a valuable reminder of the traitorous coward Jimmy was. What kind of man left his girl to deal with a pregnancy? A pregnancy he had convinced her would never happen in the first place? Yes, her mother was a pain in the backside, but she'd been right about one thing: Jimmy would break her heart and leave her in ruins.

Evelyn sighed. Well, it was done now; the first meeting was over. It was unlikely Angela would want to see her again anyway, and that was probably best all round.

As soon as Angela and Susan had left, Evelyn poured herself a generous measure of vodka, letting her secret hope of a second chance dissolve in the clear liquid.

The shot of vodka had done its job and Evelyn got up from her armchair to try to find out more about what had happened at 3A. She peered through the peephole of her front door and could see the policeman still standing there. Evelyn was torn. She wanted to ask the constable what was happening, but if her neighbours saw her talking to him…

The door of the flat opposite was still open, and if she cricked her neck to the right slightly she could just see the streaks of blood in the hallway. Just then, a man came up the stairs dressed in plain clothes – was he a detective? His beige trench coat certainly made him look like the detectives she'd seen on telly. He spoke at length with the policeman standing guard before slipping on gloves and shoe covers and entering the flat. Was he collecting evidence? Evelyn felt uneasy. It was only recently that she'd been banging on their door and shouting obscenities. Would they suspect her in all of this?

Several minutes passed with Evelyn glued to the peephole. She didn't want to miss anything. It was a good twenty minutes before the detective came back out, removing his gloves and shaking his head. He talked again to the policeman, but Evelyn was unable to catch what was said. But she didn't need to hear to know. As the policeman spoke into his walkie-talkie, a procession of wheeled stretchers left the flat, each carrying what she assumed was a lifeless body covered from head to toe in black material. Evelyn hadn't realised she was holding her breath, but as she counted three bodies in total, she understood just how serious this was. She was used to the odd fight breaking out; she'd even seen someone glassed once – incredibly unpleasant. She was used to shouting and swearing between neighbours, the secret passing of small packages as the lads plied their trade of cheap weed and God knows what else, but murder? This was something else completely, and the fact that it was happening right on her doorstep gave Evelyn a tingle that surpassed even the Christmas Day soap specials. As the police officer closed the door to the flat and started to put up the crime scene tape, Evelyn scurried off to phone Doreen.

It was while she was halfway through her description of the bodies (had she really told Doreen that one of the bodies was so badly mutilated that one of the arms was hanging off the side of the stretcher?) that Evelyn realised she would have to prepare herself for questioning by the police. Despite her enjoyment of her neighbour's rapt attention, she quickly ended the conversation and hung up before beginning to pace the kitchen.

What would she say? They would have her noise complaint on record, of course, but she didn't need to tell them about the various times she'd gone over there banging and shouting. Billy had seen her do it, though. And what about Dougie? Would it get back to the police that she'd tried to get him to intimidate them in some way? If the police questioned any of the other flat occupants about her thoughts towards her neighbours, they would all concur that Evelyn had a vendetta towards them. She hadn't exactly been discreet about it.

Evelyn could feel the sweat gather in her armpits. She had to admit that while she wouldn't wish such a gruesome death on anyone, she wasn't sorry to see them go. Perhaps a nice gentleman would move in – someone around her age who would take her out once in a while. Yes, Evelyn decided, they could do with a nice man around the place, someone to do the odd jobs and keep a protective eye out for her. Perhaps she wouldn't mention that to the police. But one thing was for sure: she would not be telling them about the spare key she still had from when the previous tenants lived there.

29

Rosemary

Rosemary dressed carefully, pulling the jumper over her silk blouse. She didn't feel like going to her monthly WI coffee morning in Cirencester but she knew it was important to keep up her own routine. It's how their marriage functioned, survived even. James had always said he loved her intelligence and independence and the fact that she wasn't waiting around for him.

The only exception had been when they'd adopted Angela. It was Rosemary who had given up her job as a civil servant then. They'd never discussed it; it was just assumed, even by Rosemary herself. And while she didn't regret it, she sometimes wondered where she would be today if she'd continued working. She didn't blame James either. His business was expanding, and he was incredibly busy. She knew James enjoyed life, but when Angela moved in, Rosemary sensed a contentment in James that she had never seen before. It was a relief really. There was always the worry that a child would add pressure, but she couldn't deny that Angela's presence brought out the very best in him. He would even come home early from work sometimes, which he had never done before during their married life.

As Rosemary sat at her dresser, she combed her hair and added a touch of lipstick. She'd used a particular light pink shade since her blond hair had started showing signs of grey. She never dyed it but she went into London every couple of months to get it cut on Bond Street, an indulgence that she was happy to pay for. Now as she looked at herself in the mirror, she saw the effort had paid off and she felt ready to face the day.

As Rosemary left Cirencester, she felt relieved she'd done her community duty. She'd undertaken the role of chairman for the WI Federation for many years, but a couple of years ago she'd decided to enjoy just being a member. There were over twenty ladies that morning, and as usual, she was sitting between Eileen and Mary.

At fifty-three, Mary was the same age as Rosemary, whereas Eileen was a few years older. She'd met Eileen in the local post office in Tetbury, her big blow-dried auburn hair and matching red lipstick almost too much against the ordinary Saturday morning of village life. But Rosemary, having learnt Eileen had just moved with her husband from Birmingham to be closer to their daughter, had invited her to the local WI group that evening and even offered to drive her there. When Rosemary picked her up, Eileen had sidled into the passenger seat in a cloud of perfume and glamour. In that moment, Rosemary, in her expensive but sensible trousers and twinset, felt old and she almost regretted her invitation. But she'd never forgotten that car journey, mainly because she couldn't ever remember laughing so much; she'd actually had to stop the car at one point. And while there had been a few side-long glances when she'd first introduced Eileen to the members of WI, by the end of the meeting, she had won them all over.

Mary, on the other hand, was and always had been a stalwart of Tetbury life, having grown up with Rosemary. Although they had each taken very different paths at the age of eighteen, they had remained close. Even when Rosemary had gone off to university while Mary had got married and had children, they had written to each other every week. Rosemary still had all the letters up in the loft somewhere. When she told Mary about her parents' disapproval of James, she didn't need to explain the reasons why; Mary already knew. Growing up together, sharing everything but the same DNA, their experiences and values were similar. And while Rosemary had married against her parents' wishes, Mary had given neither advice nor approval, but as she stood by her side at her wedding, Rosemary knew she had a friend for life.

As Rosemary, Eileen and Mary sat with four other women at their craft table, talk had turned to family, as it often did. Rosemary remembered when it was their children's lives that dominated the conversation and she still felt a thrill when she shared her own anecdotes, the stories often retold and familiar, but still comforting. But today, as if seeing the group of women for the first time, she wondered when the focus had moved on to grandchildren.

They had just celebrated the arrival of Edith's first grandchild last month and with a start, she realised she was the only one in the group who didn't have grandchildren. She felt a distasteful mix of disappointment and competitiveness. Is this how her own mother had felt? Was Angela running out of time? At twenty-seven years old, she was pushing it, but she had never so much as hinted to Angela; her own mother's impatience still stung to this day. Yet had her mother been right? Is that why Rosemary had struggled with pregnancy? The doctor had never said that in so many words but still... she had often wondered if her own ambition was the cause of her infertility. Angela had once said that she had no desire to become a mother, a statement Rosemary had ignored at the time as a combination of youthful ignorance and her experience in a children's home. All women wanted children, didn't they? But as she sat listening to Edith's description of little Matthew's feeding habits, Rosemary thought about grandchildren, wondering if history would repeat itself and whether once more she would be denied a baby in her arms.

30

Evelyn

Evelyn was pleased. She'd won two rounds of bingo and the barman had given her a drink on the house. That was a good night, in her book. Bingo was every Tuesday and Saturday, and Evelyn rarely missed it. She liked the feel of the bingo card in her hand, the rhyming slang of the bingo caller – *Knock at the door, twenty-four!* – and that tingling anticipation as she crossed out her numbers. Saturday tended to be busier than Tuesday, which meant fewer chances to win, but she still enjoyed it. If it was raining, she took the bus as it was a good thirty-minute walk, but if the weather was bearable she walked, and she normally picked up Brenda, who lived down the road.

Evelyn hadn't told her about meeting Angela, or that she even had a child at all, for that matter. It was a strange feeling because, for all their jibes and sarcasm with each other, she was her closest friend, based on a lifetime of shared love of TV soaps and bingo, disdain for the middle classes and the unwavering belief that they were the victims of Margaret Thatcher's Britain. They could spend hours talking about the news and gossip of the day, usually picked up from the daily papers.

They had been friends for years and they used to be neighbours. However, Brenda had recently managed to persuade the council to put her on a nicer estate in a ground-floor flat, due to her arthritis, although Brenda seemed to manage to get about just fine when she wanted to. Still, when her friend had shown Evelyn around her new place, Evelyn had to admit, with the small garden terrace, it had been nice sitting outside and having a cup of tea.

She'd wanted to say something then to Brenda about her birth daughter but what would she say? Evelyn wouldn't have known where to start. Besides it didn't look like it was going to go much further so what was the point in dredging it all up? No, it was better to get back to focusing on her own life.

She had gone to see Alan to put in yet another claim to the council for a better flat, but so far nothing had come of it. At this rate, she might have to develop arthritis as well, thought Evelyn. Wasn't it just the other day that her legs were playing up? Yet, all thoughts of aches and pains were forgotten as Evelyn contentedly strolled home after dropping Brenda off, the envelope full of prize money safely in her handbag. It was dark and Evelyn was looking forward to getting home and reading the magazines Doreen had dropped off earlier. They had decided long ago to buy different ones each month and then swap them as a means of saving money.

Hornsey Lane was always noisy with traffic, but still, she felt rather than heard someone behind her: brisk footsteps that echoed her own. She quickened her pace, clutching her handbag harder under her arm. A small stone hit the back of her leg, but she didn't stop. Who the hell was it? The footsteps came nearer and nearer. She was almost there – she could see the estate now.

But it was too late.

Out of the corner of her eye, a black-hooded figure was almost upon her. Instinctively, Evelyn whirled round, arms outstretched to ward him off. But the figure propelled past her, leaving Evelyn feeling foolish and breathless as the stranger fled into the darkness. Perhaps there was no intention to harm her – he or she was just impatient? Still, her heartbeat had quickened, and her hackles were raised. She had the savvy sense of a Londoner and couldn't shake the feeling she'd just narrowly avoided being mugged.

Finally crossing the estate to her block, Evelyn saw with relief the streetlamps were on. Whoever it was had given her a scare and she wasn't going to take any chances. She knew incidents happened all the time on the estate, normally between neighbours, but when they did, most people had an idea of who had done what and it was usually all sorted out. The faceless stranger had unnerved Evelyn and she quickly climbed the stairs to her flat, double-locking the door and fastening the windows before collapsing into her armchair, cigarette and vodka in one hand and Charlie on her lap.

31

Angela

It was a Saturday morning and Angela was in Tetbury again. She'd come up on the train yesterday afternoon. She was relieved to see her dad was looking much better this time. Apart from the weight loss, a stranger wouldn't suspect he was suffering from a devastating illness. But still, Angela saw him taking daytime naps instead of reading the newspaper, his moments of confusion where there used to be clarity, her mother's hearty meals gradually getting smaller and smaller as his appetite dwindled.

Some mornings James would sleep late, such as today, so Angela was having coffee with her mum. Despite it being November, it was a bright, clear day and they were sitting out in the garden, wrapped up warmly, the white wrought-iron chairs softened with cushions against their backs.

As she breathed in the air, so different from the smells of London, Angela took in the country landscape. But it was the garden that had first captured her attention all those years ago. Even today, it still took her breath away. It didn't matter what season it was, it was full of life and her parents' pride and joy. When Angela had first seen it, she had been amazed. She hadn't known such beauty could exist within reach of the capital. Her world had consisted of the commotion and clamour of the children's home and school, her only quiet escape being the school library. But here, just over a couple of hours away, was a garden from a storybook. Swathes of blooms in every colour had been planted in curvaceous flowerbeds, while long stretches of grass were interrupted with tinkling fountains, Romanesque bird feeders, and even a loveseat. It was full of life and around every corner was a surprise: the unexpected flutter of a butterfly, the ripeness of a new tomato or the first cluster of snowdrops, depending on the season. As a teenager, Angela had never tired of exploring it. In the summer evenings, her dad used to walk her round the garden telling her the names of the different plants and flowers: 'The Daffodil Jetfire, although I prefer its botanical name, Narcissus. It just suits it, don't you think, the way the flower leans over as if looking at its reflection?'

The memory made her smile. When was the last time she had walked around the garden with him? Had he asked her during one of her recent visits? Angela couldn't remember. She made a vow to walk with him before she left that weekend.

'How are you managing with the garden, Mum?' she asked now.

'Well, your father still likes to keep his hand in, but he tires after an hour. I was thinking I might get some help in, but...'

Angela looked at Rosemary questioningly.

'You know... it would feel like giving in, I suppose.' She shrugged. 'Silly really.'

'Not at all. Perhaps we can all do a little this weekend if the weather stays like this?'

Rosemary smiled. 'Yes, your father would like that. You'll have to borrow some of my overalls, though!'

Angela looked down at her outfit. Mum had a point. Even though it was a weekend, she had a silk, cerise-coloured, button-down shirt over a fitted skirt, and her small waist was emphasised with a wide belt. Angela loved clothes, and she especially loved them now that she had the money to buy them. She suspected it was a result of never owning anything when she was growing up in the children's home. Most of her clothes had been hand-me-downs – even her underwear – and there was always something wrong with them: they never fitted properly, or they had stains that wouldn't come out, or they were old-fashioned. Angela involuntarily shivered at the memory. Apart from when she had been reading her old diaries, she hardly ever thought about her time at the children's home. Those days were long gone. Yet her meetings with Susan and finding Evelyn were bringing up memories that she thought she had securely locked away. She thought back to the day before when she'd updated her parents on her meeting with Evelyn. It was the first thing her dad had asked her when she stepped through the door.

'Give her a minute, James, to get settled – she's only just got in!' Mum had exclaimed.

But it was good to see him excited about something, and they had all sat down in the living room.

'How did it go?'

Angela looked at her mum, seeing concern but also something else. Fear?

'It was...' Angela searched for the right word. How was it? Disappointing? Confusing? Shocking?

She settled for 'strange'.

'It was strange, really. Evelyn wasn't at all how I expected her to be.'

'How did you imagine her?' asked Dad.

'Well, like us, really...' Angela hesitated. 'Like me. Does that sound absurd?'

'Of course not. It's hard to imagine someone when you've never seen or experienced that person before, so your brain probably just goes with what it's used to. It's good that Susan was there to support you,' he reassured.

'Yes, she was a great help. I trust her a lot.'

Angela had recounted the conversation she'd had with Susan after the visit.

'How are you feeling, Angela? I can't imagine that was easy for you,' Susan had said as they started to walk down the hill back towards Archway station.

'No, it wasn't really, but at least it's over now.'

'I know. But the meeting went better than I expected.'

'Really?' responded Angela in surprise.

'Yes, of course,' Susan said firmly. 'I'm sure you were slightly taken aback by her character, but I suspect there's a lot more to Evelyn than meets the eye.'

'She does seem rather... tough,' said Angela, trying to find the right word.

'Yes, it's not unusual, though. Women who have given up their babies for adoption sometimes come from challenging backgrounds where there was little support. It's still a fairly taboo subject, even today, so you can imagine what it was like when you were born in 1961.'

'I suppose,' replied Angela. 'I just thought she might be a bit more... you know...'

Susan looked at her. 'Apologetic? Loving?' she suggested.

'Well, yes,' replied Angela, relieved not to have to spell it out. 'She just didn't seem to care that much really.'

'I know. It's only natural. But in all my years of doing this, I've never met a mother who didn't care. Young and naïve? Yes. Uneducated and ill-prepared? Absolutely. Ashamed? No doubt. But hopefully today is a new start – a chance to build a relationship and foster understanding. I'm not saying it will be an easy road, but you have the opportunity, which is more than most.'

Angela didn't respond. Stopping, Susan had placed a gentle hand on Angela's arm. 'At the end of the day, Angela, you are in complete control of this situation. Whatever you want or don't want to do, I will support you a hundred per cent,' she said gently.

'I know. Thank you,' Angela had replied.

'If you would like me to arrange another meeting for you, just let me know. I can be there as well, if you would like, or if you feel up to it you can perhaps meet Evelyn on your own.'

Angela had been in two minds. 'I'm seeing my parents this weekend. I might talk it through with them and then I'll let you know.'

And now here she was, in Tetbury, spending time with people who had devoted their life to her and she felt guilty that her thoughts were on someone who hadn't done that. James and Rosemary had had so much love to give and so much to share. They hadn't just wanted to fill a gap in their lives, they truly wanted to help.

'Anyway,' said Angela, 'I said I would talk it over with you and Dad first and decide the next steps.'

'Well, of course you have to see her again,' announced Dad. 'Tell her, Rosemary.'

Rosemary frowned at James before turning to Angela.

'One step at a time, darling,' her mum replied. 'What are your options?'

'Well, to meet again and try to develop some sort of relationship is one option…' said Angela, trailing off.

'And the other?' asked Rosemary.

'To leave it be.'

'I see. And how are you feeling about it at the moment?'

'Honestly, I don't know. I thought I would be a lot more interested to pursue it, but now that I've met her…' She sighed. 'We just don't seem to have a lot in common,' Angela confessed with a shrug.

'Well,' replied her mum, 'it was only one meeting and you were probably both very nervous. It seems a shame to close the door when you've come this far.'

'Absolutely,' James agreed.

'On the other hand,' Rosemary continued, 'you've met her now, so perhaps you know all you need to know.'

Angela looked up in surprise at the sudden change in tack. She was just about to respond when Rosemary got up and headed to the kitchen. 'Right, well, I'd best get the lunch started.'

And just like that the conversation was over, and Angela and her dad were left staring after her.

32

Saturday, 24 January 1976

Dear Diary,

I turned fifteen a few days ago. Kath and Ray didn't do anything, but I didn't expect them to. Peter gave me a book called *First Term at Malory Towers*, which I've hidden under my mattress to read later. It looks quite childish and he probably stole it, but it was nice of him to make the effort. He has changed a lot over the last few months. He used to be confident, with lots of backchat, but now he's quiet and thoughtful and keeps himself to himself. I think he would be quite shocked if he found out I sneaked out last night. Mark kept his promise and took me clubbing. When we got there, the music was really loud, and it was dark inside the club. But it was so cold outside I was just happy to be indoors. Mark gave me another tab, and within minutes I could feel the music like it was inside me – it was incredible. We danced all night long and missed the last bus, so we had to walk home. The strange thing is I didn't feel the cold at all on the way back.

A.

Thursday, 25 March 1976

Dear Diary,

Mark has gone. Packed up all his stuff and left. Kath informed the Inspector, but because of his age, there's not much that can be done. I can't believe he's left me here. I don't know how I'm going to survive in this place without him. Our secret meetings and nights out were the only things that kept me from going under. Where am I going to get my smokes from? Why didn't he tell me? Why has he just taken off without a word to anyone?

A.

Monday, 19 April 1976

Dear Diary,

There's a lot of excitement as Kath and Ray just told everyone that they have a couple visiting this week who wants to adopt. It will be one of the babies or the littlies that get picked as usual. I hope they pick Julia – out of everyone she could really do with a loving home. She's so frightened of everything and often comes into my bed at night. Ray says he'll be happy just to have one less brat to deal with.

A.

33

Rosemary

Rosemary tried to conceal her irritation. They had been waiting almost two hours and, after checking with reception for the second time, there was still no further update on when the consultant would see them. When James had first been diagnosed she'd anticipated the fear and the worry, but what she hadn't expected was how time-consuming it would all be. It felt like they lived half their life at the hospital, most of it just hanging around. As usual, the waiting room was busy, and every time the consultant's door opened, it was like a pebble being dropped into a pond, the anticipation as to who would be called in next rippling across the room.

She'd read all the magazines and had mentally rearranged the room to make it more comfortable and welcoming. Gone were the rows of hard seating, cheap tiled flooring and posters about the dangers of smoking. Instead, Rosemary passed the time picturing comfortable armchairs next to shelves of inspirational books and walls lined with a series of beautiful watercolours. The centrepiece would be a large aquarium, the mesmerising, colourful fish dissolving the long hours.

She looked over at James, who was reading his book, her annoyance magnified by the fact that she'd left hers at home.

'Mr Steele?' announced the nurse. Finally, thought Rosemary. Gathering up her handbag and coat, she automatically took James's hand and followed the nurse.

Rosemary considered herself an intelligent woman but even she was struggling to comprehend what Mr Redding was saying. There seemed to be no concrete answer to any of their questions. His responses were vague, reluctant to commit to anything. Instead, he spoke of optimism and living life to the full. Easy for you to say, thought Rosemary resentfully. As she watched Mr Redding shuffle through his papers, she sensed the appointment drawing to a close. She wondered how long they'd been in the room – fifteen minutes? Twenty? And all they'd learnt was that James's chemotherapy was going as well as could be expected. If she heard that phrase one more time, she would scream.

'Right, I think that's everything for now,' confirmed Mr Redding. 'Did you have any other questions before I get the nurse to do your blood tests?'

'No, Doctor, thank you,' replied James, about to get up from his chair.

Rosemary didn't move and out of the corner of her eye, she saw James hesitate and could almost hear him groan inwardly. While he just wanted to get in and out of their appointments as quickly as possible, Rosemary felt the need for more answers.

'I know there are no guarantees, but can you at least give *some* indication on survival rates with cancer of this type?' she asked now.

'As I've said before, Mrs Steele, it's very hard to tell. But look at the positives: James is healthy, this is his first major illness, and we caught it early—'

'Yes, of course,' interrupted Rosemary, having heard it all before and not caring any more that she might be coming across as rude. 'But what I'd really like to know is the chance of survival. There must be *something* you can share with us?'

'Yes, there are statistics, but I just don't know how helpful they will be to you.' He sat back in his chair, fingers interlinked, confident in his position of authority.

Rosemary waited, making it clear she wasn't moving until she'd got something out of him.

'OK, if you insist. Almost fifty per cent of people survive for at least five years after diagnosis.'

No one spoke and Rosemary wondered what James was thinking.

'As I said, Mrs Steele, the best we can do is keep going with the treatment and stay positive,' reiterated Mr Redding.

Rosemary nodded, still trying to take it in. Five years?

'Now, blood tests, Mr Steele,' said the consultant, picking up the file. 'I have your blood type listed down here somewhere. Ah, here we go – O negative. Mrs Steele, are you aware of your blood type? You also have a daughter, don't you? It's always useful to have immediate relatives on file, just in case.'

'I'm A,' replied Rosemary, 'and our daughter is O negative. She's our adopted daughter, though.'

'I see. Right, Mr Steele – the nurse will take you now for your blood tests. I'll see you for a follow-up in a month's time.'

'Thank you, Doctor,' replied James, standing up and firmly taking his wife by the hand.

34

Evelyn

'And then he barged into me as he walked past. Well, I say it was a he, I didn't manage to get a look at the face. He was wearing one of these hoodie things.'

'Bloody awful, what goes on these days,' said Brenda. 'Hooligans, the lot of them.'

'Thought he was after my bingo money,' added Evelyn. 'And there was no way I was going to give that up!'

'We need every penny we can get these days,' agreed Brenda. 'Your estate seems to be getting worse, Evie, what with the murders opposite your flat and now almost being mugged. You need to get onto the council again about getting a flat in a better area.'

As Evelyn settled herself onto Brenda's sofa (also new, she noted enviously) with a cup of tea, she knew Brenda was right. But what could she do? She'd tried with Alan, but they were both aware it was a complete waste of time.

Brenda had moved on to complaining about the increase in price of British Rail season tickets. She had a son, Neil, who lived up in Manchester. He had met and married a girl from there, much to his mother's disappointment, and she had been on the receiving end of her friend's utter incredulity that anyone would want to move to a place full of depressed people who owned ferrets. Still, despite her constant emotional wrangling with her son to move back to London, Brenda had bitten the bullet and visited – she'd had to as she wanted to see her beloved grandson, Daniel – and now regularly travelled on the train to that place where *people were too friendly for their own good*. Evelyn rarely left London and was quite happy for it to stay that way, but she enjoyed hearing Brenda's stories. She wondered what it must feel like to have a grandchild. Angela didn't have children, but if she did would that make her a grandmother? Biologically, yes... but being as she didn't have a relationship with Angela, it was unlikely she would ever get to meet a grandchild.

'Earth to Evelyn!'

Evelyn snapped out of her reverie.

'Have you had a cheeky tipple this morning, Evie?' asked Brenda. 'You seem a bit out of it – it's early even for you!' she joked.

Evelyn had in fact had a quick shot before she left the house. It had taken a while for her to get to sleep and when she did, she had nightmares about a faceless stranger chasing her with knives. Evelyn had slept with a chair wedged against her bedroom door that night.

'Of course not!' she lied. 'But you're right – with everything going on, who could blame me?'

Putting her empty cup on the coffee table, Evelyn reluctantly pulled herself up from the sofa.

'Right, I best get off then, Brenda, otherwise Charlie will be wondering where I am. I'll pick you up for bingo tomorrow?'

'Yes, I'll be ready. Shall I order us a taxi back, so you don't have to walk that last stretch on your own?' asked Brenda.

Evelyn was tempted. But then, that fiver would chip into her vodka money.

'I'll be OK,' she replied. 'He's probably long gone now anyway.'

'You're probably right,' reassured Brenda, seeing her out of the door. 'Still, give me three rings when you get home, so I know you've made it.'

'Will do. See you tomorrow.'

Whether it was because Evelyn was lost in her own thoughts or struggling to get the key in the door, she didn't hear the tread of light footsteps as they slowly crept up behind her, watching her every move. The postman had already been before Evelyn left to go to Brenda's, so she was curious about the letter that lay on the floor as she opened the front door. There was no stamp so it must have been hand-delivered. At first, Evelyn presumed it was a note from Doreen. But as she read the stark black letters, offensive against the cheap, bright white paper, the stranger paused on the landing one floor below, watching and waiting.

I KNOW WHAT YOU DID AND YOU WILL PAY.

35

Angela

Angela hadn't heard from Mitchell since they had gone out for a drink. Though she didn't like to admit it, she was disappointed – and surprised – he hadn't called. So, it was with curiosity and trepidation that she attended the meeting the following Tuesday evening. She was a few minutes earlier than usual, and as Angela went to get herself a cup of tea, she noticed Mitchell hadn't arrived yet. As she stood sipping her scalding drink, her glance kept going to the door, so she didn't hear someone come up behind her.

'Waiting for someone?' murmured a voice in her ear. She turned with a start and saw Leo. He was so close that she nearly spilt her drink over him.

'Oh, hello,' replied Angela, putting some distance between them. He was wearing the same red jacket he'd worn last time, the hood pulled up around his face. Did he ever take it down? she wondered. As he blatantly checked her out, he leant forward as if he were about to say something confidential.

'So, you met your birth mother.'

Angela stared at him.

'Heard she used to be a druggie,' he continued, his eyes shifting rapidly to the other arriving members, before coming back to land on Angela, his eyes lingering on her breasts.

'And how would you know that?' Angela asked curtly, her earlier suspicion turning to active dislike.

'I have my ways,' he smirked.

I bet you do, you creep, thought Angela. But before she could respond, one of the members had interrupted their conversation to greet them, and Leo took the opportunity to lope off, walking towards the circle of chairs. Susan called for the meeting to start and Angela deliberately chose a chair opposite Leo, so she could keep him in her line of vision. At the last moment, Mitchell discreetly slipped into a spare seat. Catching her eye, he winked at her in acknowledgement and Angela felt a thrill run through her. He was perhaps the best-looking man she had ever seen. He must have come straight from work again as he was wearing a navy-blue, single-breasted suit with a matching waistcoat underneath. Angela wondered whether he'd ask her out for a drink again, and she found herself mentally hurrying the meeting along. She also needed to finish her conversation with Leo. When it finally drew to a close, Mitchell came over to her, as she hoped he would. They chatted for a few minutes, but when no invitation was forthcoming she took a deep breath and decided to ask him herself.

'I'd love to Angela, but I already have plans to go to the gym tonight with a friend.'

'Oh, right. No problem. It was just a thought,' she replied, trying not to let her surprise show. A man had once cancelled a business trip just to have coffee with her. She wondered if he was making an excuse, but then she saw the gym bag in his hand. He showed it to her, almost apologetically, the zip half open, the contents perhaps hastily shoved in.

'Another time?' he asked, turning to leave.

'Of course!' replied Angela. She didn't think she had, but perhaps she'd misread the signals? Either way, it would give her more time in the office.

Angela peered around the corner of the street. It was dark and quiet; no one was around. Still, she would have to be quick. As she saw Leo approach, she snapped her head back out of sight. She counted to five before stepping out in front of him. He stopped abruptly in surprise.

'Hello, Leo.' She was at least a head taller and as she looked down on him, he glanced nervously around.

'Nope, just me,' said Angela. 'We didn't get a chance to finish our conversation earlier.'

'Dunno what you're talking about,' replied Leo, his nervousness now replaced with nonchalance.

'No?' replied Angela. 'Something about my birth mother. What was it now? Oh yes, you said you heard she used to be a druggie. Now, my question to you, Leo, is how would you know that?'

'Lucky guess,' he said, pulling out a cigarette and lighter.

In one swift move, she snatched the lighter from him, throwing it to the ground, and pushed him hard up against the wall, her fingers around his throat.

'Ow! What the bloody hell do you think you're doing?' he shouted.

She put her sharp high heel on his foot, pressing firmly in warning while her grip intensified around his neck.

'Listen, you little punk,' she spat. 'You so much as look at me or talk to anyone about my business, and I will have the full weight of the law to bust whatever shady crap you're up to. You understand?'

He didn't respond, and Angela pressed her heel harder. 'Leo, I'm waiting.'

'Yes, yes,' he spluttered.

Angela released her grip.

'Jesus, what the hell is wrong with you, you psycho!'

'If I were you, Leo, I'd be very careful,' warned Angela.

He ran then, not even bothering to pick up his lighter, and she watched him, satisfied he'd got the message, before turning on her heel towards the office.

It was almost eleven o'clock at night when Angela got home from work. Dropping her keys and bag on the hallway table, she saw her answer machine flashing. She pressed the playback button, then went to put the kettle on. She was desperate for a cup of tea, and as tired as she was, she knew she needed a little downtime between the office and going to bed, otherwise she would lie there for hours, her mind going over and over the day, refusing to let sleep in. As the kettle boiled, Angela could hear the answer machine regurgitating its message, but she only heard the last part clearly.

'It's Mitchell, by the way.'

As soon as she heard his name, she hurried through to the living room, quickly pressing the repeat button.

'Hi, Angela, sorry about earlier. I was in such a hurry, I wondered if I came across a bit rude? If you're free one night this week, do you fancy dinner? It's Mitchell, by the way.'

Despite her fatigue, Angela felt the excitement and, if she were honest, a tiny tingle of triumph that he'd called. She made a plan to call him back tomorrow morning. Or perhaps it wouldn't hurt to keep him guessing a bit longer and leave it until the afternoon, she thought as she got into bed. Smiling to herself, she fell asleep quickly, her tea forgotten.

Angela looked over the incredible views of the Thames, the lights glistening in the distance. She loved this city – well, the nice areas, anyway. She loved its anonymity and its eclecticism. You could reinvent yourself several times over and no one would bat an eyelid. And it was especially at these moments, satisfied with good wine, food and company, that she felt at her most powerful. It was all hers for the taking. Her ambition sometimes felt like a separate being, a mentor almost, urging her on to follow the path of success. *You are not your past,* it whispered. *This is your time.* Yes, it was tiring; yes, she had sacrificed personal relationships; but as she looked over at Mitchell, she felt it in him as well – a desire to win, to relish all the trappings that came with accomplishment. Angela had been on many dates to pubs and to coffee shops, but Mitchell had chosen to take her to The River Café. It had just recently opened and was one of the most talked-about restaurants in town. As they dined on wild sea bass and artichokes, the conversation flowed as easily as the crisp Italian white wine. They talked more about being adopted and he encouraged her to meet Evelyn again.

'The first meeting I had with my birth mother was difficult, too. It was another year before I saw her again. I wished I hadn't left it that long,' admitted Mitchell.

'What happened?'

'She still believes she was right to give me up for adoption,' he said simply. 'No regrets whatsoever.'

'That must have hurt,' replied Angela.

'It did, but over the years I've learnt to live with it. She had her reasons, I know, but still… Anyway, what has helped is being able to talk to her. While we're not as close as I'd hoped, she's an interesting and intelligent woman and I'm glad I persevered. The hardest thing was accepting her for who she is. Once I got past that, it was easier.'

Angela thought about Evelyn. Did she want to give up so quickly? It wasn't in her nature, and besides, it was important to her dad. Perhaps she would call Susan in the morning to ask her to set up another meeting.

They also talked more about his work at Saatchi & Saatchi as a business development director. She knew a little about the world of advertising, mainly from the significant number of takeovers and buy-outs that had occurred as major corporations globally expanded. It was a topic he felt passionate about.

'I've worked in advertising my whole career, but over the last few years there has been so much opportunity,' he replied when she had asked about his job as they tucked into their main course. She could sense he was keen to impress her. 'I'm currently the youngest development director in the company,' he continued.

'So, you must work a lot then?' asked Angela, with a flirty wink. 'It's not just me.'

'Yeah, absolutely. But a lot of my job is entertaining clients so I'm often at dinners or having drinks in the evenings. It doesn't really feel like work a lot of the time!'

'Same here. But I also do a lot of research and support the

partners with their clients. I'm hoping to get promoted soon,' she added, conscious that she was also keen to impress.

'Really? Well, that's a celebration in itself and definitely worthy of another glass of champagne!'

Angela had laughed at his spontaneity and now, as they walked along the Thames, she found herself hoping they would see each other again soon.

'Are you sure it's not too late to go back to the office?' he asked as they walked.

'No, it's fine. Don't worry, I'll only be half an hour – I just need to finish preparing some paperwork for tomorrow and then I will take it directly to the client in the morning.'

'Well, I'm walking you back to your office then,' he asserted. 'No, I insist,' seeing her about to protest. 'Besides, you owe me.' He winked.

'Owe you?' replied Angela. 'What on earth for?'

'This,' he whispered, and with that, he gently leant down and kissed her. Afterwards, she'd sat at her desk as if in a dream. Mitchell had walked her to the office and even come up in the lift with her. His last kiss had been lingering.

'Right, go or you're going to be here all night,' he had teased. 'Are you sure you don't want me to wait for you?'

'No, I'll be fine. I don't live far away.'

Forcing herself to concentrate, she pushed away the thought of Mitchell and got down to work.

36

Friday, 4 November 1988

Dear Diary,

I'm shattered. Travelling to Tetbury at the weekends is tiring and the cold weather seems to have come earlier this year. I'm always relieved when the weekends are over and I'm back in London.

A.

Friday, 11 November 1988

Dear Diary,

Evelyn and I look nothing alike. I wonder what she does all day. The estate was pretty run down. There were several blocks all linked and accessible from one central concrete area. The centre was quite a large open space and the architect probably imagined little old ladies sitting on the park benches gossiping, toddlers playing on the grass islands watched by their loving mothers, and polite, young teenagers playing basketball and tennis on the courts. The architect would have been disappointed. Gangs of young teenagers were smoking against a backdrop of graffiti-covered walls while the tennis and basketball courts remained empty with the exception of a trail of rubbish left by a few pickpocketing seagulls.

A.

Friday, 18 November 1988

Dear Diary,

That kiss outside the office – I will always remember it. The way he stood tall and strong, his expression as he leant in – it was like something out of a film! So handsome and the look on his face – smitten!

A.

37

Angela

Angela paused outside Archway Tube station after work on a Monday evening. Around her, people swarmed like bees, relieved to be emerging from the underground. She checked her watch again. She'd taken Mitchell's advice and had arranged to meet Susan outside Evelyn's council estate block at seven o'clock. It had just gone six forty-five. Beyond, Angela could see a stream of double-deckers and hoped the W5 had not left yet. Hurrying to the bus stop, she was relieved when she saw it slowly turn the corner and trundle towards her. Having stepped on and paid her fare, Angela stood holding onto the bright yellow bars, as the bus strained up the incline. Evelyn's flat was only fifteen minutes away, but walking uphill in high heels was not something she relished. She was not normally a bus person. She could have taken a taxi, but they were difficult to get during rush hour. She alighted and walked down the dark street, the light from the sporadic lampposts her only guide. Approaching the fringe of the estate, she was surprised not to hear the Morse code of skateboards on the steps and as she drew nearer to Evelyn's block, she saw Susan hadn't yet arrived.

Angela was still a few minutes early. She looked up at the empty stairwell. Should she? Why not? She climbed the stairs and hovered on the landing just below Evelyn's, watching and listening. Everything was quiet, but if she strained, she could hear a television. Evelyn's? Then out of the corner of her eye she saw movement down below. Leaning over the barrier, she saw Susan approaching the block and Angela quickly descended the stairs, circling round so Susan wouldn't notice the direction she'd come from.

'Hi, Susan!'

She saw the older woman jump.

'Sorry – did I startle you?' said Angela, putting a hand on her arm.

'Oh, no, it's fine. Have you been waiting long?'

'Not at all. I just got here as well.'

'Shall we go up?' asked Susan.

'Yes, absolutely,' replied Angela. 'I'm ready.'

38

Evelyn

Apart from letting Charlie do his business on the grass outside, Evelyn hadn't gone outside very much. She told herself it was because it was cold – she could already see frost climbing her bedroom window each morning – but she knew that really it was because she was scared. Although she'd ripped up the anonymous letter immediately, she could still remember every word of it. Someone had found out she'd called the police, but who? Who would send such a thing?

The neighbours opposite her were dead. Dougie would be her first guess, although an anonymous note wasn't really his style. She doubted whether he could even put pen to paper. No, if it had been Dougie, wouldn't he have sent round one of his sons? What about Billy? Unlikely. He was a complete nutjob, but he wasn't a coward. If he had something to say, he would say it, even in his underwear. Evelyn continued going through everyone on the estate. Suddenly, she felt alarmed: what if the letter and the person who had followed her on her way back from bingo were linked? It had to be a coincidence, surely.

The worst thing was she couldn't talk to anyone about the letter because then they would know that she'd called the police. Even Brenda. She would be horrified that she'd involved the pigs. Evelyn sunk down in her chair while Charlie tried to jump onto her lap. Not even he could alleviate her fear and Evelyn started to feel the walls close in on her.

The only good thing that had happened over the last few days while she was hiding at home was Susan's call. Much to Evelyn's amazement, Angela wanted to meet her again. This time, Evelyn was determined to do better. This was her second chance and she wasn't going to mess it up. That day she had cleaned the flat from top to bottom, but she hadn't been to the shop to get milk and they were due in two hours. She had meant to go earlier but she'd kept putting it off and now it was dark.

This is ridiculous, thought Evelyn. I can't stay a prisoner in my home forever.

Getting up, she grabbed Charlie's lead and went to the front door with every intention of leaving. But as she saw her own letter box, she imagined an anonymous hand slipping through, cloaked in a black glove, and suddenly she knew she couldn't go out there. What if he was waiting for her? In the end, she'd called Doreen upstairs to see if she could borrow some milk and biscuits.

'I'd come up for them but my legs, Doreen, they've been giving me so much grief the last few days. I'm struggling to walk to be honest,' complained Evelyn, hoping she would offer to bring them down.

'Ah, Evie, sorry to hear that. Give me ten minutes, and I'll drop them down so you don't have to struggle with the stairs.'

'Thanks, Doreen. I owe you one,' replied Evelyn.

She put the phone down with a sigh of relief. She'd have to go out at some point but for now she was safe. Going into the kitchen to put the kettle on, she paused mid-step: what if the sender of the anonymous note had been Doreen? She pushed the thought away immediately; she was becoming paranoid.

A few minutes later, she opened the door to her neighbour, gratefully taking the items off her.

'Thanks so much again, Doreen. I'll return them as soon as I'm up and about again.'

'No rush, Evie – hope you feel better soon.'

As she watched Doreen climb back upstairs, Evelyn caught sight of a shadow on the stairwell below and quickly closed the door, heart hammering. She had to pull herself together. Charlie was waiting for her, enticed by the packet in her hands, and she hurried through to the kitchen to put the biscuits on a plate. Charlie followed. He wasn't used to being ignored and eventually lay down, resting his head on his front paws and looking up at her.

'Sorry, Charlie,' said Evelyn, giving him a quick scratch between the ears. 'These aren't for you. Here, have some of your own while I turn the TV off.'

In the living room, Evelyn took one last look in the mirror over the fireplace. She was ready. At that moment, she heard Angela and Susan at the door. Inviting them in, she led them through the hallway and settled them into the living room while she served tea, trying not to spill anything on the now gleaming coffee table.

'Did you find out what happened to your neighbour?' started Angela, making conversation, as she took one of the biscuits Evelyn offered. The remnants of police tape still criss-crossing the front door had served as a vivid reminder of their first visit.

'Murdered!' announced Evelyn. 'Well, you saw the blood on the walls, no doubt. Can you believe it? Apparently, someone broke in and stabbed them.'

'Them? How many were there?' asked Angela.

'Quite a few, I think, from the racket they used to make. I saw three bodies come out of there.' Evelyn, encouraged by their shocked faces, told the tale of the bodies being removed on stretchers.

'Why would anyone do such a thing?' said Susan, disbelief on her face.

'Well, Doreen upstairs said she thought it was something to do with the drugs business. They trashed the place at some point as well.'

'I hope the police catch who did it,' said Susan.

'They were round 'ere, the bobbies, asking me if I'd seen anything strange. Been here twenty years and there's been some right goings-on, but I've never seen murder, not in all the time I've been living 'ere.'

As the conversation moved on, Evelyn thought Angela seemed more relaxed this time. She'd tried not to take offence when Angela had eaten only one biscuit, but she supposed it would take a lot of discipline to keep a figure that slim. Angela asked her plenty of questions: what she liked to do in her free time, when she'd moved to the estate, and how long she'd been playing bingo. Evelyn was pleased at the interest and felt more comfortable now that the topic was no longer focused on the past. She found herself intrigued by Angela, especially her job, and wondered aloud if Angela could help her get a new flat (she would try, but she dealt in criminal and corporate law); was it anything like *L.A. Law*? (no, nothing as dramatic), and did she get paid lots of money (yes, she got a decent wage but she worked very long hours and the profession favoured men). She also asked Angela about her adoptive parents, whom she thought sounded very posh – James and Rosemary – but then listened sadly as Angela told her about James's illness.

The hour passed quickly and the conversation drew to a close. Then Evelyn was struck by a thought.

'Will you be coming back 'ere any time soon?' she asked as Angela put on her coat. 'It would be nice to see you again,' she added.

Angela paused, caught off guard, but pleased to be asked. 'Yes, of course, if you would like me to.'

'Well, I need a favour. I've lost my spare key – God knows how I've done it – but I need it recutting. I'd ask one of these lot round 'ere but you just never know… and with recent events… Anyway, I'm pretty sure a fancy lawyer's not going to fleece me!' she laughed.

Angela ignored the flash of disappointment. 'Of course. I'll get it cut for you and bring it back next week,' she said, slipping the key into her purse. 'Just a thought, though: if you've lost it, is it not better to change the lock?'

'Nah,' replied Evelyn. 'The key doesn't have my address on it. I probably lost it at Tesco – gone forever. No point paying out when I don't need to.'

Perhaps there could be a real chance for them after all, thought Evelyn. When Angela agreed to do her a small favour and get her key cut, Evelyn realised just how useful it might be to have a grown-up daughter in her life: someone to look after her in her old age, like she did for her own mother. Someone to help shop, cook and clean, although of course Evelyn would be a lot more gracious than her own mother and certainly a lot more appreciative.

But it was when Angela opened her purse to put the key inside for safekeeping that Evelyn saw the photo. It was in a clear plastic wallet on the inside flap and showed a young teenage Angela sitting in a garden seat with a woman's arms around her from behind, the two of them smiling widely for the camera. But it was the man on the left of the girl, his warm embrace circling the two for that perfect family photo, who made the breath leave Evelyn's body. It couldn't be, could it? Yet, the evidence was staring her in the face. It must be a mistake.

Quickly seizing the opportunity, Evelyn faked a smile. 'That's a lovely photo. Is that you with James and Rosemary?' Both Angela and Susan froze at the question, Susan recovering much quicker. But Angela handled it well and answered with obvious pride in her voice.

'Yes, it is. This was taken over ten years ago now but it's still one of my happiest memories.'

'How lovely,' replied Evelyn. 'What did you say the family name was?'

'I didn't, but it's Steele.'

Evelyn swallowed hard.

Susan was watching the exchange carefully and Evelyn knew she would have to be quick. She leant in to Angela, taking the purse in her hands, and looked closely at the image. There was no doubt in her mind.

'It looks a beautiful garden – where was it taken?'

'Thank you. At our house in Tetbury, by one of our neighbours, if I remember correctly.'

'Tetbury? I don't think I've ever been there. Do they still live there then?' asked Evelyn, her voice sounding strained to her own ears though she focused on keeping her questions light and casual.

'They do,' replied Angela. 'I don't think they'll ever move – they love it there.'

'Well,' said Evelyn, handing the purse back to Angela, 'it's always nice to keep these memories, isn't it?'

Susan smiled her approval and Evelyn was pleased that she'd managed to disguise the shock of seeing him in the photo.

After they left, Evelyn leant against the wall, mulling the picture over in her mind. How was it possible that he was even *in* the photo? And why was Angela referring to him as her dad?

All of a sudden, Evelyn felt weak. She walked unsteadily into the living room, using the wall for support. What had he done? Collapsing into her chair, she closed her eyes and leant her head back, trying to think of an explanation other than the one assaulting her. He wouldn't do that to her, would he? Not without telling her? Opening her eyes, she picked up Charlie from where he sat at her feet, holding him close as if he could protect her from the dawning realisation of Jimmy's actions. However he'd done it, she knew she needed to get to the bottom of it, and once she did, he would pay – and she wasn't just talking about a bit of a fright from Dougie and his bulldog. Oh no. Cancer or no cancer, he would pay severely if it was the last thing he did on this earth.

39
Angela

Angela almost didn't make it to the adoption meeting. One of the partners, Dereck Lyndhurst, had approached her late afternoon to do some research for an urgent case. He was a quiet, methodical man, whose habit of thinking for several seconds before responding to a question frustrated the newer associates. Yet Angela had discovered it was often worth the wait. While Lyndhurst had none of the loud-mouthed brashness of the other partners, he was well-respected by his clients and peers alike, and whenever Angela worked with him she always learnt something new.

Last-minute requests didn't bode well for her personal life, though, and she didn't think she would finish in time. Luckily, one of the interns, eager to show willing, had helped her and she had the typed-up report ready in hand just under three hours later. Dropping it off with Mr Lyndhurst's secretary, Angela was looking forward to seeing Mitchell and she did a quick stop in the ladies' toilets to refresh her lipstick before hurrying out of the office.

Arriving at the church hall, she was just in time, slipping

into her seat as Susan called for the meeting to start. She saw Mitchell and her sense of anticipation increased as their eyes locked.

She also saw some of the now familiar faces: Katie, Linda, Simon, Tracey and Ken. She knew them, in some ways, better than she knew her own friends. Despite her initial reluctance to attend the support group, she had to admit she was glad she'd made the effort. They were all so different from each other yet had an understanding that could have surpassed even the deepest of friendships. She thought of Lucy and felt guilty. Although her friend had left several voice messages on her answer machine, Angela hadn't called her back as she'd had so much going on, and when she did have the time, late at night, she knew her friend would be catching up on some much-needed sleep. Digging in her bag, she pulled out a notebook, writing a reminder to call Lucy on Saturday morning.

As Susan began, Angela was pleased to see Leo wasn't present.

'Evening all. Everyone ready to begin?' called Susan as the noise began to die down. 'We'll have our usual sharing of updates and questions, and then I want to talk a little bit about a new programme that Family First is about to launch, which some of you might be interested in.'

As each member took their turn, Angela shaped her own contribution in her mind. She noticed there were a couple of new members – an older man of about forty called Geoff, who walked with a stick, and a woman called Lindsey, who didn't look anyone in the eye.

'Angela? Anything to share?' asked Susan, when it came to her.

'Yes,' she replied. 'I met Evelyn, my birth mother, for the second time last night and it went well – better than last time, anyway. I'm glad I decided to try again with her as the first meeting wasn't easy.'

'Well done, Angela,' said Ken, who was sitting on her left and always liked to comment after each person spoke. There were rumours he was training for a group lead role similar to Susan's.

'Thanks,' she replied. 'I feel sure we can meet just the two of us now,' continued Angela, more to Susan than anyone else. 'It's been great to have you there but hopefully we're in a good place.'

'That's good to hear, Angela. I trust you'll keep us all updated with how you're getting on?'

'Of course,' Angela nodded, recognising the not-so-subtle request to keep attending the meetings. Luckily for you, Susan, I have another reason to attend the meetings now, thought Angela, sneaking a sliding glance at Mitchell.

'Leo says she was a druggie,' piped up Katie suddenly, 'is that true?'

'Katie!' exclaimed Susan quickly. 'I really don't think that's an appropriate question, do you?'

'Why not?'

'Because—'

'It's all right, Susan,' interrupted Angela, rearranging her face into a tight smile. Clearly, her message to Leo hadn't been strong enough if he was spreading gossip around the group.

'Evelyn's been clean for over ten years now, Katie. It's an incredible achievement.'

'Once a druggie, always a druggie,' said Katie resolutely to no one in particular.

What is her problem? seethed Angela silently. All she has

to do is hold her baby and keep her mouth shut about other people's business.

'That's enough, Katie,' replied Susan, sharply. 'Angela, anything else?'

'No, I'm done,' she replied.

'Right, well, thank you, everyone. So next on the list is the new programme that Family First is launching. This is basically a mentoring programme to help young adoptees settle into their new families. Of course, we need mentors, and who better than all of you?'

As Susan passed around the leaflets and the group started chatting, Angela narrowed her eyes at Katie, struggling to control her anger.

As the meeting came to an end, Angela quickly picked up her bag, about to approach Katie.

'Come on,' whispered Mitchell, coming up behind her. 'Let's get out of here and go and get a drink.'

Giving Katie one last cold look, Angela followed him out onto the street. He took her hand and they walked away from the church hall. As soon as they were out of sight, he leant in to kiss her. Angela responded, wrapping her arms around him, her earlier fury forgotten. As they entered the bar, the warmth surrounded them, and Angela knew there was nowhere else she'd rather be – not even at the office.

'So, you met Evelyn again,' acknowledged Mitchell as they sat down with their drinks.

'I did. I took your advice,' replied Angela.

'Well, I'm glad it went well,' he said, squeezing her hand. 'Ignore Katie – she can be a pain in the neck when she wants to be.'

'Yeah, I know. But like I said, it's not a problem, although I'm glad Leo wasn't there tonight.'

'Yeah, he's a strange one. Anyway, enough about them. My plan is to keep you here as long as possible, so you can't go back to the office!' said Mitchell.

'I wish,' replied Angela with a sigh, thinking of everything she had to do.

'You know,' said Mitchell, 'you're the only person I've met who works harder than I do! It's very sexy, you know,' he added suggestively, putting his arm around her waist.

Angela laughed away the compliment but she felt herself falling for him.

It was almost eleven thirty when Angela got on the Tube. She'd only just caught the last train on time. It didn't matter that she was exhausted and only had a few hours to sleep before having to get up and go into work again. All she could think about was Mitchell. They'd had a glass of white wine each and a quick bite to eat before he'd walked her back to the office.

'Don't stay too late,' he'd cautioned, as he left her with a lingering kiss.

But Angela had a lot to catch up on. With her time spent at the meetings, Mitchell, and her frequent trips to Tetbury, her billing hours had reduced – not by much, but enough to capture Clive's attention.

'You were the best-performing associate for six months straight. What happened?' he asked at their weekly progress report meeting earlier that day. 'You broken up with your boyfriend or something?'

Angela bristled at the unnecessary remark.

'Get your billing back up,' he had told her directly.

'Yes, Mr Mooring,' she'd replied quickly, not even bothering to explain about her other commitments. He wouldn't be interested anyway. Raymond had smirked at her from across the room, and Angela had stared down the humiliation, knowing she would have to deal with him at some point – he was becoming intolerable. In the meantime, she had vowed to work harder than ever before. She had spent two hours behind her desk that evening and was planning to do more work at home. The office was still a quarter full when she left.

But as the soothing white noise of the Tube accompanied her home, Angela felt the lure of sleep take over. Leaning her head against the glass partition, she thought she would just close her eyes for a few minutes. Drifting off into a light snooze, she dreamt of Mitchell's intense kiss, the graze of his stubble as she leant in towards him, his hand coming round to cup the back of her head. Waking with a start, she realised she was almost at her stop. As the train slowed, Angela reached down for her bag but the space between her feet was empty. Shock and disbelief mingled together, a powerful concoction that put her on full alert. She quickly scanned the few remaining passengers and was met with a barrier of newspapers and books. Would they have seen anything? A young woman next to her, who was dressed as a punk, was the only one not reading. Instead, she was listening to her Walkman. Angela turned to her to ask, but the punk ignored her, seemingly too lazy to remove her headphones. God, London could be so unfriendly sometimes, she thought, but at the same time she knew it was her own fault – she shouldn't have fallen asleep.

There was nothing to do except get off the train and report the theft. She recognised the hopelessness of the situation, though. The thief would be long gone by now. How could she have been so stupid? Her life was in that bag – her Filofax, her purse, and, oh God, some of her notes for work. Damn it, she would have to rewrite them. She also remembered that Evelyn's keys were in there. She had got the key copied and was going to give them both to her. She would have to call and tell her. At least they weren't labelled. Luckily, Angela had taken her own keys out of her bag on the Tube, so they were in her hand ready to use.

Annoyed, she made her way to the stationmaster's office to report the crime, where she knew she would have to fill in paperwork the length of *War and Peace*. Sighing, she doubted she would get much more work done that evening.

40

Wednesday, 23 November 1988

Dear Diary,

It was just a combination of factors really – tiredness, the wine, and people are so engrossed on the Tube. It's so easy for things to get stolen – thieves target the Tube all the time for that very reason. They can hide amongst all those people. Of course, true Londoners should know better. Thank goodness for Mitchell. I've never been so busy. Between the office, the adoption support group, and Tetbury – it's exhausting. I'm never at home these days.

    A.

4I

Evelyn

Evelyn hadn't known where Tetbury was and she hadn't liked to show her ignorance by asking, but she had managed to find out by dropping the place name into conversation with Brenda. According to her, it was in the Cotswolds and it was a very fancy area – lots of antiques, apparently. Evelyn wondered about Tetbury and what the Steeles' life together had been like. It was one thing to see a photo of Jimmy – or James, as he clearly now liked to be called – but the urge to see him and confront him about his lies was almost overpowering. Tomorrow, she would call the railway station and find out how much a train ticket to Tetbury cost. As long as she was back from Tetbury before dark, she'd be fine.

Despite her determination to get to Tetbury, Evelyn didn't want to get on the train by herself, so she persuaded Brenda to join her on the pretence of a day out. When Brenda had asked why Tetbury when they could go to Brighton, Evelyn was prepared. She'd discovered that Highgrove House was close by and Brenda was nothing if not devout in her passion for the Royal Family. It was arranged for the following week: they would travel there on the train, visit the Royal Gardens and have a wander around the village. Evelyn had written down the address and telephone number for James and Rosemary from the phone book, and on the morning of their departure she could barely think straight.

'Evelyn, for goodness' sake, whatever is the matter with you?' Brenda asked when Evelyn kept fidgeting and sighing on the train.

'Nothing,' replied Evelyn sullenly, irritated at being spoken to like a child. 'I'm going to get a cup of tea – do you want one?'

'Yes, please. Just make sure it's hot and not that lukewarm stuff they usually serve,' complained Brenda.

As Evelyn waited for the tea in the buffet car, she wondered what she would do when she got there. Would she just knock on James and Rosemary's door and introduce herself? Of course she couldn't. There had to be a better way.

Think, Evelyn, she urged herself. What excuse could she come up with to see James in person? She wasn't worried about him recognising her. The young girl she had once been had long disappeared, changed beyond recognition by a life of hardship, disappointment and debauchery.

Evelyn was quiet all the way back to London from Tetbury. For once, she didn't mind Brenda's constant prattle – it gave her time to think. Despite the photo, she was still shaken when she saw Jimmy – James – strolling through the town with a smartly dressed woman she recognised from the photo in Angela's wallet as Rosemary. Evelyn saw her reach out to take his hand, and when she saw how much love exuded from James towards her, the injustice of it all floored Evelyn.

He'd left her pregnant and alone to cope with the mess he'd caused, but had somehow managed to find his daughter, adopt her with a new woman and live an idyllic family life. It should have been her, she thought. Why wasn't it her?

But here was her opportunity to find out. She couldn't believe it had been so easy to see him. If that wasn't a sign to confront him, she didn't know what was. Yet as her feet went to move forward, something held her back. While he looked incredibly well-to-do and still had a hint of that rakish charm, she recognised a dying man when she saw one. While Brenda was browsing one of the antique markets in the Market House in the centre of town, Evelyn discreetly followed James. As she watched him walk down the High Street, clearly struggling with the effort, she took in his expensive-looking blue jacket and checked shirt. He even had a little handkerchief peeping out of his top pocket. Oh for goodness' sake, thought Evelyn to herself crossly; he looked ridiculous.

Still, Evelyn felt herself smile. They'd had some good times. As the years rolled back, memories flooded her mind: the excitement of sneaking out to meet him, the music as they swayed together, his hand taking hers as he led her up to a bedroom. He'd made her feel special and she'd fallen for it all. He must be over fifty now, and look where they'd both ended up: he battling cancer, and she ravaged by drugs and drink.

She watched him go into a coffee shop, and turned away to find Brenda. Remembering the look of love on his face towards Rosemary, she knew what she would do.

*

Evelyn wandered through the house, its welcoming but fancy accessories giving it a farmhouse feel. A huge fire was lit, its flames giving off a warmth that drew her to sit in front of it. As she looked around, she could see family photos. There was Angela with James and Rosemary, all on their skis ready to go down the slopes. Angela on her graduation, with her father's arm wrapped around her. Angela dressed up for her sixth-form disco. There were so many. Evelyn counted twenty-four photos scattered across the living room walls and on various cabinets. Twenty-four occasions Evelyn had missed out on. The door opened and she turned, coming face to face with Jimmy. He didn't look surprised to see her, just sat down on the sofa and watched her.

'You aren't fit to be a mother, Evelyn,' he said.

Evelyn tried to defend herself but she couldn't speak. She watched in dismay as Rosemary entered the room and joined James, cuddling into him, a baby nestled in her arms. Evelyn stood up to get a closer look at the infant but James put an arm out to prevent her.

'You aren't fit to be a mother, Evelyn,' he said again. 'But Rosemary is. We'll take it from here.'

All of a sudden, Evelyn is lying on a bed, her legs held open in stirrups. She can't move but her body is straining to sit up and get a glimpse of her child. All she can see are shadows moving above her as the anaesthetic brings her back under its spell. But just as her eyes are about to close, she briefly sees her baby screaming and grimacing at the wrench from the womb. She hears the midwife say it's a girl before they take her away and Evelyn lies back, relieved that the baby's healthy. They bring her back, quiet now, placing her little body in one of Evelyn's arms as she tries to fight the haze of the drug. But the pull is too strong and Evelyn falls limp as they take her away for the last time.

Evelyn woke from the dream in her own bed. Her mouth was dry and her head was pounding. Looking around her, she tried to remember when she went to Tetbury. Yesterday? Or the day before yesterday? Covering her face with her hands, she made a vow to herself that this time she really would give up the drink.

42

Rosemary

The day had started off well. James had woken up relatively early and seemed to be in good spirits. They'd had breakfast together and even taken a stroll round the garden. They'd talked about next season's planting and what they would look forward to seeing in bloom. They hadn't made any plans for a while; it seemed pointless when the two of them were so focused on getting through each day, each week, but that morning as she felt a hint of normality return, Rosemary felt optimistic. When James had mentioned going for a walk in the village after lunch instead of his usual nap, she even went so far as to hope he'd turned a corner. But they'd only been walking for ten minutes before James slowed his pace to lean on the wall. He was breathing heavily. Gently guiding him into the nearest café, Rosemary had ordered a large pot of tea, fighting the disappointment with cheery chatter. An hour later, they were safely back at home, James in his chair, head to one side, gently snoring. It was then that the phone had rung, and Rosemary quickly hurried to answer it before it woke him.

'Good morning, is that Rosemary Steele?'

'It is. Who's speaking, please?'

'This is Evelyn Harris.'

Rosemary's hand unconsciously went to her chest, her fingers clasping the gold locket that lay there.

Evelyn Harris.

During the adoption process, it was James who had dealt with everything. He had visited the children's home several times to sort out paperwork and approvals, while Rosemary had visited only once. Even though it was years ago, she still remembered it vividly.

As soon as the large front door of the children's home had opened, James and Rosemary were met by clamouring toddlers, their little starfish hands begging for them to be lifted. Unable to resist, she had picked up one child, a beautiful little boy with huge brown eyes. Rosemary's heart had contracted with sorrow while the searing heat of disbelief that abandoned children even existed pressed against her throat.

'What's his name?' she'd asked Matron.

'Hughie,' she'd replied.

Holding him in her arms, Rosemary felt the urge to protect him, insistent and physical. They fitted together perfectly, his arms gently resting around her neck, and when he leant his head on her shoulder, it took everything Rosemary had not to turn and walk out of the front door with him. She caught James watching, a strange expression on his face before he quickly replaced it with an encouraging smile.

'Come on, love, Angela will be waiting for us.'

Nodding, Rosemary buried her cheek against Hughie's, as if breathing in his scent could make him hers. Reluctantly, she put him down, his chubby legs still wobbly like a new-born lamb, making him grasp for her hand. As Rosemary watched it dawn on him that she was leaving, Hughie let out a sob which crescendoed into a series of howls. As one of the carers led him away, Rosemary bit her lip hard, focusing on the pain to harden herself and prevent her own tears from falling.

Following James, Matron showed them through to an office on the other side of the hallway. It smelt of furniture polish and bubble gum, presumably the former used to disguise the latter. A large wooden desk with chairs dominated the space, and Matron indicated for her visitors to sit down. On the desk waiting for them was an adoption consent form and as James picked it up, Rosemary caught sight of the black typed letters, bold and official: '**BIRTH MOTHER: EVELYN HARRIS**'. Underneath was her illegible, scrawled signature. After years of trying for a child, in the end all it took was a few ink marks. Matron left, presumably to bring Angela, and James grasped Rosemary's hand.

'I can't believe this is finally happening!' he said. 'In just a few days, we'll be parents. After all these years...'

He appeared lost in thought but suddenly he turned to her, his eyes wet.

'I know it's not a baby, Rosie love, but I just know you're going to make an incredible mother. Thank you for this.'

Rosemary smiled, her heart full of love for James. She would do anything for him, and if they weren't allowed to adopt a younger child, then Angela would be perfect, she told herself firmly.

Since that day, Rosemary had thought about Evelyn – of course she had. Who was this woman who had given up her daughter? What were her circumstances? What was her medical history? If Angela ever mentioned her, she referred to her as her birth mother. Rosemary guiltily remembered reading Angela's diary once and was both horrified and gratified to see Evelyn referred to as *that bitch who gave me up*, the teenage angst clearly apparent in the heavy underlined script. But apart from that, Evelyn's name was rarely mentioned.

Until now.

Still holding the receiver in one hand, Rosemary peered into the living room to make sure James was still asleep. Normally, the sight of him evoked sympathy, but with Evelyn on the end of the line Rosemary felt the irritation rise again that he had persuaded Angela to bring this woman into their lives at such a time.

'Good morning,' Rosemary finally replied, closing the living room door behind her. 'How can I help you, Evelyn?'

'Oh, well, you can't really,' she replied, seemingly oblivious to the polite rhetoric. 'I was just giving you a ring to say thank you for doing such a wonderful job raising my daughter. Angela tells me it was you and Ji— James who encouraged her to get in touch with me.'

Despite Evelyn's pleasant tone, Rosemary felt the words like barbed wire on her skin. *Her daughter?*

'I'm sorry,' said Evelyn into the silence. 'I hope I haven't taken you by surprise. I did mention to Angela that I would be in touch. Don't tell me she forgot to tell you! Kids these days, eh?' Evelyn laughed, her attempt at camaraderie falling like a deck of cards.

'Indeed,' replied Rosemary. 'Well, it was lovely to hear from you, Evelyn.'

'Any time. It would be nice to stay in touch, wouldn't it? I'm sure Angela would be pleased to see everyone getting on so well. She says you come to London regularly. Perhaps we could all meet for a cup of tea next time you're here. That would be nice, wouldn't it?'

'That would be very nice, now I really—'

'By the way,' Evelyn interrupted, 'there *is* one thing I wanted to talk to you about. A delicate matter, what with James being Angela's real father and everything. I'm presuming Angela doesn't know – I suppose you and James were waiting for the right time to tell her?'

Rosemary gripped the receiver, pressing it hard against her ear until it started to smart. Closing her eyes tightly, she resisted the urge to hang up.

'I'm sorry, Evelyn, you must be mistaken. The information about Angela's father was never shared with us at the time of adoption.'

'But—'

'Look, I'm very sorry, but I must go – I have a pan boiling over. It's been nice talking to you.' And before Evelyn could respond, Rosemary replaced the receiver, finally cutting off the endless prattle.

Rosemary slammed around the kitchen, banging cupboards, pans and drawers. She couldn't remember the last time she'd felt so enraged. How dare Evelyn call her? And saying James was Angela's real father? It was ludicrous. She would tell James about the call; how brazen Evelyn had sounded, how she had referred to Angela as *her* daughter. She no longer cared whether she woke James or not – she wanted to wake him as a punishment – but as he stumbled through in a sleep-laden fog, she felt a sliver of remorse. He looked so tired. But then she remembered his persuasive patter about how finding Evelyn would be in Angela's best interests, especially with the news of his cancer. And who could deny a sick man, thought Rosemary bitterly, as she threw salt into the pan of potatoes. At the time, it had all seemed to make sense, but now she wished she'd stuck to her initial reaction.

'Rosemary!' he said, the use of her full name indicating his annoyance. 'What on earth is wrong and why are you making so much noise?'

Rosemary turned to him. 'I just got a phone call. From Evelyn Harris.'

'Who?' replied James, bewildered. 'Evelyn? As in Angela's birth mother?'

'The very same. Apparently, she told Angela that she was going to call to thank us for raising *her* daughter. *Her* daughter!' flared Rosemary.

'Now, calm down, Rosie. While the wording's not great, I'm sure the intention was—'

'And do you know what else she told me, James?' she interrupted, bending down to get the place mats from the cupboard. 'That you are Angela's real father! You!' she emphasised, her voice lost in the back of the cupboard. 'Can you imagine? Didn't Angela say something about her once being on drugs? She must have been if she's managed to concoct that story. Honestly, James, I said at the time it wasn't the best idea to go looking for her...'

Standing up, place mats in hand, she was surprised to see him pale.

'James! What is it? Are you all right?'

'Yes, yes, of course. It's nothing. Just felt a little dizzy, that's all. I'm fine.'

James walked over, turning down the heat on the pan of potatoes. Then he placed both hands on Rosemary's shoulders, gently guiding her to sit down at the dining table.

'Now tell me again about the conversation with Evelyn,' he said calmly. 'But this time a little more quietly,' he added with a grin.

As he listened carefully while she talked, her anger dissipated as it always did when James directed his full attention on her. After all, Evelyn's life was sad and lonely – surely she could let such an insensitive comment about *her daughter* pass? As James had pointed out, Evelyn was probably just a lonely old woman who liked to make up stories.

43

Evelyn

So, Rosemary didn't know then. Jimmy had kept his wife in the dark about being Angela's real father. Evelyn wasn't surprised: he was a secretive snake who only thought about himself and she hoped the pretentious bastard was getting an earful right at this very moment. Evelyn wasn't sure what she would have done if Jimmy had answered – probably resisted the urge to give him an earful herself, hung up and tried again another day – but she'd been lucky on the first try.

As she heard Rosemary's Queen's English down the phone, she'd understood exactly how Angela had grown into the sophisticated woman she was today. Nurture had trumped nature on that one, that was for sure, thought Evelyn, looking down at herself critically. It sounded like Jimmy had done very well for himself. From an East End council estate to a posh town favoured by royalty, no wonder he hadn't given Evelyn a second thought. Resentment, jealousy and relief wove together. Her decision – or rather Mother's – to give her daughter up for adoption had been the right one but that didn't make it any easier, and Evelyn felt regret settle in the pit of her stomach.

After several more days in self-imposed incarceration at home, Evelyn knew she had to get out. The walls were starting to close in and the anonymity of the letter writer was becoming more frightening than the threat itself. If she could find out which of her neighbours had written it, then they could thrash it out and that would be the end of it. Job done. Over a breakfast of dry toast and black coffee (lack of food being just one more reason to get out) she hatched a plan. She would take a walk around the estate and see how her neighbours treated her. If any of them acted suspiciously, she could approach them. What she would do from there she had no idea, but a confrontation in broad daylight was better than letting her imagination get the better of her.

Evelyn put down the piece of toast, suddenly frightened. It wouldn't be a confrontation – more like a beating – but at least it would be over with. She balanced the thought of never-ending worry and claustrophobia with a fifteen-minute punch-up and made her choice. Getting up from the table before she could change her mind, she left Charlie fast asleep next to his dog bowl and quickly left the flat.

It was late on a Saturday morning and Evelyn could smell bacon in the stairwell, which was a welcome change from the stink of the bins. She normally loved a fry-up, but that morning it made her feel queasy. As she passed Billy's flat, she willed him to open his door and shout some obscenity just to reassure herself that everything was normal. She'd even put up with his mooning if she had to. But his door remained closed. As she reached the first floor, Evelyn paused, her hand holding the stair rail tightly. Her whole body was telling her to turn round right now, go back upstairs, make a cup of tea, stick the telly on and spend the day at home. But she knew she would go mad. As if being led to the gallows, Evelyn reluctantly started her descent.

At first, she saw and heard no one, and the concrete communal area seemed to be empty. There wasn't even the usual pump of a boom box. She was sticking close to the walls, trying to maintain as wide a view of the area as possible. She didn't fancy being taken by surprise. Leaning with her back against the wall, Evelyn nervously lit a cigarette and pulled on it thankfully. She was dismayed to see her hands shaking. Come on, Evie, she said to herself, you're tougher than this. After a few drags, she felt brave enough to leave the comfort of the wall and walked across the grassy area. There were several benches and she headed for the one furthest away, which gave the best vantage point. Her heart pounded and with every step she imagined the muffled sounds of a hood being placed over her head as she was carried away to one of the flats to answer for her decision.

But nothing happened.

Sitting down, she felt as exhilarated as if she'd climbed Mount Everest.

'All right, Evelyn,' muttered a voice behind her.

Shit. Dougie.

He was walking Floyd, the bulldog roaming free, the empty dog lead held in his right hand like a whip.

Evelyn swallowed.

'All right, Dougie,' replied Evelyn.

The silence stretched between them and she knew it was a waiting game. Suddenly, she jumped as she felt Floyd sniffing at her ankles under the bench. Had Dougie instructed the dog to attack her, wondered Evelyn frantically. She froze as the dog's wet nose pushed up her leggings, and Evelyn had a vision of her leg being ripped off, Floyd holding it between his jaws like a trophy. She knew she had to lean down and stroke him to appear normal but every fibre in her body resisted.

'Hungry, is he?' called out Evelyn, forcing herself to chuckle.

'He shouldn't be, the amount of bacon he's just eaten, the fat bastard,' replied Dougie. 'Floyd!' he called sharply. 'Get over here now!'

At the sound of his owner, Floyd pushed past Evelyn's feet towards Dougie, who leant down to put his lead back on. His goodbye came in the form of a brief nod, and Evelyn almost cried with relief. Dougie – with the protection of his sons – pretty much ruled the estate, so if it wasn't him, surely she couldn't have too much to worry about. It was probably just one of the lads on a dare. They would do anything for a fiver, that lot.

Evelyn sat back on the bench and looked up at the sky, feeling ridiculously grateful to be alive. Sitting up, she decided to make the most of her new-found freedom; she would go to bingo tonight – she would call Brenda as soon as she got home – but first she needed to get to the shops.

Evelyn struggled up the stairs to her flat, but not even the weight of the shopping bags could dampen her mood. She'd spent a little more money than she normally would on groceries and even treated herself at M&S Food, which she hardly ever did. She was looking forward to a nice curry lunch and an afternoon nap. Evelyn unlocked the door and dumped the shopping bags in the hallway, placing her handbag and keys on the table. As usual, Charlie came to meet her.

'Hello, boy!' she said, bending down to give his tummy a rub. 'I missed you. But we'll go out for a long walk later. You'll enjoy that, won't you?'

Evelyn picked up the shopping from the floor and it was then that she noticed the envelope. She looked at the letter box as if her mind could conjure up the person who had delivered it. In disbelief, she stared at it, hoping that it was nothing more than junk mail. But as the white envelope, addressed to her, lay on the carpet, Evelyn already recognised the handwriting as the same as on the last one. She debated whether to just throw it in the bin without opening it, but as she picked it up she could feel a small, slim rectangular shape inside. As she lifted the flap, a packet of white powder fell into her hands with a note attached. Hardly daring to unfold it, she braced herself, slowly exhaling as she read.

GO ON. TREAT YOURSELF. WHO KNOWS IF IT WILL BE YOUR LAST CHANCE BEFORE...?

Evelyn felt a scream claw its way up her throat. Her mind raced as she tried to think who could be sending her these notes. Her next-door neighbours were dead. It had to be someone who knew about her past and her history with drugs – otherwise, why send an eighth of coke through the door?

44

Angela

Angela arrived in Tetbury much later than planned. She was hungover, had missed the train due to delays on the Tube, and had had to wait an hour and a half to catch the next one. She'd gone out with Lucy for a late dinner and drinks the night before. They were supposed to go clubbing but her friend had made her excuses and left early. Angela had been disappointed and as a result had drunk slightly more than she'd intended to after Lucy had left.

While waiting for the train, she found a seat in a café in Paddington near the departure board, and tried not to take out her irritation on the waiter. It was valuable time that she could be in the office. It wasn't just that, though. She was fed up with the snide comments from Raymond.

'Leaving early *again*, Angie?' he'd sniped as she tried to slip out of the office unnoticed.

She didn't know which angered her more, his overfamiliar use of her shortened name or the fact that he was keeping tabs on her. The other week she'd caught him loitering around her desk. She'd left the office for the night but had come back as she'd forgotten her umbrella. As she'd approached her desk, she could see him hovering over her desk planner. When she'd asked him what he was doing, he'd said he'd misplaced a file, but he'd looked shifty. On Monday, she'd do something about him once and for all. A tearful chat with Lisa in Human Resources would do the trick. She knew the manager was particularly gung-ho about sexism in the workplace. Perhaps Raymond had got a bit handsy one evening with Angela when they were working late – nothing too dramatic, of course, just enough to get him suspended for a bit.

Satisfied she had a plan, she sipped her hot tea along with two paracetamol and tried to focus on something else, her gaze finally falling on the new bag on her lap. Shopping for it had been the only consolation for the theft on the Tube. She hadn't planned to spend so much money, but browsing Selfridges she had spotted the soft red leather and been drawn to it immediately. Slipping the flap between her fingers, she had caressed it appreciatively. Nearby, a saleswoman had hovered, recognising desire when she saw it.

'Would you like to try it?' she'd asked, slipping the bag from its stand. Not waiting for a response, she'd continued her sales pitch, unaware that it wasn't required.

Angela had let the words flow past her as she gently held the bag in her right hand, admiring the gold clasp and matching zip as she walked to a nearby mirror. As she'd seen her lean elegance reflected back at her, undoubtedly enhanced by the luxurious bag, Angela knew she had to have it.

The saleswoman nodded in agreement. 'It was made for you,' she'd concluded smoothly. 'Shall I wrap it?'

'Yes, please,' Angela had replied.

Handing over her credit card, she tried not to look at the price on the till. It was expensive, even for her. But it would last for years, justified Angela to herself, trying to ignore the fact that red wouldn't go with everything. After the sales assistant had prepared her purchase in an endless spray of tissue paper and placed it in the distinct yellow shopping bag that Angela had envied for years growing up, Angela took a perverse pleasure in the envious glances that came her way.

Angela heard her train being called. Engrossed in her paperwork, the tea cold beside her, she gathered up her things and put them in her bag, the thrill of her *investment*, as she liked to call it, still fresh. At this rate, she wasn't going to reach Tetbury until after nine o'clock. She should have used the payphone to update her mum. Oh well, it was too late now.

Settling down into her seat, she watched a small crowd of commuters dash past her window, all keen to get on the train and back to their suburban lives. Angela grimaced. As much as she loved Tetbury, she was always happy to return to the city and simply couldn't imagine living in the commuter belt. She thought of Mitchell – if their relationship continued, is that what would eventually happen to them? Would he want children? She hoped not. The predictability of it all repelled her, mainly because it would be her career that would fall by the wayside. Maybe her feelings would change in the future, but she didn't think so. *It's different when they're your own*, said countless ex-colleagues who'd all given up work for their little darlings. How often had she heard that? It wasn't just about her career; she simply didn't feel the need.

With Evelyn now in the picture, however, and the opportunity to find out more about her background, would that change things? Her gut said no. She was still thinking about it when she finally arrived in Tetbury.

Her mum, clearly ready for bed, opened the door before Angela had a chance to slip her key in the lock. It was late for her parents and the silent warning of her mum's finger to her lips indicated her father was already asleep. As Angela said goodnight, she went to her own bedroom, quietly getting undressed, brushing her teeth, and, in her nightie, slipping beneath the covers. She would unpack the rest of her case tomorrow.

Perhaps her reluctance to have children was because she knew just how many unwanted children there already were in the world, she thought as she remembered Susan's words from one of the meetings. Closing her eyes against the darkness, she didn't delve too deeply. It distracted her from the present moment and her future plans. And Angela had always succeeded by moving forward.

45

Friday, 25 November 1988

To say I was hungover is the understatement of the century. After I got back home, I must have drunk almost two bottles of wine last night, judging by the state of the coffee table. Even my normal hangover cure of paracetamol, coffee and a bagel didn't work. That's the problem with approaching thirty – I used to be able to drink several nights in a row and feel fine, but the hangovers are definitely starting to get worse.

A.

46

Rosemary

Rosemary had put off sorting out the loft for as long as she could, but she knew she had to face it someday. And she'd rather do it now than later, especially with Angela visiting, as she could keep James company while she got her jobs done. Rosemary didn't like to think too much about what would happen if James died, but her practical nature urged her to sort out their paperwork. The majority of it was in order, of course – James had seen to that – but she was conscious she hadn't been as organised as usual recently. Over the years, she'd become more and more involved in James's business, starting off helping him with the books. Before they'd retired, James often asked her for help, consulting in areas such as strategy, finance and growth. She'd enjoyed it as well as being good at it. After every project, he always told her how invaluable her advice had been and when the business grew and became a major name in the industry, Rosemary felt proud that she'd helped. Of course, James oversaw everything, but still...

It had been her recommendation to franchise the business, which was one of the most profitable outcomes for the company. More than profitable, in fact: it had made them very wealthy. She'd spent weeks researching and preparing the proposal and costings. Her gut instinct told her it was a good move, but she needed the numbers to work, otherwise it would be a non-starter. When James came home a few weeks later, telling her his board of investors had approved the proposal, Rosemary had been thrilled, and had pulled out a bottle of chilled champagne.

'My wonderful, gorgeous, brainy wife!' James had said, grabbing her in a hug. 'I would be nowhere without you!'

Rosemary had laughed – it was all talk, of course; James was prone to dramatic exclamations – but she couldn't help hoping that he might invite her to oversee the franchise development now that it had been approved.

'But what about Angela?' he'd objected when she'd mentioned it. 'She's about to do her GCEs, then sixth form, and then university. She's going to need you at home, not gallivanting around the country meeting potential franchise partners. Besides,' he'd added, 'I've already appointed Lenny Duncan to manage things. You remember Lenny, don't you, Rosie love?'

She knew he was right about the timing with Angela's exams, but still, Rosemary couldn't help but feel disappointed. And Lenny! Yes, she remembered him – one of the old boys in James's network. He knew the product, that was for sure, but he hadn't spent weeks researching the market trends, understanding franchising and projecting the costs, had he? It hadn't become a point of contention between them because Rosemary hadn't let it. Their roles had been clear since they'd adopted Angela. Still, even if the business paperwork was no longer her responsibility, she always liked to keep an eye on things at home.

Which is why she found herself amongst the dusty beams and boxes of the loft. She'd had to get the stepladder to reach the hatch, pushing the white square piece of wood so she could peer into the dark hole. As she pulled herself up, a roll of rubbish bags tucked under one arm and her legs dangling from the ceiling, she flapped her hand aimlessly in the dark to find the cord to switch on the light. Her fingers grasped the small, bell-shaped plastic and she gratefully tugged on it, blinking at the sudden burst of light on her surroundings. At one end, old suitcases were lined up like dominoes ready to fall, while at the other, a series of large boxes were stacked, their battered corners showing their age. She sighed, regretting not bringing a radio to help pass the time.

Two hours later, Rosemary, surrounded by mounds of papers and files, was almost enjoying herself. Her approach was simple: empty the container, throw out the rubbish, and put everything back in alphabetical order. Once she'd got going, she'd worked quickly, and it was when she was about to repack the last box that she saw she'd missed something. A brown envelope, its edges bleeding with coffee-coloured stains, lay at the bottom. It was addressed to James and, opening it up, she pulled out a piece of yellowed paper. She smoothed it out, its official status marked by the faded red symbol of the Royal Crest.

It took just seconds to read the birth certificate and Rosemary felt sick as the truth of Evelyn's words glared back at her. The paper fell from her hand, fluttering into the open box before landing face down. Rosemary looked around her as if to escape. It had to be a mistake. James would never do such a thing – not to her.

Tears clouded her vision. Wiping them away, she picked up the document and read it over and over, her brain taking its time to believe what she suspected she already knew. No, she told herself resolutely, because if she had known, she would have asked him about it immediately. Wouldn't she? Rosemary thought about the photo of James and Angela, their similarities so obvious even the delivery man saw it. As Rosemary held the paper in her hand, she realised it wasn't cancer that she needed to worry about separating her from James, but his lies.

47

Angela

It was Angela's second night in Tetbury after arriving late the night before. Angela watched from the table as her mum stood in front of the Aga and heated up some milk. It was an age-old tradition that Rosemary used whenever she needed a pick-me-up, the warm and sweet aroma of the hot chocolate soothing her. So, Angela knew something was on her mum's mind when she handed her a cup and sat down opposite her at the well-worn table.

'You look tired, Mum,' she said. Angela had tried to sound sympathetic but somehow it didn't come out that way.

Rosemary didn't reply, simply nodded, and Angela wondered what was on her mind.

'Have the doctors given you any more updates?' probed Angela.

'Not really,' replied her mum. 'They just keep reassuring us that we're almost finished with the chemotherapy.'

'Well, that's good news,' Angela said, but her mum didn't appear to share her enthusiasm.

'If I'd had any idea what this cancer would do to us... how it would change everything...' murmured Rosemary, almost to herself. She placed her head in her hands so Angela couldn't hear the rest of the muffled words.

'What's that, Mum?' Angela waited patiently, unsure what else to do, but when her mother looked up she saw her eyes were dry.

'I said, sometimes you have to wonder if he would be better off dead.'

Angela went to her own room and looked at herself in the large mirror as she removed her make-up. Smoothing night cream into her skin, she tried to make sense of her mum's words: *better off dead*. What had she meant exactly? Euthanasia? Or was there something else going on? Had she wanted to gauge Angela's reaction? If so, she must have known that Angela would be horrified by the statement. She waited until she heard her mum go into her bedroom before getting into her pyjamas. She wasn't used to going to bed so early but perhaps it was what she needed. What they all needed.

She turned out the light and lay in the darkness, trying to rationalise her mum's words. Closing her eyes, she decided to see how both her parents were in the morning and go from there. Surely her mum would feel better after a good night's sleep.

48

Evelyn

It was three days before Evelyn listened to the message on her answerphone. She didn't really know how to use it, but the flashing light was driving her to distraction and she pressed one of the buttons in frustration. Listening to Angela's message, she called her back immediately, wondering what could be so urgent.

'Ello? Angela?'

'Hello?'

'It's Evelyn.'

'Hello. How are you?' Evelyn could hear the low hum of background noise. She must be in her office.

'Can't complain. I just got your message. Sorry, it's a bit late but I didn't realise the message was from you. It's normally those irritating telesales people trying to sell me something.'

'Well, I was ringing you because I wanted to let you know my bag was stolen and unfortunately it had your key and the copy I had made in it.'

'What!' exclaimed Evelyn. 'How the hell did you let that happen?'

Angela smiled briefly. Evelyn clearly agreed with her that it was only tourists who were daft enough to be the victims of petty crime.

'Buggers, I tell you,' continued Evelyn. 'The amount of theft that goes on is just—'

'I'm at work at the moment but I'm going to call the locksmith now and get them to change your locks. There's no record of your address in the bag so it's unlikely that anyone could use them, but it would make me feel better. Of course, I'll pay for it as well…'

'Well, that's very good of you,' replied Evelyn. 'Thank you,' she added, remembering her earlier vow to appreciate her daughter more than Mother ever did.

'OK, I'll let you know what time once I've confirmed with the locksmith. Speak soon.'

And with that Angela hung up. Evelyn replaced the phone thinking how busy she sounded. She imagined her in a big fancy office – did it overlook the Thames? wondered Evelyn – before heading off to court to argue cases in a fancy wig. It was so far from Evelyn's own reality that for a moment she felt off balance. It was bizarre to think that just a few months ago she couldn't have even pictured Angela, yet here they were, reunited, and they seemed to be making progress.

As she went to sit down in her chair, despite the cold she decided to keep the living room door open so she could hear the phone when Angela rang back. If the locksmith was coming to change the locks, she might get him to add an extra security lock for a bit of extra peace of mind. The anonymous letters still haunted Evelyn, especially at night, and even though she'd told herself repeatedly that it was only the lads daring each other, the inclusion of the small amount of coke had unnerved her. It was just a bit too personal.

49

Rosemary

There'd been lies before, but smaller things that James always managed to rebuff with the classic *but I didn't want to worry you*. They were minor business matters usually, and you could hardly really describe them as lies, more omissions. He occasionally told fibs about what time he got in after a night out at the pub but what man didn't? Rosemary knew that the odd white lie between couples was normal – if not a necessity – for a marriage to survive. But this level of deceit was something else entirely. It wasn't just that James had lied to her about who Angela really was, but that he'd got a girl pregnant and left her. Why hadn't he done the right thing and married her? What if it had been her in that situation?

'That's exactly why I wanted to adopt her! To make it right!' blustered James after she'd confronted him the same evening in bed. They'd been going over it for hours, Rosemary refusing to yield to his deft sales patter. 'I was young and stupid, Rosie. Surely you can understand that?'

Or ambitious and inconvenienced, Rosemary thought, the deception still raw, making her vicious. And while the sheer exhaustion of arguing for so long had eventually made her nod her head in acknowledgement, she didn't understand. Not even a little bit. The irony hit hard: years of trying and wanting a child of their own, and all this time James already had a daughter.

Whom he'd abandoned.

Rosemary didn't know how she was going to get past it. It changed everything. And then there was Angela herself. They would have to tell her – how would she react?

It had been several days since she'd confronted him. They hadn't discussed it since – there seemed very little left to say – but as she went about her days, looking after James, she began to thaw. The prospect of losing him to cancer gradually overshadowed his lie, and death played its part by placing the deceit in context.

50
Angela

Saturday dawned bright and clear. Sounds and smells from the kitchen floated through to her and Angela wondered where she was at first. After the strange conversation with her mum last weekend, she sensed there was something not quite right because the next day her parents had sat in stony silence, and by the afternoon Angela was ready to go home. Whatever was going on, they would work it out.

During the week, though, it played on her mind and she mentioned it to Mitchell as they enjoyed a mid-week dinner at an Italian close to her office. She'd liked the way he listened to her without interrupting, his head slightly cocked to one side.

'Well,' he said, after she'd finished, 'I had hoped to whisk you away somewhere romantic along the coast this weekend, but it sounds like you should visit your parents.'

For a moment, Angela forgot everything except the thought of a weekend away with him. She imagined them cosied up in bed, drinking wine, listening to music...

'Angela?' said Mitchell.

'Sorry,' she smiled. 'You're right – I probably should go and see them, although a weekend with you is certainly tempting,' she added flirtatiously.

'Well, in that case, how about I book something for the New Year?' he suggested.

'That would be wonderful,' she said, leaning over to give him a kiss.

So instead of waking up with Mitchell in a luxurious hotel, she found herself in her old bedroom again. She'd arrived in time for dinner last night and she could easily imagine the conversation from last weekend with her mum had never happened. Her parents seemed back to their normal selves, but then she saw a look in her mum's eye when she thought no one was looking.

Angela looked over at the clock: it had just gone seven forty-five. She could hear her parents having breakfast and decided to join them. Reaching for her old towelling dressing gown, she wrapped herself up and went through to the kitchen.

'Angela!' exclaimed her father. 'Good morning! Did you sleep well?'

'Good morning. Yes, I did thanks.'

'Good morning, darling,' greeted her mother. 'Would you like some eggs? Poached, scrambled or fried?'

'Poached, please.' Taking a chair, Angela enjoyed the pleasurable feeling of being cooked for again while discreetly taking in her father's plate. He hadn't eaten very much.

'Not hungry?' she asked enquiringly.

Her dad looked at her with a silly grin. 'Let's put it this way – I may have had a midnight snack.'

'Oh, Dad, do you think that's a good idea? You shouldn't be groping around for the light switch – what if you fell?'

Her dad laughed. It was good to see. 'Angie darling, you know I've been doing this for years. It's the only time I can enjoy my sweets with a bit of peace and quiet without your mum around to nag me!

Rosemary placed the plate of eggs in front of her silently and Angela tried not to notice her unusual lack of response to James's jest.

'So,' attempted Angela brightly, looking at both of them. 'What shall we do this morning? It looks too cold for gardening.'

'How about a little drive and an early pub lunch?' suggested her dad.

'Sounds good to me!' replied Angela. 'Mum?'

'Well, I still have a few things to do yet...'

'Come on, Rosie. It will do you good to get out,' James encouraged her.

'Will it not be too much for you, James?'

'Of course not! I'll be fine.'

'OK then. Why not?' agreed Rosemary, but Angela sensed her reluctance.

'Great. I'll read the paper and then we'll get off.'

As her dad went through to the living room, the paper tucked under his arm, Angela quickly finished her eggs. As she was about to take her last mouthful, her mum said, 'There's no need to rush. Your dad will be a while yet.'

'But he said after he read the paper – I still need to have a shower and get dressed.'

'That's OK, he normally has a little doze after the paper, so you have a good couple of hours yet.'

'OK.' Angela stood up and went to wash her plate and cutlery in the sink while her mum wiped down the countertops.

'You OK, Mum?' asked Angela.

'Yes, of course. Why?'

'No reason, just checking. I know you have a lot on at the moment,' she added tactfully.

'I'm fine, darling. Why don't you go and take a long shower – you must be exhausted from the journey.'

Feeling dismissed, Angela left the room.

It was after ten that morning when they left the house, Rosemary driving slowly down the High Street past the Market House and through the winding lanes of the Cotswolds. When she stopped the car by the side of the road to take a stroll, Angela took in the landscape. While the shades of crimson, amber and gold had mostly disappeared with the arrival of December, it was still breathtakingly beautiful. She was not a religious person but sometimes she wondered how such scenery could be explained, if not for God.

The three of them walked in silence, Angela holding onto her dad's arm. On some level, she knew they were creating a memory – a memory that would help heal her grief in the months to come. After thirty minutes, James was visibly exhausted, and they went back to the car. As she leant over to help him with his seat belt, Angela heard him puffing hard.

'You OK, Dad?'

'Yes, yes, fine. Just need a moment to catch my breath, that's all.'

'Oh, James, I told you it would be too much for you,' said Rosemary crossly.

'I'm fine, Rosemary. Please don't fuss, for goodness' sake.'

They drove the long way round to a nearby pub, and by the time they arrived, her father seemed to have recovered. He ordered his usual pie and chips while Angela and her mother ordered some soup and rolls. It was a cosy place called The Potting Shed. In summer, it would be filled with tourists, attracted to its traditional Cotswold stone walls, historic fireplaces, and classic wooden furniture made comfortable with cushions.

As they settled down to their food, Angela started telling them about her meetings with Evelyn.

'It's been much better since the second visit,' confirmed Angela, in response to her dad's question.

'That's good, Angel. I thought it might be. I'm so glad you decided to give her another chance.'

'Yes,' replied Angela, 'me too.'

'Well, I'm so pleased that you're starting to develop a little bit of a relationship. I think it's very healthy for everyone,' concluded James. 'Don't you think, Rosemary?'

Angela's mother nodded before taking a sip of her wine.

Angela decided to change the subject. 'So, I was thinking I might join you on Monday for your doctor's appointment, if that's all right?' she asked, as the waitress cleared their plates away.

'Well, what about work, love?' asked James. 'The appointment isn't until three o'clock.'

'It's OK, I can take one day off.' She couldn't really – she would have to work even longer during the rest of the week to achieve her target billing hours – but if she didn't do this, she knew she would regret it.

'Well, of course, darling,' added Rosemary. 'You're more than welcome, but your father and I know how busy you are at work and—'

'It's fine, really, Mum,' interrupted Angela determinedly. 'I'd like to come. Maybe we can spend some time in the garden in the morning before we go, and I'll get the first train back on Tuesday morning.'

'Of course it's OK,' said her dad warmly, squeezing her hand. 'I appreciate the support.'

Angela sat in the waiting room, a cold cup of tea abandoned beside her, the polystyrene cup offensive against her lips. They were waiting for the doctor and had been waiting for over an hour now. Her parents seemed accustomed to it, both having brought their books. Angela wished she had brought some work to read but it hadn't seemed appropriate to be working while her dad's prognosis was being discussed. Eventually, a nurse arrived and called them through to the consultant.

A man of about fifty greeted them.

'Mr Steele. How are you? Mrs Steele,' he acknowledged. 'Please do take a seat. And I see you have brought someone else today,' he added cheerfully, indicating Angela.

'Yes, my daughter, Angela,' said her dad with a touch of pride. 'Angela, Mr Redding.'

'Welcome,' said the doctor warmly.

'Thank you.'

'Right, Mr Steele,' started the doctor, as they all settled into their chairs. 'How are you feeling?'

'Good, good... a little tired but you said that would happen.'

'Yes, that's perfectly normal, especially as the chemotherapy gets more intense, but we're almost there now – just a couple more sessions to go.'

'So, it's normal then?' asked Angela, unable to stop herself.

'What specifically?' asked the doctor.

'The decline as the chemo goes on.'

'Well, it really depends what you're referring to. If you're talking about the side effects – such as tiredness, weight loss, hair loss in some cases, weakness, sickness, nausea – then yes, that's normal. Is there anything else you've noticed?' he asked, turning to James.

'No, no... just everything you've described,' replied her dad.

Angela should have felt relieved. The doctor sensed her need for reassurance.

'Everybody reacts to chemotherapy in different ways, and of course those over fifty will have a more difficult time than those in their twenties and thirties. While there's a lot we don't know about cancer, there are still a lot of reasons to be optimistic. Of course, there are never any guarantees, but I would say the prognosis so far is encouraging.'

Angela felt her shoulders relax at the doctor's reassurance.

'So, looking at the results of your last course, so far, so good,' the doctor continued, changing the subject, rifling through the file in front of him. 'Your blood counts are showing improvement...' Mr Redding frowned as he continued to read. Then, looking up, he smiled. 'There's just a small concern with the protein levels in your blood.'

'What does that mean?' asked Angela, her previous relief forgotten in a flood of anxiety.

'Well, it could mean a variety of things. Most likely it's just an anomaly in the results. I would suggest we test again.'

'And if it's not an anomaly?' Rosemary asked, echoing Angela's thoughts.

'Well, it could mean the start of an infection, and if it is, we'll have to medicate accordingly. But let's not jump to any conclusions,' replied Mr Redding firmly. 'Let's redo the test, and we can go from there.' He issued a set of instructions to a nurse and James was then led away for a blood test. Rosemary got up to leave and Angela followed suit. The appointment was over.

'It was a pleasure to meet you, Angela,' said Mr Redding.

'Thank you.'

'I know it's difficult, but try not to worry too much,' he added as he opened the door for them, seeing them out.

Nodding, Angela followed her mum back into the waiting room.

51

Rosemary

A lie was a bit like cancer, thought Rosemary as she finished preparing the meal for Angela's final night that weekend. Unseen, but deadly if it wasn't contained and eradicated. And like a surgeon, Rosemary wanted to cut it out as soon as possible before it had the chance to spread and do even more damage. Rosemary had been pushing James all weekend to tell Angela about his being her real father, but he had avoided it. Now, after coming home from the doctor's appointment, they only had a few hours left.

'James, you need to tell her before she goes back to London,' she said now as he walked into the kitchen.

'I know, I know...' replied James. 'I will. As soon as we've finished eating.'

Rosemary nodded, wondering whether he would do as he promised. Well, if he didn't bring it up, then she would, she decided, and then there would be no more lies. She could understand why James was worried. She knew Angela would feel similar to how she did: betrayed and deceived. But how could Rosemary help her through it when she was still struggling with it herself?

Rosemary tried to finish eating the succulent roast chicken before giving up and putting her knife and fork together on her plate. It was just after eight thirty and she was apprehensive. James and Angela had both finished eating and were talking about Angela's upcoming week at work. She could see that James had absolutely no intention of breaking the relaxed mood. She tried to catch his eye, but he studiously avoided her.

'James,' she said eventually. 'Wasn't there something you wanted to talk to Angela about before she left?'

'Was there?'

'Yes, there was,' replied Rosemary pointedly.

'Oh?' said Angela. 'Sounds intriguing!'

Rosemary waited for James to speak. Surely he wasn't going to leave it up to her?

'Angela,' he began eventually, clearing his throat. Rosemary had never heard him sound so nervous. 'There's something I've been meaning to tell you for quite a long time now, and I know this is going to be a shock. But I honestly believe you'll understand why I had to do it.'

Rosemary watched Angela. She sat perfectly still, already aware that the news was serious.

'Angie, love, how would you feel if you also met your birth father?'

Rosemary held her breath, waiting for her response, but she could already sense Angela's curiosity.

'I thought the home didn't have that information?' replied Angela, finally. 'Are you saying you know where he is?'

'I do,' replied James. Taking his daughter's hands in both of his, he twisted in his chair, so he was facing her.

'He's sitting here, right in front of you, having loved you from the moment he discovered you were born.'

Rosemary saw Angela swallow, the only hint of her true feelings.

'I'm just sorry I couldn't get to you sooner,' continued James. 'I tried for so long…'

Silence descended around the table and Rosemary braced herself for impact. She'd seen Angela explode several times over the years and it was a harrowing experience for anyone in her path. What would she do? Shout? Scream? Storm out of the house? Cut them off? All of a sudden, she realised she'd been wrong forcing James to tell her. Angela didn't need to experience betrayal. She was about to reach out and take her in her arms and tell her it was all one big mistake when Angela surprised them both.

She launched herself at her father. But instead of the violence Rosemary was expecting, Angela was hugging him hard, tears rolling down her face.

As James gathered her up in his arms, soothing her as if she were a child who had a scraped knee, Rosemary could hear the faint words almost lost in James's shoulder.

'You came for me. I knew you would.'

52

Angela

Angela got back into London early Tuesday morning and went straight to the office. She'd barely slept a wink the night before but as she sat at her cubicle, she felt invincible. As her dad had held her in his arms, the two of them sobbing, for the first time in her life Angela felt like she belonged. She wasn't just some random mistake – she was wanted. Wanted, searched for, and rescued. She thought back to her little girl's dream; now her wish had come true and she let the tears of overwhelming relief and happiness spill over. The other associates looked at her in shock, surprised at her unusual show of emotion.

'You OK, Angela?' asked Nigel tentatively. He sat in the cubicle next to her and he looked like he'd rather be at the North Pole than having to deal with her.

She turned to him with a big smile, the tears still rolling. 'Absolutely – couldn't be better!' Grabbing some tissues, she wiped her face and headed to the toilets, feeling slightly hysterical from happiness and lack of sleep. Looking at herself in the mirror, she could see now why Nigel had been petrified.

Her mascara had streaked down her face and she was grinning like a teenager on weed. She carefully rinsed her face before patting it dry with a paper towel. Yesterday, she had been adopted; today, she had a *real* father who had rescued her from the depressing, pitiful nothingness of a children's home.

When she and her dad had stopped crying, her mum had shown her the birth certificate – as if she needed proof, thought Angela now. She felt it – she knew it – to be true, instinctively. He was everything she'd dreamt he'd be: generous, kind, funny, handsome, successful, rich. It was the fairy-tale ending she'd always hoped for, and it was all hers. Suddenly, she knew she had to tell someone. She hurried back to her desk, noting the relief on Nigel's face as she sat down, and called Mitchell.

Angela was on a roll. Despite her exhaustion, she'd attacked her work and was flying through it. She'd already billed three hours that morning when Clive walked up to her desk.

'Ah, Angela, good to see you. Enjoyed your little holiday?' His tone was laced with sarcasm, but Angela was immune.

'Good morning, Mr Mooring. It was excellent, thank you!'

Expecting her to be more subservient, Angela noted with satisfaction that Clive looked taken aback.

'Anyway, you're back now. Where are we on Sedgwick? Get ready for a briefing in ten minutes,' he instructed, not waiting for a response before turning on his heel. Knowing that would be the first thing he would ask for, Angela had already prepared. Picking up her files, she went to wait for him in the meeting room, unable to stop smiling.

★

Looking at her watch, Angela saw it was already two o'clock. It had been an interesting morning. During the briefing, she could tell Clive had been impressed with her, as she shared another potential legal strategy to present to the Sedgwick board. He had listened carefully as she went through her proposed plan on employment agreements for him to present. If they were successful and the client agreed, it would mean another quarter of a million pounds per annum. At the end of the briefing, Clive sat back, thinking. After a few minutes, it appeared he had come to a decision.

'Why don't you take the lead on this one, Angela, and present this proposal to Sedgwick?'

Angela's heart had quickened at Clive's tone, indicating it was a statement rather than a question. As far as she was aware, no associate had ever presented to a client this large, especially when the stakes were so high. The potential income for the firm was huge and it would all rest on her. If she made just one mistake... well, Angela didn't even want to think about the consequences. Her dream of promotion to senior associate would be just that – a dream. Her career, while not over, would be stagnant. No one would forget a mistake that significant.

'Do you think you can do it?' he asked. 'I think it would be an excellent way to assess your readiness for the next stage in your career.'

He was testing her, she thought. Sink or swim. She knew, though, that while he was bullish, he was also smart. He wouldn't risk so much if he didn't believe in her. It was his reputation at stake as well here. Angela took the bait and looked him straight in the eye.

'I'm ready, Mr Mooring,' she said firmly.

'Good girl,' he replied with a wolfish smile. 'Do the

research and changes I suggested for the proposal and have a jaw-dropping presentation ready. Arrange the meeting asap – we need to get this done before their board breaks for Christmas.'

So here she was, planning, researching and polishing her presentation. She knew bias would be against her from the beginning. Clients certainly didn't like to be handed over to an associate, and she knew that, as a woman, she would have to work even harder to impress. Sedgwick's board was made up of older men, typically between forty-five and fifty years old. She had never once seen a woman on the board. But this was her chance. She had to get it right if she wanted that promotion. She tried to ignore the fact that the male associates would never be tested in such a way. Angela had seen Clive present many times. His style was flamboyant, entertaining, and he walked the thin line between arrogance and confidence. Clients bought into him because of his reputation and network. Angela knew that if she tried to emulate that she would fail. She had to showcase her skill and knowledge another way – her own way. She knew the mechanics of the proposal inside out; knew that it was solid, and that she would be able to answer any questions the board put to her. But how could she make herself memorable? How could she get them to take her seriously? And most importantly, how did she get them to trust her? She had a lot of work to do. If she managed to pull this client presentation off and get the signed contract, it would be a major achievement and the senior associate position would be the icing on the cake. Her dad would be thrilled.

'Angela Steele speaking.'

'Gawd, it's like Fort Knox, trying to get through to you. She was a right cow to me, your receptionist.'

At first Angela thought the receptionist had put the wrong person through.

'A million questions – asked me if I was a client! No, I am not a client, I said. Please put me through now.'

'Evelyn!' replied Angela, finally understanding. 'Is everything OK?'

'No, everything is not OK. The pains in my legs are something else, Angela. Keeping me up all hours.'

'I'm sorry to hear that,' she said.

'But that's not why I called you. Did you book the locksmith?'

Angela mentally swore to herself. She had completely forgotten about it.

'I tried to call,' she lied, 'but I couldn't get one on such short notice. Let me try again for you and call you back.'

'OK. Thank you.'

The line was silent. 'Everything OK, Evelyn?' asked Angela eventually.

'Yes. Sorry. If you could arrange the locksmith… the sooner the better, to be honest. All the goings-on have me jumpy, and I don't scare easily.'

'What goings-on?' asked Angela.

'I don't know,' replied Evelyn vaguely. 'There's a lot of noise. And someone knocked at my door late at night, but when I got up there was no one there.'

'I'm sure it's nothing, Evelyn. I'll call the locksmith right now and get it sorted.'

'Thank you.'

'Oh, by the way, will you be free one evening next week? I'd like to come and see you. I have a bit of news.'

'Of course. Any night apart from bingo night. Just let me know.'

'OK, will do.'

Angela put down the phone thoughtfully. She picked up the phone book and paid extra for the locksmith to visit within twenty-four hours. Having called Evelyn back to confirm the locksmith, Angela got back to work. She would have to skip the adoption support meeting tonight – a shame because she would have liked to have shared her news. The secretary had booked the meeting for Thursday morning with Sedgwick, which meant Angela had less than two days to prepare.

For a few moments, she felt panicked at the enormity of what she had agreed to do. Everything she had worked so hard for could be lost in an instant if she didn't get this right. And getting it right meant getting the client to buy in and part with their cash. It meant getting them to sign on the dotted line. Angela's job was to eliminate all potential doubt from the client's mind. Taking a few deep breaths, Angela told herself she could do this. She just needed to stay calm.

Angela could feel herself sweating despite the rapidly dropping temperature of the cold winter. She had practically lived at the office the last two days, only going home to shower and sleep. She had practised the Sedgwick presentation over and over again until the information had seeped into her bones. She had prepared for every single question the board members could challenge her with and done endless mock presentations using the interns as her audience. Instead of trying to disguise the fact that she was a woman in a so-called man's world, she decided to take advantage of it, focusing on one of the most important things in their lives for the majority of the board

– their wives and families – and how having robust, revised employment contracts in place would protect and benefit not only the employees themselves but also the company. She was also advising them that if they implemented her proposal, they would be the first company in the UK to do so, signalling their innovation and progress to the rest of the industry. Well, it never hurt to leverage their ego, thought Angela. Ultimately, it was personalised and professional but it was also very different from the norm.

She had arrived at the client's office early to set up the transparencies. She would deliver the information verbally and she had her printed handouts ready. She had gone home at around nine the night before, intending to choose her clothes, have a bath and get a reasonably early night. She surprised herself when she woke up the next morning to her alarm at five – she didn't think she would have slept so well. Feeling refreshed, she made some coffee, took a hot shower and got dressed. She had chosen a well-cut navy suit to match the corporate culture of Sedgwick but she had added her own style with a striking, canary-yellow blouse underneath. Unbuttoning her jacket now, she was glad the shirt material was light against her skin. She looked around for a window to open to try to cool down a bit. Seeing none, she took a sip of water and checked her watch. Where was Mr Mooring? He had promised to be here. As the board members strolled in, she could see a few of them were wondering the same thing. As each one entered, she greeted them by name, shook their hand and informed them they would be starting in a few minutes. She could tell most of them thought she was Mooring's assistant, which she supposed she was, in a way. But not today, thought Angela.

As the board helped themselves to coffee and sat down,

she knew she would have to start without him. Damn him, she thought to herself. She would bet any money he'd done this on purpose to unnerve her. Another test. She thought about her dad – her real dad, she corrected herself happily she would have to get used to that – and how hard he'd worked for his success. She could do this. Angela forced herself to breathe three times. She was ready.

She didn't even notice when Mooring finally entered the room and, thinking back, she didn't remember any of the board members being distracted by his entrance either. They were rapt. Introducing their families into the mix had been a risk that could have backfired, but it had paid off. She'd added a touch of humour and within ten minutes, she knew it was going to be a success. She had done the hard part – getting them to like her – and she had gained their trust with the quality of information and being able to answer every single question in detail. Not only had they signed a letter of intent on the spot for her to undertake her proposal starting January 1989, but the managing director had requested a second proposal to take it one step further. At the end of the presentation, it was her the members had gathered around, not Mooring, as she'd expected, and as she left the office with him, the letter of intent safely in her briefcase, she struggled to tell what he was thinking. It was only when they got out onto the street that he turned to her.

'I think a celebratory lunch is in order, don't you?' he asked.

'Well, I still have quite a bit—'

'Don't be ridiculous – you can take an hour out for lunch. Besides, you deserve it. It looks like you made quite the impression.'

'Thank you, Mr Mooring. Lunch sounds good.'

'Excellent. Shall we do Sheekey's? I know it's your favourite restaurant,' he said with a wink.

'Lovely,' replied Angela, wondering how they would get into the popular restaurant at such short notice; surely not even Mr Mooring had such influence? But it turned out he did, and as Angela clinked glasses with him in celebration, tipsy on triumph, she realised she could get used to this lifestyle that Raymond had enjoyed so often.

It was Friday afternoon, the day after Angela's presentation to Sedgwick, and the rumours about promotions were circulating thick and fast. There had been a management meeting that morning and Angela could barely concentrate. It was the last meeting of the year: an important one with business decisions being finalised for 1989, and new promotions were a key agenda item. If she got it, it would mean a massive jump in responsibility, and with it a significant increase in salary. She would have her own team of associates and interns as well as her own office, rather than the cramped cubicle.

What if she'd got it all wrong, though? Angela didn't think she'd be able to swallow it if Mr Mooring gave the role to Raymond. But even with her complaint to HR hanging over Raymond, Mooring might – she'd seen it happen often enough. The problem with her industry was that it was often more about connections and influence than it was about winning cases and accounts. The phone rang, and Angela jumped. It was Mooring's latest secretary asking all the associates to gather in the boardroom. Angela replaced the receiver. She'd done her best; there was nothing more to be done. She hoped it was enough.

53

Tuesday, 6 December 1988

Dear Diary,

I've been so busy, but things feel like they're really coming together now. I can't believe how much my dad and I look alike – I don't know why I didn't see it before. Perhaps I did on a subconscious level. Was Matron at the children's home in on it? Did she keep his secret when they went through the adoption process? I also wonder how Evelyn felt about it all. At least, though, he did something about the situation – what did she do? Nothing! Anyway, it was nice to have a drink at Sheekey's restaurant – very fancy. Mooring can be quite charming when he wants to be.

A.

Wednesday, 7 December 1988

Dear Diary,

Not long until Christmas and still so much to do. I wonder what Mitchell does during this time of year? A Caribbean cruise? An all-inclusive in a luxury resort in Spain? Imagine the two of us relaxing on our sun loungers. I would be wearing a red bikini that sets off my dark hair and Mitchell would dutifully arrange the umbrella, so my skin doesn't burn. We would spend our days lounging and swimming, occasionally ordering a glass of champagne from the bar to cool down. After lunch, we would head back up to our suite where we would make love before falling asleep in each other's arms. After a nap, we would order afternoon tea, enjoying delicate sandwiches and fresh strawberries on our balcony overlooking the ocean. I would then take a long bath while Mitchell goes to the gym (well, he has to keep that body in shape somehow!) before I slip into a sexy dress for dinner. Bliss – how nice would it be not to have to spend Christmas in this dreary weather?

I took a walk down Oxford Street this week. I saw a watch in the Ernest Jones window that would be a perfect Christmas present for him. It might be a bit much, though.

A.

54

Angela

As she emerged from the Tube station at Archway, Angela could see the back of the W5 bus as it left the bus stop, trundling up the hill. Damn, she thought, she would have to walk. It was twenty minutes later when she stood outside Evelyn's door. She listened carefully to see if she could hear anything, but the block of flats was silent.

Angela knocked and Evelyn answered the door after several moments, all the while telling Charlie to calm down.

'Hello, Evelyn!'

'Hello. Come on in.'

'Everything all right?'

'Yes, yes, all fine. It's nice to see you again. Thanks for organising the locksmith as well,' she added.

'No problem. I'm glad it got done eventually,' replied Angela.

'Sit, sit. Do you want a biscuit?' Evelyn asked as Charlie settled himself at her feet.

'No, I'm fine thanks,' said Angela, sitting on the sofa opposite her. The same magazines were still on the coffee table, but tonight there was also a crossword puzzle book splayed facedown, its spine a river of tiny cracks.

Angela picked up the book.

'Seventeen down,' commented Evelyn. 'It's niggling me. Maybe your brain can work it out.'

Angela looked at the clue: *Cold drink in prisons (6)*

She drew a blank. Crosswords weren't exactly her forte.

'What – that university education not paying off?' Evelyn laughed.

Angela had to smile at her outspokenness. It was hard not to.

'Well, if you're not having a biscuit, can you get me one? I would do it, but my legs are playing up.'

'Of course.'

'While you're up there, can you also pop the frozen lasagne in the oven? The oven should be hot enough by now.'

Evelyn wasn't shy in asking, thought Angela to herself, as she removed the lasagne from its wrapping. You had to admire her in a way, though: Evelyn was a hustler. Having put the food in the oven, Angela found the biscuits, then washed the few dishes in the sink and wiped down the surfaces. There, she thought, it looks better already.

'There you are – thought you'd got lost in there,' said Evelyn.

'No, I'm here,' Angela replied as she put the plate of biscuits in front of her. Evelyn had put the fire on and the lamps created a warm glow in the room. The TV was on low, the flickering images capturing Evelyn's attention every so often. Angela sat on the couch letting the heat massage her feet from the walk from the bus stop.

'I brought you a Christmas present,' said Angela, handing over the gift.

Evelyn looked surprised. 'Oh, thank you. I'm sorry I don't have one for you. As you can see, I don't really do Christmas.' She indicated the absence of a tree and decorations.

'Oh, why not?' replied Angela, the admission strangely bringing back memories of the meagre Christmases at the children's home.

'Well, after my father died, Mother never wanted to celebrate. I suppose it was her way of coping. And since then... well, I've just never bothered.'

'Well, I hope you like the gift,' Angela said, at a loss how to respond. She'd struggled to know what to buy. In the end, she'd chosen a soft, warm cashmere scarf that would be useful for when Evelyn walked Charlie.

'I'm sure I will. So, you said on the phone the other day you had some news?'

'I do,' replied Angela, and started to tell Evelyn about the events of her last visit to Tetbury.

'I couldn't believe it when he told me. I'm still in shock, actually,' admitted Angela when she'd finished.

'I'm not surprised,' replied Evelyn. 'It's a lot to take in.'

Angela waited for her to continue – it wasn't like her to hold back.

'It's incredible that in just a few months I've found my real parents – it's surreal,' filled in Angela. 'And for my dad to come and find me and rescue me from the children's home – well, I dread to think where I would have ended up!'

Evelyn's beady eye caught Angela's, an uncomfortable silence filling the room at the implication. Angela had surprised herself with the remark. She didn't know where it had come from. While it had been a bit close to the bone, it was still true, wasn't it?

'Yes, you've been lucky. It could have gone either way,' replied Evelyn, unwilling to be drawn into the conversation further. 'So, how's work going? By the way, would you like a cup of tea? No? Well, I might just get myself one, if that's all right.'

Angela was about to tell Evelyn about her promotion but as she watched Evelyn struggle to get up, Angela offered to make it for her.

'Thank you, that's very kind,' replied Evelyn, immediately sitting back down.

'While I'm up, do you mind if I use your loo first?'

'Feel free,' replied Evelyn before taking a bite of the chocolate digestive. Locking the door behind her, Angela looked at herself in the bathroom mirror. She knew the harsh strip lighting wasn't the most flattering, but she thought she looked more tired than usual. After the initial jubilation at her father's confession, it was dampened by his illness, especially since the result of the blood protein tests had come back. Unfortunately, it wasn't an anomaly, which meant additional medication. While her father had reassured her that the doctor was still positive and the test result should be considered just a minor setback, Angela had a distinct sense of foreboding. It was unusual for her. She dealt in facts, not feelings.

Angela turned away from the mirror to dry her hands on the small, pink towel. In doing so, she accidently knocked a small basket off the side of the sink, the contents spilling over the floor. Kneeling down on the bathmat to pick them up, she felt something under her knee. The contents of the basket completely forgotten, Angela lifted up the mat. Underneath, the linoleum had been carelessly cut into a flap, which when lifted, revealed a small gap in the floorboards. Within the gap, Angela could see the edge of a plastic bag sticking out – just enough to grip between thumb and forefinger. Angela paused. It really wasn't her business what Evelyn kept hidden in her bathroom. But after a slight hesitation, Angela pulled out the small plastic bag. Evelyn had said she'd been clean for years now – that was one of the conditions of Susan facilitating the meeting. So why was Angela now holding a bag of white powder?

As Angela stood on the escalator taking her down into the depths of the Underground, she turned over the possibility that Evelyn was back on drugs. That would perhaps explain why Evelyn was getting things confused: hearing strange noises in the night and so on. It made sense, thought Angela as she stepped onto the train. She was surprised to find herself feeling worried about Evelyn. Angela stopped herself. It wasn't her responsibility. All she could do was help out where she could, but she knew that if someone chose that lifestyle it would be very difficult to prevent it. All she could do was bear it in mind next time Evelyn had one of her turns, as Angela had now begun to think of them, and not take the drama too seriously.

55

Wednesday, 14 December 1988

Dear Diary,

I have started to wonder about St Matthew's. Is it even still there or has it been demolished to make way for new houses? Ray and Kath must be long gone now, but if it is still in operation who is running it? Could I go back there and see? What would it be like walking down the gritty streets of Hackney? The home was at the crossroads of Mile Street and Newsome Avenue, set back from the road. It was a red-bricked, three-storey building surrounded by wasteland and trees. The wire fencing all around was supposed to keep us in, and everybody else out. I wonder what happened to Nelly. She's the only one I haven't been able to track down. Does she remember nights snuggled in our dorm? It's been years and I know it will be painful, but perhaps it's time to revisit the place.

A.

56

Evelyn

Releasing the smoke from her lungs, she stroked Charlie absent-mindedly, thinking about Angela's news. She wondered how Rosemary had reacted. She must have confronted James. What had he said? She hoped she'd given him hell for his lies. Angela seemed happy enough, though – delighted in fact. And why wouldn't she be? James probably retold the events as if he were her knight in shining armour. Bastard.

It was thoughtful of Angela to bring her a Christmas present – beautifully wrapped it was as well, thought Evelyn as she checked the door was locked. She probably felt guilty about losing the key. It was unthinkable. Only tourists were daft enough to let thieves on the Underground get the better of them. Still, perhaps she was tired; it sounded like her work kept her very busy. Didn't she say she spent more time at the office than she did at home?

Well, it was a different time compared to when Evelyn was younger. All that was expected of a woman back then was to get married and produce babies, and here Angela was in her power suit probably earning more in a week than she got from the council in a year! It was all different these days.

Evelyn got up from her chair and went to check the door again.

With December in full swing, it was perhaps no surprise that Evelyn had had one too many drinks one Saturday night. She could normally hold her booze, but when she woke up the next morning she couldn't remember how she'd got home. She certainly couldn't remember getting into bed. She was still fully dressed when she woke up, so she presumed she must have come straight into the bedroom and crashed immediately. But it was when she went into the living room, the pounding in her head almost unbearable in its intensity, that she almost passed out in fear.

Someone had entered her house while she was unconscious and moved things around. Nothing seemed to have been stolen, but the dining table had been put upside down, and the TV had been unplugged and moved to the other end of the room. Evelyn forced herself to think. Had she left the door unlocked? No. She was being extra vigilant these days. But how else would they have got in? And why hadn't Charlie barked? Another thought pierced the pain in her head: had she been so drunk she'd done this herself? It would explain why Charlie hadn't caused a fuss and, if someone had broken in, surely the lock would be broken? Yes, that was it. Perhaps she'd come home, worse for wear, and decided to rearrange some furniture. It was a new one for her – she usually liked to sing when she'd had a few drinks – but it was true she'd been thinking about her décor for a while since seeing Brenda's new flat. Evelyn began to feel the horror of intrusion recede as the possibility presented itself. She must have had an awful lot to drink. There was only one way to find out: she would have to phone Brenda.

'Honestly, Evie,' laughed Brenda. 'I can't imagine what you were thinking, turning your dining table upside down! You must have had your own party when you got home because you weren't that bad when you left me!'

'Oh God,' replied Evelyn. After telling Brenda she would call her later, Evelyn hung up and tried to think.

Had she come home and started drinking? If so, the bottles must be somewhere. She frantically searched the flat but came up empty-handed. Perhaps the drink was starting to affect her more than she liked to think? She'd said it many times before, but she really would have to start cutting back.

Then she thought of the threatening letters, the drugs, and the stranger pushing past her on her way back from bingo. Evelyn didn't believe in coincidences – was the moved furniture somehow linked? Another way of sending a message? But how could someone get into her flat? It was impossible – she'd just had the locks changed! And then she thought the unthinkable: was Angela somehow involved in this? She was the one who had arranged the locksmith.

Evelyn thought back to the timeframe of events. They had only started happening after she'd met Angela. Angela knew where she lived, had her details. But why? Evelyn shook her head dismissively, trying to clear her mind, but fear began to creep its way back in, pushing at the edges of her hangover, making her pace frantically.

57

Rosemary

Rosemary quietly opened the front door in case James was still sleeping. She'd been to help Eileen sort out the leftover things from the WI Christmas jumble sale, which had been held the week before. Tetbury was a generous town and while they'd had a good sale, there were still a lot of things left that would need to be taken to a charity shop. However, with the two of them, they worked quickly.

'Thanks so much for helping me,' said Eileen. 'Fancy a spot of lunch as a thank you?'

Rosemary was tempted. 'That would have been lovely, but I'd best get back. I don't like to leave James for too long.'

Eileen nodded in understanding. 'How's he doing?'

'He's doing well. Still very tired but...'

Eileen squeezed her arm sympathetically.

'Anyway,' replied Rosemary, 'I'll see you soon.'

'Take care, Rosemary, and love to James.'

Arriving home just after midday, she was ready for some lunch and hoped James had prepared a salad. Instead, she found the stepladder placed under the loft but with the hatch closed. Where was James? Surely he hadn't gone up there by himself? And if so, why would he close it? After searching the house and the garden and finding no sign of him, she climbed the ladder.

'James,' she called, pushing aside the hatch covering. 'Are you up there?'

Finally able to see into the loft, Rosemary looked around her in dismay. It looked like someone had burgled them. All the boxes that she'd carefully organised were unpacked, the papers strewn everywhere.

James turned to her in surprise. 'Aren't you supposed to be with Eileen?'

'James!' replied Rosemary, ignoring the question. 'What on earth are you doing up here?'

'I, er, I was just trying to help.'

'Help?' replied Rosemary. 'How?'

'Well, you know, just make sure all the paperwork is sorted. I know you've been wanting to have a clear-out for a while.'

She tried not to lose her patience. 'OK, well, can you put everything back and come down?' she asked, retreating down the stepladder. 'It's not safe for you to be coming up here when I'm not home. What if you fell?'

She didn't hear James reply, but she was pretty sure he sounded cross. Heading to the kitchen, she went to make them some lunch, the absence of a freshly prepared salad only adding to her irritation. It was a good twenty minutes before James came down and as she heard him plant his feet on the stepladder, she went to make sure he got down safely.

'Rosie love, all sorted and everything is back in its place,' he announced cheerfully. 'How's Eileen?'

'She's fine. She asked about you.'

'Did she? That's nice of her.'

'It was. Come on, I've made you a salad and there's a little bit of pie left, if you want it.'

'Sounds good. I'll just put the stepladder back in the shed and wash my hands and I'll be through in a minute. Perhaps after lunch I might go and see who's in the pub and read the paper. Is that all right?'

A few days later, Rosemary was sorting through her jewellery box. Over the years, she'd gathered quite a collection. There was the black opal ring she'd inherited from her mother, passed down through the generations. She rarely put it on but occasionally she took it out and held it in the palm of her hand, imagining the women of the past who had worn it. There was a thin gold chain with a diamond pendant from James, which he'd given to her when they'd adopted Angela, and a silver cross, tarnished with age now, but still special as it had been the first piece of jewellery James had ever bought for her. It had three diamonds in it – one for each month they'd been together, he'd told her.

Removing everything, she decided to give the box a clean and it was then that she noticed the hinge was coming loose. James had gone to meet one of his friends in the village to talk cars and business, so she would have to wait for him to come back to fix it. Rosemary looked at the collection of rings, necklaces and earrings spread across the table in different piles. She hated to leave the job unfinished. James did pretty much all of the DIY around the house and she was happy for him to do it. She went into the shed once a week just to tidy it up a bit so she knew where all the tools were kept – it was such a small job, she really didn't need to bother him with it.

She would unlock the shed and get the screwdrivers and fix the jewellery box herself.

The shed door swung open as the key turned in the lock and Rosemary shuddered at the sight of a large spider's web across one corner of the doorframe. Stepping inside and looking around, she was disappointed to see that everything was a bit of a mess despite only tidying a few days ago. A workbench to her right was covered with a plastic sheet on which oil canisters, tools, nuts and bolts lay haphazardly, while a cylinder block was trapped in a vice. On the other side, a lawnmower and rake were propped up against an old chest of drawers. On the bench right in front of her she saw the black tool box, which she knew held various screwdrivers of different sizes. On top of the box, a folded piece of paper was threaded through the handle, most likely a warranty left there by James as a reminder to file it away. Breathing a sigh of relief, she picked it up and locked the shed door, safe from all the creepy-crawlies.

Back at the house, she opened the box, checking the contents, then sat down at the table, screwdriver in hand. Rosemary felt a ridiculous sense of accomplishment, mending the broken hinge. She put the screwdriver back in the tool box and had closed the lid when she caught sight of the folded piece of paper again and decided to file it. Unfolding the paper to check the contents, she immediately saw that it wasn't a warranty or a manual but a letter she had never seen before.

After a few minutes, she placed the paper slowly down on the table. Calmly, she picked up her now-fixed jewellery box, examining it from every angle. Through the glass cover she could just see the silver cross, the three diamonds blinking back at her. With a strength she didn't even know she had, she raised the jewellery box high over her head and brought it crashing down on the table in front of her, scattering its contents in an explosion of grief.

7 September 1974
Dear Mr and Mrs Steele,
APPROVAL FOR ADOPTION
It is with great pleasure that I inform you that the assessment of your suitability for adoption, carried out on 16 July, has been successful. Please find enclosed a copy of the report for your reference.

As a next step, we would like to invite you for a meeting on 18 September at 10 a.m. to finalise the arrangements for adoption. We have recently taken in a two-month-old baby boy and believe he would be an ideal addition to your family.

I look forward to discussing this matter further on 18 September and would be grateful if you could confirm your attendance by return mail.

Yours sincerely,
Matron Ward

58

Evelyn

Evelyn felt the familiar crawl of her skin signalling her need for vodka. She'd been dry for only a few days, but she could see the slight tremor. The shock of waking up to a rearranged flat and having no recollection still traumatised her. As much as she tried to reassure herself that she'd simply overdone it on the drink, she couldn't deny the number of strange incidences. It was becoming difficult to know what was real and what was in her imagination. The last time she'd gone out, she'd convinced herself that someone was following her. She'd broken into a run then, so petrified she hadn't even noticed the pain in her legs; her only thought was to get to the safety of home. But she didn't even feel safe there any more. Evelyn resisted the temptation of the clear liquid and lit a cigarette instead, hoping she could summon up the courage to go outside.

Evelyn looked furtively about as she walked Charlie around the estate. It was all quiet. Still, she slipped her hand in her pocket, her fingers wrapping themselves around the handle of the small kitchen knife, although she didn't believe her tormentor was someone on the estate any more. She took the knife with her everywhere she went now, always making sure it was concealed but easily accessible in her pocket. She knew Brenda would think she was being ridiculous, but she felt safer with it. She just couldn't shake the feeling that she was being watched. It started with a prickle on her neck, working its way across her scalp like a spider. She hated it. It only really went away when she was at home. But even then, she had to go through an elaborate checking process before she felt truly secure. She'd taped up the letter box, much to the annoyance of the postman, who had pushed the post through anyway, easily tearing the flap away from the Sellotape. After that, she'd used superglue and packing tape and that had seemed to do the job. The postman couldn't get the mail in and she could hear him muttering as he knocked on her door. She'd shouted through to him to leave it on the mat and when she heard the tread of his steps fading she'd looked through the peephole before opening the door and picking up the post.

She was also vigilant – probably excessively so – about making sure the front door was locked all the time, and every night she checked all the windows were secure. She had been sleeping with a chair against her bedroom door, but recently she'd taken to moving the dresser, its heavy presence a reassuring barricade against any intruder, as an extra precaution. The only problem was moving the damn thing when she needed to use the bathroom.

Evelyn felt the insistent tug of Charlie on his lead. They had already been out a good half an hour and the cold temperature wasn't agreeing with Evelyn.

'Come on, boy, let's go,' she said now, eager to get back home to her morning TV shows. But Charlie was resolute, foraging amongst the bushes, barking and dancing. He was a lazy dog so what on earth had caught his attention to get him so excited?

Unable to pull him away, Evelyn went to have a look. She'd expected a dead bird or a squirrel but instead several pieces of cooked meat on the bone lay in a heap. Charlie was already at it, using both front paws to hold it steady while he got his jaws around it. Who would dump so much cooked meat? thought Evelyn. There must be something wrong with it. Pulling a disappointed Charlie away with promises of dog treats when he got home, she thought nothing more of it, her only desire being to get home.

Evelyn inspected the bottom of her burgundy velvet slipper curiously. A thick substance covered the sole, its cloying texture emitting a foul smell. Recoiling, it was only when she saw Charlie lying on his side that she realised he'd been sick. Leaning over him, Evelyn stroked his matted fur, his eyes looking up at her beseechingly. His breathing was rapid, coming in short bursts. Scooping him up in one arm, she didn't hesitate. Pausing just long enough to slip on her boots and jacket, she raced out of the door, slamming and locking it behind her, before flagging a taxi to take him to the vet. She would clean up the mess later.

'My best guess would be poisoning,' announced Mr Mills, who had been treating Charlie since she had found him abandoned on the construction site. As usual, his white jacket sleeves were rolled up to reveal his hairy forearms as he gently examined Charlie's limp body.

'Poison! From what?'

'Some kind of chemical, I suspect – rat poison, or something similar – but we'll have to run a blood test to be sure. In the meantime, it's a good sign that he's been sick already, so we'll start an antidote and keep an eye on him.'

Rat poison? Where on earth would he find that? She deliberately took him for walks in the green areas and normally the council would inform them of any pest control. She recounted their walk earlier that morning and remembered the cooked meat.

'Charlie found some cooked meat in the bushes earlier today. He only managed to get a few licks before I pulled him away, but could the meat have been rotten and caused this?'

'Possibly, but I would say his symptoms are more indicative of a chemical rather than food poisoning. Unless the meat had been sprayed with weedkiller or something similar. You say it was found in the bushes?'

Evelyn's thoughts came at her rapidly like bullets. The council never put weedkiller down in winter – they always did it in spring. Her heart started pounding and she slipped her hand in her pocket, feeling the reassurance of the sharp knife.

59

Rosemary

Rosemary lay in bed staring at the ceiling, not wanting to be awake but unable to sleep. She could hear the Macmillan nurse in the kitchen, putting the kettle on and preparing breakfast; James's greeting as he was met with coffee and boiled eggs.

After a few moments, she sat up and looked around the guest room. When they'd first moved in, all those years ago, Rosemary knew the space would be perfect as a nursery. As they'd unpacked, she'd designed it in her mind: the white crib placed on the far side, an armchair in the corner by the window overlooking the garden, and a chest of drawers filled with tiny clothes, clean and pressed, ready to slip on. But as the years passed, the room remained empty and, reluctantly, Rosemary turned it into a guest room. She'd bought a double bed with matching side tables and a mirrored dresser. In the corner, there were two chairs with a small coffee table, and she remembered being pleased that she'd been able to match the wallpaper, bedspread and tablecloth so that hundreds of tiny little flowers covered the room. Looking around now,

Rosemary wondered if she would ever feel like decorating again.

The day she discovered the letter seemed like a lifetime ago. She didn't remember how long she'd sat on the floor sobbing, amongst the strewn jewellery and broken glass. Eventually, she'd stood up, put the letter back exactly where she found it, and went to the shed. As she stood there amongst the oily smell of machinery, James was all around her but she felt removed from his presence, shock making her numb. She put the tool box back where she'd found it. She'd then gone back inside, telephoned Macmillan Cancer Support, and retreated to the guest room, telling James she was ill and couldn't risk passing anything on to him when his immune system was so weak.

This was her third day in bed and she knew that she wouldn't be able to hide forever. She had slept most of the time, unable to face the inevitable breakdown of her marriage. It all made sense now; she had never been involved in anything to do with the adoption process, leaving it all to James to handle, and when he'd told her the home had called to say they were too old to adopt a baby, she'd never questioned it. They'd been married for over two decades and not even her wild imagination could have predicted such a betrayal. He had prevented her from having the one thing in life she truly wanted: the silky satin of a baby's cheek pressed up to her own, the warm curl of a grasp on her finger, the contented sigh from a rosebud mouth. Rosemary clawed at the bedcovers, doubled over in physical pain at the thought of the baby she could have had. What she had lost. What had been denied to her by a man who had put his own needs above her own.

Rosemary could hear James calling her, his words soft and mellow. She heard the gentle tap of a cup placed on the bedside table and felt his kiss on her forehead. When she didn't stir, he left the room, closing the door quietly behind him. As she heard his footsteps recede, she rolled over, letting the pillow soak up her tears.

When James said he was going to call the doctor if she didn't improve soon, Rosemary knew she had to get out of bed. Despite the irony of the room's original intended use, she'd found, if not comfort, then at least a place for her grief amongst the flowery pillows and sheets. It was Friday and as she washed and dressed, she wondered what she would say to James, where they could possibly go from here. But as she walked into the kitchen, she was surprised to see James at the table, a couple of documents laid out before him. She couldn't see the contents of the papers but the yellowing of them told her they were old. As he spotted her, he rose, coming over to wrap his arms around her. Rosemary forced her arms to reciprocate.

'Rosie, love, you're up! How are you feeling?'

She heard the kettle being switched on and was disconcerted to see the Macmillan nurse making tea. She'd almost forgotten about her – what was her name again? Sarah? Sam?

'Good morning. Would you like a cup?' the nurse asked now.

'No problem, I can make it,' Rosemary replied, glad of the excuse to extract herself from James. 'Thank you so much for your help this week,' she continued. 'I'm feeling much better now so I can probably manage from here. I shall definitely be in touch again, though.'

The nurse quickly picked up the hint. 'It's been no problem at all. A pleasure, in fact.'

'Thank you very much,' added James, with exaggerated politeness as if trying to make up for the abruptness of his wife.

Rosemary saw the nurse out before returning to the kitchen.

James looked at her in concern. 'Are you sure you're well enough to be up, Rosie?' he asked.

'I'm fine,' she replied, making herself busy in the kitchen. Anticipating he would pry further, she was surprised when, instead, he sat back down and started looking at the documents again. He seemed preoccupied. With a start, she realised he was going to tell her about the letter himself. Is this what a potential life-threatening illness did – enticed you to right wrongs? And even if it did, would it make a difference to the way she felt about him and what he'd done? Could there be hope for their marriage after all?

That afternoon, Rosemary was sitting in the living room with a pot of tea. She felt lethargic and couldn't even drum up the energy to pick up a magazine. James came through and sat next to her. She'd left him to his own devices that morning, struggling even to look at him.

'Rosie love, there's something we need to discuss. Do you think you're up to it today? I'd rather do it sooner than later, to be honest.'

Rosemary looked at him closely, sensing his apprehension and... was that fear?

'Of course,' she replied, relieved that the moment of truth had come so quickly. 'Let me just put some fresh water in this pot and then we can talk.' She needed a few moments.

Returning, she saw the documents in James's hand and braced herself. She imagined him tentatively showing her the letter, the apologies tumbling like a waterfall. Since the morning, she had tried to plan her response, hoping that her rage wouldn't get the better of her. Would she tell him she already knew? Would they cry together? In the end, like the hope she'd felt earlier, Rosemary decided to let her instincts take over.

60

Angela

Angela slowly opened her eyes and it took her several moments to realise she was in a hospital. As consciousness took over, she remembered. The frantic phone call from her mum late Friday afternoon saying her dad had been rushed to hospital, the race to leave the office, and the endless train journey. She had been planning to go home for Christmas for a few days that afternoon anyway, now her promotion had been made official, so she already had her weekend case with her. With a quick explanation to Mr Mooring, she had left the office.

She moved her neck, which was now stiff from sleeping in a chair, and looked over at her dad. He was sleeping and looked peaceful, but the tubes and beeps and the foreign noises alarmed Angela. How could this be happening? Angela closed her eyes again, eager to block it all out. She had told her mum to go home on Friday evening and rest for a few hours in her own bed. She looked more than exhausted – she looked ill.

'It's OK, Mum. He's here now and being well taken care of.'

Rosemary had nodded. She'd barely spoken since Angela had arrived.

'Have they said when he's likely to wake up?' asked Angela.

'No. The consultant on duty just told me he's comfortable for now and to let him rest. Oh, Angela, do you think he will be all right?'

'I'm sure he will,' replied Angela, clutching her mum's hand. 'I'm sure he will.'

Knowing she wouldn't be able to sleep any more, Angela got up and went to look for a coffee machine. As she approached the nurses' station, she decided to ask what time the doctor would come.

'Good morning,' she said to the tired-looking nurse, whose name was Christine, according to her name badge accentuated by a touch of red tinsel.

'Good morning,' replied Christine, smiling. 'How did you sleep?'

'Fine, thanks,' Angela said, trying not to grimace.

'I know, those chairs are not the best for sleeping,' empathised Christine. 'The canteen is open, though, if you would like to get some coffee.'

'You read my mind,' replied Angela gratefully.

'Go straight down the corridor and take the lift down to the first floor,' instructed Christine.

'Thank you.' Angela turned away.

She followed Christine's directions. She began to feel the poundings of a headache, but soon the doctor would be round and would give them an update. And then when her dad woke, she could tell him about her promotion to give him something to cheer him up. He would be absolutely thrilled for her and so proud.

But Angela never got the chance. Her father died that night, Christmas Eve 1988, without ever regaining consciousness.

The call had come at two in the morning on Christmas Eve. Angela had been asleep in her childhood bedroom in Tetbury, her mother refusing to leave her husband's bedside that evening. Perhaps she had known then, thought Angela later. The doctor's visit that morning hadn't provided any real update. It was simply a case of patience. Angela had stifled the urge to scream, '*Do something!*' The voice in her head was persistent, but when she spoke to the doctor outside in the hallway, the doctor said simply that they'd done all they could and now it was a waiting game for her father to wake up.

The phone's shrill tone had interrupted a nightmare in which Angela was on a cruise and the boat had started to capsize. She had had the dream frequently since the Zeebrugge disaster the year before, in which almost two hundred people had died. Why it affected her she had no idea, but her overactive brain insisted on imagining herself as a trapped passenger struggling to breathe as the water level rose higher and higher. She imagined the feelings of panic and fear as it slowly dawned on her that there was no escape and the end was inevitable.

And now it seemed to be the end for her father. Dread flooded her as she picked up the phone, praying that it was a wrong number. But her prayers went unanswered and her mum's voice came down the line asking her to come to the hospital.

*

There was nothing more to be done, said the consultant sympathetically but professionally. James's body, already weak from chemotherapy, was unable to cope with the trauma sustained. When the machines alerted them that he had gone into cardiac arrest, resuscitation had failed.

He could have been just napping, he looked so peaceful. Angela reached for his hand, trying to avoid looking at all the machines around him. Their noise had pierced her sleep the night before but now they were silent, as if in respect for her father. There had been so many of them, all needed to keep her dad alive, and at that moment Angela would have given anything to hear the machines' beeping rhythm, that chime of hope.

When she'd first arrived at the hospital, her mum hadn't said very much except that he'd tripped and fallen and it had been enough to knock him unconscious. Angela had seen her dad only last weekend and he'd been in good spirits. She was in disbelief that in just a few days everything had changed. Seeing him now, lying at peace in a hospital bed, she was in shock. She held onto his hand tightly, her head bowed, trying to find the courage to say goodbye. She couldn't. Not now, not when she'd just discovered their true relationship. She had no idea how long she'd been there when Christine gently led her away.

'Mum,' said Angela softly. 'Have you had anything to drink?'

Rosemary shook her head, looking on the verge of collapse. Angela cast a worried glance at her.

'Let me go and get us some tea. Just wait here and I'll be

back in a minute.' She added sugar to her mum's cup even though she didn't take it and hurried back. She was relieved when she saw her mum take a sip of the hot drink. They sat drinking in silence until Angela saw her put the cup down and sit back in her chair.

'What happened, Mum?' asked Angela, trying to hide the despair in her voice.

Angela wasn't sure her mum was going to respond at first but then Rosemary answered, slowly and quietly.

'I'd only been gone a few minutes, before I heard an almighty thump,' she said. 'It was so loud, I didn't think it was your dad at first. I thought someone was trying to get into the house – you know, like a burglar or something. But then I didn't hear anything else. I went to look and there he was... lying on his front, sort of twisted...' Rosemary gulped back the tears at the memory of it, visibly horrified. 'I called 999 as soon as I saw him, and then I just... waited. They told me not to move him and the girl stayed with me on the phone until the ambulance got there. It was good of her to do that.'

61

Friday, 23 December 1988

Dear Diary,

I'd been close to the office when it had happened. I wasn't sure what did happen exactly, but I knew one thing was for certain: it wasn't good news. Despite it being mid-morning, the train station was heaving. There was no time for browsing the shops or picking up a coffee – it was a case of scanning the noticeboard and seeing what time the next train left. Luckily, there was one within a few minutes. Everyone was fighting to get a seat, due to all the delays and cancellations. Bloody British Rail. Luckily, I managed to get a seat and I read the paper.

Tetbury wasn't the end destination though, and as I arrived at Cirencester Hospital I was running through the various possible scenarios in my mind. What had happened exactly?

I made it eventually but there was an awful lot of waiting around. In the end, I went to find the maternity unit. It was a ridiculous thing to do now in hindsight but, like always, something drew me there. I sat outside the ward for a long time, watching couples leave the hospital with their babies for new lives as families. It was always the same expression on the parents' faces – part shock, part relief, but always love. There was never any doubt about that. I had been to dozens of maternity wards and you could almost reach out and touch it, the love felt so tangible.

A few years ago, after making small talk with one of the new mothers, I asked her how she was feeling. While she was clearly exhausted, her face lit up as she talked about her new daughter. When she told me how well I was doing to be up and dressed after the birth, I quickly left, promising myself to give up the ridiculous habit of visiting maternity wards. It was unbelievable that someone hadn't reported me to security. Yet, there I was again, gazing at beautiful new-borns, wondering why Evelyn hadn't felt the same.

A.

62

Rosemary

Rosemary hadn't slept properly for days. The rush to the hospital the day before Christmas Eve, the emergency doctor identifying the internal injuries, the hours of waiting... Rosemary had lost all sense of herself in the adrenalin. Why did nobody ask what had happened? Perhaps they did – what had she told them? She couldn't remember. The time in the hospital was a blur. When the doctor stepped out of James's ward to tell her resuscitation had failed, Rosemary simply didn't believe him and she told him as much, even going so far as to order him to go back in and try again. It was then that she'd collapsed, her knees giving way. She'd felt herself lifted and was vaguely aware of someone holding her up. Was it Angela? But by that time it was too late. James was dead.

Rosemary sat in the shed wrapped in a blanket. Through the small window, she could see the moon, its iridescent sheen the only thing able to hold her attention for more than a minute. She wondered if this was what madness felt like – a searing need to rip off your own skin, to morph into another person, to be anyone but oneself. She put her head on her knees, closed her eyes, and pulled the blanket closer, hoping sheer exhaustion would soon take over.

It had taken everything she had to get through the following days. But at least she'd been busy, her mind consumed with organising the funeral. Over a hundred of their friends, family and neighbours had passed through their home, offering their condolences, eating, drinking, and hugging. Many had assumed it was the cancer that had taken him and she didn't bother to correct anyone. It was the longest day in Rosemary's life and there were even moments when she forgot what she had done. But then she remembered, and the terror was paralysing.

It was worse at night when she was alone and Angela was sleeping, which is why she had started coming to the shed. Here, as she remembered finding the letter of approval for a baby, the guilt lessened just a fraction, or at least enough for her to sleep a little. She wondered if anyone had ever died from lack of sleep. Insomnia was a cruel bed-partner.

She tried not to think about Angela. Her devastation was etched on her face at the loss of her dad, but Rosemary couldn't help her. Every time she saw her, she was reminded of James – his look of sheer desperation, their last conversation ringing in her mind like a never-ending alarm.

'I know this is going to be difficult for you to hear, Rosie love, but I do think it's the right thing to do,' he'd said.

And as he showed her his updated will with everything, except the house, to be left to Angela, Rosemary wondered if it was some kind of joke.

'You'll not go short, of course you won't, as you still have everything from your parents, and of course this house,' James had reasoned.

Rosemary stared at him as if he were a stranger, slowly realising that this was no joke. After years of marriage, he was choosing his daughter over her.

'But I supported you in that business!' protested Rosemary. 'Who was the one who helped you? Gave you the funds to get started?'

'I know,' he placated. 'Of course, I know that. And I can return that to you. It's just Angela has a good business sense – she knows how to run it, get the best out of it. It's worth a lot of money—'

'I know it's worth a lot of money!' shouted Rosemary, 'because it was my franchise plan that made so much money! Why do you think I'm so upset about it? And what about the savings? Am I to be left with nothing?'

'Of course not,' said James. 'You'll have the house and I'm sure we can arrange an allowance of some kind.'

'Are you out of your mind?' Rosemary was now screaming but she didn't care. He was supposed to be begging her forgiveness for his lie about adopting a baby. 'I gave up my life for Angela and you think I would be happy relying on her for money?' screamed Rosemary.

'Rosie, will you just calm down—'

'You have just changed your will and given away your ENTIRE inheritance to Angela and left me with nothing. Nothing! The house was already mine, you bastard!' The expletive felt foreign on her tongue – she rarely swore.

'Rosemary, you're hysterical. I'm not going to have this conversation with you,' he'd said then, and Rosemary felt the violence within. She might not have done it if he hadn't walked away from her towards the back door.

But he did.

At that moment she realised her parents had been right about James all along: he wasn't good enough for her, not by a long shot. He was a liar.

'James!' she'd said, approaching him. He'd already opened the back door and she guessed he was going to his precious shed. What other secrets were in there?

'For God's sake, Rosemary,' he said wearily, turning back to face her. 'Let's just give it a rest for a bit.'

But as he left her, his misplaced arrogance visible in the lift of his chin, she snapped.

And just like that, she'd pushed him.

Hard.

In the back.

With both hands. She'd watched him fall, her hands still able to feel the soft cotton of his shirt. His feet had gone out from under him and in that millisecond between disbelief and reality, his head had turned to her and she saw his eyes wide with fear, reaching out for her.

And she'd just stood there.

As his head slammed against the stone-paved steps leading up to the garden with a sickening crack, Rosemary knew they had both gone too far.

63

Angela

Angela watched silently as her father was lowered into the cold, damp ground. She stared straight ahead, her chin slightly raised, well-practised at keeping her emotions in check. Her mother stood beside her, pale and sunken, while Mitchell was on her right, tall and upright, head bowed in respect. The homily floated around her. The words were meaningless, but their mesmerising drone tempted recollections to resurface from a time when she'd had to attend church every Sunday, morning and evening, forced to stand for ages listening to the priest as he talked about redemption. Even a slight waver in concentration could result in a backhand from Matron afterwards. Sometimes the girls would stop off at Woolworths on the way home from school, pilfering a Revlon foundation and giggling helplessly as they streaked it on their cheeks to disguise the remnants of red fingerprints. To this day, Angela was still incredulous at how, even in violent situations, they still managed to laugh, their glee a triumphant revenge on Matron.

As the priest led the congregation in the Lord's Prayer, Angela saw her mum bow her head in prayer, her lips silently moving. Neither of her parents had been devout Catholics but they had attended church most Sundays and she knew her mother found solace in the religion and its community. It gave Angela a degree of comfort to know that her mum had this support around her. Yet her parents had never questioned Angela when she stopped attending after they adopted her; they simply respected her decision and told her she was always welcome if she changed her mind. During her early years, however, Angela had seen another side to religion and she had decided a long time ago that the only doctrine she would ever follow would be her own.

The wake, held at her parents' home, passed her by in a blur of canapés and well-wishers. She repressed her own grief until she could deal with it alone. She almost admired anyone who could be so open as to share their darkest times with other people. To Angela, it just felt wrong – there was no other way to describe it. She couldn't think with so many people around, all squeezing her arm in sympathy and asking how she was coping. She stood with her back to the window in the living room and near the door. Her strategy was that people would come in and move further inside the room to mingle and she would only have to greet people rather than engage in small talk. She could see Mrs Henderson and her husband approaching down the hallway. They were an elderly couple who used to invite Angela over to their house to play board games when she'd first arrived.

'Hello, Mr and Mrs Henderson. Thanks for coming,' said Angela automatically.

'Angela! You beat us to it! Not surprising really, a couple of old dodderers like us.'

Angela smiled politely and turned to the next set of neighbours who had just arrived.

Mitchell had brought her a glass of wine and she clutched at it thankfully, its sharpness making everything just that little bit more bearable. Both he and Lucy had been so supportive, helping her and Rosemary with the arrangements. Angela watched her mother now, moving from group to group, always with a tray of something or other. As she looked around at the number of people who had come to pay their respects, she felt reassured that her mum would be well supported. Secretly, Angela was slightly envious. Despite the genuine warmth of the people around her, many of whom she had known for years, she felt closed off, remote, and unreachable.

She longed to get back to her flat, to simply lie down, close her eyes, and let the pain swallow her whole. Later, she would emerge, get up, go to work, come back, lie down, and let the pain wash over her again. She felt compelled to compartmentalise in order to cope. She knew people wouldn't understand it. At best she would be referred to as dignified, at worst aloof, but she didn't care enough to correct them, or to try and convey the depths of despair she felt as she imagined never being able to talk to her father again; never having the chance to see him again. Angela felt her breathing constrict.

Forcing her shoulders back, she went to see if there was anything that could be done in the kitchen to help her mother.

64

Thursday, 29 December 1988

Dear Diary,

Yesterday was the funeral and it was cold and slightly drizzly, and I had to take an umbrella with me against the rain. I wore a black funeral veil over a pillbox hat. It was a bit old-fashioned, but that didn't matter. I shouldn't have been surprised at how many people attended but I was pleased by the turnout – it made everything easier. The atmosphere was sombre, and the priest went on and on, his words lost in the dusty old beams of the church. I wondered how many people were listening, how many people were taking comfort from his words or, like me, were just waiting for it all to be over.

    A.

65

Evelyn

Evelyn pulled up the collar on her black wool coat against the cold as she walked down the steps of the church to the graveyard. She hadn't worn this coat in ages, and she felt awkward and constrained by its formality. She had debated for days whether to attend Jimmy's funeral after Angela had called her to let her know he'd passed away. She'd been too frightened of Angela to pick up the phone, but she had left a message, her sadness magnified through the speaker. Evelyn had wanted to attend, but she knew she didn't belong there. Theirs was a past long swallowed up by time. Evelyn still couldn't believe it could be Angela who was behind everything. In the end, she decided to get the train, discreetly attend the service and just slip in at the back. She wouldn't go to the wake, despite the appeal of free booze.

Evelyn walked, invisible amongst the large groups of black-clad figures, all unknown to her. Would there be as many people at her funeral? She didn't think so, and she was surprised to find the thought distressed her. Jimmy, for all his wrongdoings, had left legacies – a family, a business, and clearly a lot of goodwill, going by the sheer number of attendees. She'd been worried that some of Jimmy's family might recognise her, but as she'd looked at the lines on her face in the mirror before leaving home she knew she didn't need to worry. She didn't own a black hat, so instead she wrapped a black scarf around her head and, as luck would have it, there was a slight drizzle so her umbrella provided a little more camouflage. She could have been anyone.

She didn't see the casket as it was lowered into the ground, only heard the priest's words as they floated loud and clear over his congregation. She was standing right at the back and knew that Angela and Rosemary would be by the graveside. But when she saw her daughter just inches in front of her, her pillbox hat and veil making her look almost royal, Evelyn had fled, hoping that she hadn't been recognised.

66

Angela

It was a few days after the funeral, and Angela and her mother were in the living room, the only voice in the room being Bob Holness on the television as he quizzed his contestants on *Blockbusters*. Every so often, Angela got up to answer the door or the telephone. The flowers, letters of condolence and calls of regret were still trickling in. Angela looked at her mum worriedly. She had picked up a spiral notebook and pen, presumably to write down her own answers to the quiz show, but they lay untouched on her lap while her eyes glazed over, whether from tiredness or grief Angela didn't know.

After the wake, Mitchell had gone back to London. He'd called regularly since then and it was the highlight of her long days in Tetbury. He had cancelled their weekend away and promised her he would rebook it whenever Angela felt up to it. She would look forward to it, but for now her focus was on her mum. Her grief was harrowing to watch, and Angela was at a loss to know how to support her. She'd expected tears, sadness, days when she didn't want to get out of bed. But her mum seemed – she didn't want to say it – slightly crazed. The day after the funeral, she found her by the back door, opening and closing it repeatedly. One morning, when she'd gone to her mother's room with her breakfast, she wasn't there. She'd searched everywhere, the panic rising, until she found her lying on the floor of the shed, a blanket covering her.

'Mum! Oh, Mum,' she had cried, waking her. 'Are you all right?' She couldn't get the sight out of her mind, and as she gently helped her up, she noticed the strong smell of body odour. Had her mum not been showering? She led her back indoors, sitting her on the sofa in the living room with a cup of tea before running a hot bath.

'Mum, I've run you a bath – why don't you come and have a good soak?'

Her mother didn't respond, simply staring off into the distance.

'Mum?' she said again, more insistent.

Angela was relieved to see Rosemary slowly get up and follow her into the bathroom. She left the door slightly ajar, so she could hear her call if she needed anything. An hour later her mum emerged looking, if not better then certainly much cleaner.

Then there were times when she couldn't keep up with her. Rosemary would go into a frenzy of cleaning, ironing, shopping and cooking, although Angela noticed she didn't eat much of what she cooked.

'There's no need to do all that, Mum. Betty will sort out the cleaning and I can make you whatever you fancy eating.'

But it didn't make any difference and Angela watched helplessly. In the end, she put it down to lack of sleep.

'Mum, if you're struggling to sleep, we could go and see the doctor if you like, and get something to help. What do you think?'

'No, no – no need for anything like that. I'm fine,' she responded, and Angela hadn't liked to push it any further. As she herself knew, grief was messy, complicated and unpredictable.

But when she saw her mum reach for a glass of wine before it was even noon, Angela wondered what to do. Rosemary was not a big drinker: just the odd glass of wine with dinner and even that was only on weekends. She decided not to say anything, but as the bottle started to empty, Angela began to feel uneasy.

'Shall I make you a cup of tea, Mum?' she asked, picking up the wine bottle and going to put it in the fridge.

'Leave it!' Angela jumped at the sound of her mum's harsh voice. 'No, I don't want a bloody cup of tea. I just want to be left alone.' Her words were slurred and Angela realised she'd never seen her mother drunk before.

'OK,' she pacified. 'I'll be in my room if you need me.' She felt Rosemary's eyes on her back as she retreated and hoped a little space would help. Lying on her bed, Angela pushed her own pain aside as she grabbed her diary and started a list of possible solutions to help her mother. She couldn't go back to London and leave her in this state.

Angela woke and looked at the time; it was early evening and she hurried to go and check on her mum. The house was silent, and Angela found her asleep in the guest room. Picking up one of the fallen pillows, Angela held it close to her chest and watched as Rosemary slept, her chest rising and falling. A few minutes later, she closed the door gently and went into the kitchen. There was only one empty bottle and Angela was relieved she hadn't opened another one. Tomorrow, she would talk to her again and see if she could get her some bereavement counselling.

Angela had been dreading the next morning. However, she woke to the smell of eggs and bacon. Padding into the kitchen, she saw Rosemary cooking and drinking coffee.

'Hello, darling, how did you sleep?'

'Fine, thanks. You?' Angela replied, astonished but relieved to see her mother somewhat back to her normal self. Coming over to the table, she placed some breakfast in front of Angela before sitting down herself with a boiled egg and some toast. Angela watched her take a bite.

'Sorry about yesterday, darling. I do appreciate everything you've done.'

Angela's shoulders sagged in relief. This was the Rosemary she knew.

'You don't need to apologise, Mum. It's a really difficult time. I can't even begin...' Angela tailed off, feeling tears at the back of her throat.

'Your dad would be so proud of you, you know that?' Rosemary said.

Gulping, Angela nodded.

'As am I. And your promotion – well! He would be thrilled.'

'He would,' replied Angela. 'I'm just sorry I didn't get the chance to tell him.'

'I feel sure he knows,' said her mum. 'And now you need to get back to work and continue making us proud.'

'But what about you? I'm worried...'

'I will be fine. And if it makes you feel any better, I will go and see the doctor about some help with sleeping and bereavement counselling.'

Angela looked at her mother. She looked better than she had in days.

'OK, but please just let me know if there's anything you need and I'll be here.'

'I will, darling. I promise.'

'And you'll call the doctor today and make an appointment?'

'Already done. Anyway, how about you? How are you holding up?'

'I'm fine, Mum. Just worried about you.'

'I know, darling.' She was quiet for a moment, but then added, 'Try not to worry too much about me. I know I went a bit strange for a while, but your father and I had a lot more time to prepare for the worst than you did.'

As Rosemary slipped her arms around her daughter, Angela felt herself start to grieve.

'I miss him so much, Mum.' It was all she could utter before the open wound inside her released a torrent of tears.

It was on the morning that her mother was having her sewing circle coming round that Angela headed back to London. Mitchell would meet her at Paddington. Rosemary had decided to leave the sorting of James's belongings until she felt a bit stronger, she told Angela as she left.

Promising to call her every day, Angela stepped onto the train and into 1989 – a brand-new year – and a year without her father.

67

Rosemary

Rosemary had just wanted Angela gone. Out of the house. She couldn't bear to see her any more, nor hear her misguided belief in a man who was nothing more than a liar. She knew Angela had adored him from the moment she'd been adopted, but the discovery that he was her real father had visibly transformed Angela before her eyes. She now saw him as some kind of hero and his death had only martyred him. Her presence was intolerable; checking up on her, watching her every move. Rosemary couldn't breathe when she was around.

A thought suddenly occurred to her: what if Angela knew what she, Rosemary, had done? Rosemary thought back to the other night when she'd woken to find Angela watching her while she was sleeping. She'd been holding a pillow – had she been planning to use it on her? Rosemary chided herself: she was losing it. If she could just sleep! She needed to pull herself together, and quickly. It was the only way to get Angela to go back to London. So she had made the doctor's appointment; had dutifully gone and reported back, sleeping pills in hand. Not that she planned to take them. She needed her wits about her as the incident with the wine had told her. What if she started talking when she was drunk? No, to get through this she would have to stay as level-headed as possible. But sleep still eluded her and when it did come, all she saw was James falling, his skull cracking like an egg. She would wake, sweating profusely, too afraid to close her eyes but so exhausted it was painful.

So she would get up and roam the house, but there was no escape from the memories. Their life together was displayed in every room: the beautiful watercolour they'd picked up from a market stall in Greece, James's chair where he used to nap, his car keys hung on the hook near the door. Everywhere she looked he was there and with it came her crime. If she hadn't pushed him, James would still be alive today. Had she pushed him? It was all so hazy in her mind. She went to the back door, opening and closing it over and over again, unable to stop herself. At least Angela had gone – finally.

It was Tuesday and usually she'd be at a WI meeting but she knew she'd never attend one again. Elaine and Mary had called or visited every day. In the end she'd had to tell them firmly that she needed some space to grieve. She remembered the look of hurt on their faces but surely she was entitled to a bit of peace and quiet? She just needed some time to think. To plan what to do. To stop the panic and the fear. She just needed some time. Why couldn't anyone understand that?

68

Angela

'The boss wants to see you in his office, Angela. Sounds serious,' announced his assistant down the phone. She had no idea of her name – Clive Mooring went through assistants like hot dinners. His office, thought Angela as she put down the phone. That was never a good sign. She could do without it. She'd overslept that morning and was late in, meaning she had been playing catch-up and fighting fires for the last few hours, rather than doing any real work.

'Angela,' he barked, as she stepped into his office, 'why the hell did I have Sedgwick's managing director on the phone to me for thirty minutes just now, complaining about God knows what?'

'I don't know, Mr Mooring,' replied Angela honestly.

'Well, you should know!' he retorted, shouting. 'Get it sorted NOW and report back to me asap!' he bellowed.

Angela hurried back to her office, mentally going through the account. There should be no issue. She had been so careful, double-checking, if not triple-checking every piece of work. She thought back to the amount of leave she'd had. Could something have happened while she was away? Surely they wouldn't hold her responsible? But of course they would. It wouldn't matter if she were on her deathbed – it was still her job to make sure the client was happy, and right now the client wasn't happy.

Angela gathered her team and updated them, firing instructions in quick succession. She was a senior associate now: whatever had happened, she would fix it, even if it meant staying all night. But first she had to call the client.

Angela stared at the document in disbelief. There was her signature, approving one of her associate's proposals. Had she been so preoccupied she'd signed it by mistake? She thought back to the last few weeks and realised it was a possibility. It hadn't been easy, and it had taken the whole day, but she'd managed to find a way to resolve the situation. But still, it was bad timing. She needed more wins to cement her new position, to prove to management that they hadn't made the wrong decision. Sedgwick's managing director clearly didn't trust her a hundred per cent if he called Mooring when something went wrong. And sometimes things did go wrong, thought Angela, trying to reassure herself. Of course they did – she just wasn't used to making mistakes.

The pain was still raw from the death of her dad. People in the office had been sympathetic but it wasn't as if she had a close confidante whom she could talk to; she had never been that sort of employee. She experienced a passing moment of regret that being constantly on her professional guard may have cost her genuine friendships, but if she had spent time gossiping in the kitchen or having lunch with the other associates would she be where she was today? She didn't think so. It was already late, and she hadn't touched the work that she had planned to do that day. Usually, she would thrive on this sort of pressure, so it was worrying she felt so unmotivated. Susan had warned her that her emotions could be complex following the death of her father and it might change her perception and priorities. At the time, she thought she was referring to Evelyn, not her work. She wished she'd had the chance to tell her dad about her promotion before he passed away. He would have been so proud. The youngest associate in the company to have been promoted – and a woman at that! But perhaps he did know, as her mum said. Perhaps he was looking over her shoulder right now, smiling to himself at how far she had come. The thought gave her some comfort and, with that, Angela picked up her pen and began in earnest.

'I know you're probably not in the mood to celebrate but I didn't want your birthday to pass by without doing a little something,' said Mitchell, as he leant over to pour her another glass of wine.

'This is perfect,' replied Angela, looking around the intimate but casual restaurant. The lights were low and when they'd been shown to their table there was a bouquet of roses on her chair. She inhaled their scent and kissed him before settling down with the menu.

After the main course, Mitchell had handed her a small box wrapped in gold birthday paper. She'd opened it, feeling something close to happiness for the first time in a while. Inside, a delicate silver bracelet with a tiny charm of a hummingbird sat against the suede cushion.

Angela gasped, surprised and pleased. 'How did you know I loved hummingbirds?'

'I didn't. But it was something you said at dinner once – that you thought they brought good luck.'

Angela couldn't believe it. It had been such a small comment – a throwaway detail that he'd remembered. She kissed him, gently at first, and then more passionately, the feel of the silver bracelet on her arm cool and expensive.

'Thank you,' she said, when they drew apart. 'I love it.'

69

Friday, 20 January 1989

Dear Diary,

I'm now 28 years old. It was a lovely restaurant – expensive too. A little quieter than I usually like them but perfect for the occasion. It was very thoughtful, all things considered. Throughout the night, I kept wondering what would happen afterwards – would it just be a goodnight kiss or was it time to take the relationship to the next level?

A.

70

Angela

Angela hadn't seen Evelyn since before Christmas. When she'd called to arrange a visit, Evelyn had sounded strangely reluctant to meet. In the end, Angela had just turned up on her doorstep, knowing it could take days for her to pick up the phone or listen to a message.

It was a Thursday evening, the last week of January. Angela hadn't been there long before she asked to use the loo, an excuse to check under the bathroom floorboards again. Evelyn seemed even more paranoid and on edge than usual, and certainly looked the worse for wear. Susan had asked Angela if she thought Evelyn was using drugs again, and that's how Angela found herself on her hands and knees, trying to lift the floorboard without Evelyn hearing and without damaging her manicure. She had to be quick: there was only so long she could spend in the bathroom. When she pulled out a half-bag of white powder, her suspicions were confirmed. As the small packet rested in her hand, Angela wondered how long Evelyn had been using again.

Tucking it back into its hiding place, Angela recalled

Susan's advice: 'If someone has a drug problem, you're not the one who can help them. They can only help themselves.'

Despite this, Angela went back into the living room, where the TV was blaring, determined to get a definitive answer from Evelyn. Turning the volume down, Angela sat on the sofa.

'Oi, what did you do that for? I was watching that,' protested Evelyn.

'I know, but I just wanted to ask you something,' replied Angela, all of Susan's advice going out of the window.

'What is it?' replied Evelyn, letting go of Charlie as he jumped down from her lap.

'Are you using again, Evelyn?'

'What? Of course not. What do you take me for?'

'Well, it's just that you've seemed a little paranoid these last few weeks,' replied Angela, not wanting to own up to the fact that she had been snooping in her bathroom.

'Well, wouldn't you be with everything that's been going on around here? There've been murders across the hall, I'm getting threatening letters, someone broke into my house, and now someone's trying to poison Charlie. Who could blame me if I needed a little something to relax these days?'

'So, you *are* using again?' persisted Angela, ignoring her complaints.

'I didn't say that,' replied Evelyn testily. 'I said there's a lot of strange things going on around here, and if you want to start throwing accusations, you better look in the mirror, missy, because all this weird stuff only started happening when you came into my life.'

'That's ridiculous,' replied Angela.

'Is it? Think about it. I gave you a key to get copied and everything goes to shit.'

'Evelyn, we changed the locks.'

'Yeah, but how long did that take? Anyway, it's not just that. Sometimes I get the feeling I'm being followed.'

'Followed? By who?'

'If I knew that I wouldn't be stuck at home terrified to go out, would I? Is it you?'

'Of course not! When have you been followed?'

'I haven't seen anyone, it's just more like a feeling,' answered Evelyn.

'It's your imagination,' reassured Angela. She had read that prolonged drug use could lead to some terrifying mental ordeals. Who knew the damage Evelyn had inflicted on herself?

'Are you calling me a liar?' Evelyn shouted.

Angela felt her impatience rise. 'I'm sure if you stopped taking drugs you wouldn't have these experiences,' she said a little more harshly than she'd intended.

'Who the hell do you think you are, coming in here and telling me what to do?' shouted Evelyn, jumping up from the chair, her gold hooped earrings swaying as her spittle landed on Angela's jacket. 'You come here with your do-gooding ways and your fancy-shmancy job, telling me how to live my life.'

'Of course I'm not! All I meant was—'

'You have no idea – *no idea* – what I've been through, so don't come in here telling me what to do. I'm not paranoid. I know what I saw and I know there's some weird stuff happening around here. Is it your doing? Eh? Is it payback for giving you up for adoption?' Evelyn was now in front of Angela, her bony forefinger prodding Angela's chest with each word.

'Of course not!' replied Angela.

'Well, I'm telling you,' said Evelyn menacingly as she took a step closer to Angela, 'since you came back into my life, things just keep going wrong.'

71

Sunday, 29 January 1989

Dear Diary,

I haven't been able to find the courage to go and find St Matthew's, but yesterday I knew I had to do it. My digging at the library told me that the building was still there and, unbelievably, was still being used as a children's home. That threw me, but I took the bus anyway to see for myself. I had a bit of a walk once I got to Hackney and I was worried I would get lost. After a few minutes, though, the streets started to look familiar and I realised that it was just round the corner. The building was just as imposing as when I was a child and I was glad I'd skipped breakfast. I must have stood looking at it for ages. The curtains were closed on the upper levels, but the downstairs windows were naked apart from some net curtains that fell halfway down the window. I touched the main gate, its red paint fractured and peeling under my hands. I wasn't sure I wanted to go inside but I'd come this far. I pushed it and was surprised to find it unlocked. That would never have happened back in my day. I walked to the front door, but then I saw a face at the window on the second floor. Someone was peering down, probably wondering who the hell I was. As soon as they saw me look up, they dropped the curtain and a few moments later the front door opened. A woman stood there, a welcoming smile plastered across her face. She looked a bit startled when I told her I used to live there.

We chatted on the doorstep and I wasn't sure if she was going to invite me in or not. In the end, I had to make up something about needing to use the bathroom and then she invited me in. Her name was Charlotte and she showed me where the children did their homework, ate their meals, and slept. She was one of those very annoying bubbly types that kids love. She seemed intent on proving to me how much the children enjoyed living there. And maybe it was true. The beds looked comfortable, there was central heating, and the dining room was already set for lunch. Some children were reading, some lounging on their beds, some playing games outside. They seemed happy enough. The last place Charlotte showed me, though, was the kitchen, and there they were: eight wooden spoons and utensils of different sizes hung from their familiar place on the wall.

A.

72

Evelyn

Evelyn felt something was wrong the moment she put the key in the lock. But it was when she opened the door that she knew for certain. Even if he had been sleeping, Charlie always ran to the door to greet her. Where was he? Perhaps he'd just got stuck in the washing machine. It had happened once before – he'd jumped in to investigate and then couldn't get out. He'd not been near it since.

'Charlie, here, boy,' she called.

Nothing.

'Charlie!' She went into the kitchen where the washing machine was – empty.

'Charlie, come on. Where are you?' She checked the living room and the bathroom, moving quickly.

The last room was her own bedroom and with a start she saw the door was ajar. Had she left it open? She was pretty certain she hadn't because she knew, if she did, Charlie would be in there and on her bed. But she must have done – there could be no other explanation. Charlie was in there on her bed, marking his territory. But as she opened the door and saw him on the white duvet in a pool of blood, she let out an ear-piercing scream.

'What did you do?' A version of Evelyn's voice came down the phone that Evelyn herself had never heard before.

'Evelyn, is that you?' replied Angela.

'I said: What did you do?' replied Evelyn.

'Evelyn – what do you mean?' Angela sounded taken aback. *Lying bitch.*

'Charlie is dead.'

The silence was deafening.

'He's dead,' repeated Evelyn. 'And you killed him.'

Evelyn was in the hallway when she saw the front door handle slowly turning and she knew then her time had come. The day before, she'd buried Charlie in a patch of grass on the estate and she couldn't believe he'd gone. It had been a warning.

Evelyn had always been afraid of death – ever since she went to her father's funeral as a little girl and saw him being lowered into a grave. She had felt her throat constrict at the thought of being buried in a box in the ground. What if her father were still alive in there? How would he get out? She had to be sure and her childish impulse was to let go of her mother's hand and save him. But her mother held onto her hand tightly, her black leather glove like a vice around her pudgy four-year-old fingers.

The door opened slightly and Evelyn saw with horror a pair of heavy-duty bolt cutters slip through the gap to cut the security door chain. As the gloved hands holding the cutters disappeared and the door slowly opened, she simply stood there, waiting for the intruder to come in.

Evelyn woke up groggily. Her mouth was dry and her head felt heavy. Surely she hadn't been on a drinking binge? Her thoughts were scrambled and she could smell burning. With a start, she realised her hands were tied and she was strapped to a chair. As she took in the scene around her, she tried screaming but her mouth was gagged. She couldn't move or speak, but as she became more lucid she saw her living room had been transformed. Gone was her armchair and in its place was a structure of some sort, held together by wooden poles and covered with a blue tarpaulin. Photographs of individual children of different ages were stuck onto the structure with sticky tape to create a makeshift gallery. The television was upended and the screen smashed, while on the coffee table lay a selection of wooden spoons and cooking utensils, including several large knives. It was only when Evelyn realised that her back was to the electric fire and felt the heat on her body that her fear gave way to a trickle of urine, which soaked through her leggings. In front of her, lounging on the sofa, was her daughter sucking on a lollipop. Evelyn closed her eyes and thought of God. She never asked him for much but now as her daughter increased the temperature of the electric fire and picked up one of the knives, she prayed for her death to be swift.

'I hate lollipops,' observed her daughter, looking at the one in her hand closely. 'They're just so sickly sweet. In fact, I think this is the first one I've had in years. Do you like lollipops, Evelyn? I know you have a sweet tooth.'

Evelyn opened her eyes but couldn't answer. She was trying to understand where all this was going, but, more importantly, she was wondering if she could escape. Her daughter looked utterly serene, as if they were having an everyday conversation about the weather, but the madness in her eyes told her otherwise.

'Well?' she demanded.

Evelyn shook her head cautiously. She had no idea what the right answer was.

'What is it? The flavour? The hardness? Why don't you like them, Evelyn? Never mind. I really don't care. Shall I tell you why I don't like them?'

She was pacing the living room now, agitated as she talked.

'I don't like them because at the children's home, they were what Ray – that's the man who ran the place – used to entice and reward the littlies with when he abused them. That's right, Evelyn – you left me in a home that was managed by a paedophile.'

Evelyn swallowed hard.

'Every day. Every single day, he abused one of us in a den similar to this one,' she said, pointing to the structure with the blue tarpaulin. 'To the older ones he gave gifts and to the littlies, such as Julia here, he gave lollipops.' She indicated to one of the photos stuck onto the structure: a beautiful girl of about four years old with blonde hair and blue eyes.

'Do you know what happened to Julia?'

Evelyn shook her head again, her heart pounding.

'She committed suicide. Jumped in front of a bus because she couldn't take it any more. She was fifteen years old.' She threw the lollipop on the floor in disgust.

'I'm so sorry,' tried Evelyn, but the words were lost, the gag pulled tight across her mouth.

'You do not get to speak,' said her daughter quietly. 'It's been about you for too long. Now it's my turn.'

She took a few deep breaths as if trying to find the cold malice she'd had when she entered the flat.

'This is Peter,' she announced, indicating a photo of a good-looking boy who looked about fourteen. 'He was beaten so hard one night that Ray broke both his arms and he couldn't see because his eyes were so swollen from Ray's fists. Recently, I found out he's also dead – he died from a drug overdose.

'And Maureen,' she continued, pointing to a girl with her hair in plaits. 'She lasted a little longer than Julia but also committed suicide – on her twenty-first birthday, by jumping from a balcony.'

Tears ran down Evelyn's face. She'd had no idea of the conditions her new-born child would be placed in. St Anne's had simply told her she'd be placed for adoption. In her dreams, Evelyn had envisaged a faceless, childless couple cooing over her baby, giving her everything that she could have ever wanted. Was she so damaged, despite the love and care of Jimmy and Rosemary? A silent scream of frustration flashed through her head. This was not how it was supposed to end.

'You'd think someone would notice what was going on in such a flimsy structure,' she said now as she kicked the den with her foot as if to prove her point, 'but no one gave a damn about us. Not the teachers, not the inspectors. We tried to tell them but they didn't care.' She sat back down on the sofa, crossing her long legs. 'But then why should they? We weren't really their responsibility, after all. No, Evelyn, I don't blame them – not Ray with his wandering hands, nor Kath with her vicious temper and wooden spoons. No, Evelyn, I blame you, and now you're going to pay.'

*

Evelyn wasn't sure how much more she could take. The soles of her feet stung from where they'd been lashed and her back was starting to burn. Her lip had been split open with one of the wooden spoons and she wondered when her daughter would be satisfied. She feared her tormentor might never be. There was a part of Evelyn that just wanted to give up. If this is what her daughter had endured as a child, then perhaps Evelyn should be punished?

But something inside Evelyn fought back. If she could just untie her hands then she might have a chance of escape. She worked the knots, trying to ignore the blistering heat on her fingers. But slowly, they were becoming looser, and she was able to feel the fastening holding her to the chair. It had a buckle and Evelyn realised that it was a belt. It seemed to take forever, but slowly she managed to undo it. Her daughter was pacing up and down the living room, still talking about the home. Gone was her calm sophistication – she was deranged.

Evelyn was just about to make a run for it when her daughter turned, and Evelyn was struck once again by her beauty. She walked towards the living room door, blocking the exit, Evelyn's hopes of escape dwindling. But then she moved towards the window and Evelyn took advantage of her turned back, got up and ran as fast as she could to the front door. But she wasn't fast enough and she felt a long arm reach out and grab the back of her baggy jumper in the hallway, just inches from the front door, and she fell heavily. Evelyn turned on her back to fight her off, but the other woman straddled her, pinning her down, youth giving her an advantage. As she held her mother's hands with one of her own, the other hand holding a knife, Evelyn couldn't believe that this was the same polite, professional woman who had visited her for the first time all those months ago.

73

Wednesday, 1 March 1989

Dear Diary,

It had all been quite easy in the end. After months of secretly following Angela and Evelyn's movements, I knew their routines as well as my own. It was a 24-hour job and I spent far too many hours in the freezing cold but it was so worth it. I trailed Angela everywhere – when she went to the office, her dates with Mitchell, when she went to the adoption meetings, and even all the way to Tetbury at the weekends. I was her secret shadow and she never even knew.

It was a risk getting so close to Angela on the Tube to steal her bag, but the lost key for Evelyn's flat helped and I came and went as I pleased. Sometimes, I pretended to be Angela to get information from Evelyn – good job she's such a talker – and the rest? Well, let's just say Leo and I became quite good friends and he was willing to do pretty much anything for a tenner. The letters, the break-in, her dead dog. And the finale – coming face to face with Evelyn and inflicting all the pain I was subject to in the home. I can still see her eyes now, begging me to stop. Well, Evelyn, I wanted it to stop too, but it was worse for me because I was a child. Evelyn was an adult and she should have to take responsibility for the hell she put me through. How could she not have known that she'd given birth to twins? Her pathetic excuse of being knocked out with drugs during the birth is exactly that – pathetic. She deserved everything she got.

And James? Well, at least he tried to find one of us. Shame he didn't bother to check if he had any more children. Still, he served his purpose. Every day, I would wait outside Angela's office, but it was pure luck that I had arrived early the day James had gone to hospital and saw Angela leave the office in a hurry. I knew something was up when I saw her face – she looked distraught. I followed her all the way to Cirencester Hospital.

I shouldn't be surprised at what people are willing to do when they're hurt and angry, but I have to say I never expected prim and proper Rosemary to kill him. I do feel sorry for her, in a way, but it was easy to make sure she found the adoption letter. I knew I had to do something when I had secretly watched James go into his man cave with a document and suspected it might be important. I couldn't see where he'd hidden it of course, but after an hour digging around I found it behind a false panel – sneaky. To think Rosemary could have had a baby after all? Anyway, who cares about her. I have never felt so powerful – everything is going to plan.

Amanda.

74

Evelyn

That was the thing about Evelyn's neighbours – they could be interfering, noisy, loud and offensive, but when times were tough, they all rallied round.

It was Doreen from upstairs who had called the ambulance. She had come downstairs to drop off her magazines and had seen the back of a woman with dark hair running down the stairwell. But when she saw the door ajar, she was suspicious. Evelyn didn't hear her friend's screams as she took in the blood, or see her shaking hands as she dialled 999. She didn't remember Doreen removing the gag or feel her hands as she pressed the wounds to stop the bleeding. She had no memory of the ambulance crew arriving and lifting her onto the stretcher. And she certainly had no memory of grabbing Doreen's hand and saying the name Angela over and over again. If she had, perhaps she would have watched in fascinated horror at the attempt on her life, which could have been straight out of one of her favourite TV shows.

If she hadn't been in hospital she would have enjoyed recounting the drama to Brenda. Brenda would have had to come round to her flat for a change to see 'the scene of the crime'. And did Brenda know that Doreen was actually an ex-registered nurse? Had worked at Great Ormond Street, no less. Well, she would have seen some sights in her time, no doubt about it, and it had served her well.

Evelyn would relish telling Brenda just how savage the attack had been. It was brutal – there was no other word for it. There was blood everywhere and it even looked like Evelyn had been tortured beforehand. There were markings and bruises all over her body. It was truly a despicable act and the police had done nothing to help. It was the second violent attack in the building in a matter of months. When was it going to stop? Why hadn't the police done anything when the first murder was reported? But if the police didn't care, why should anybody else? Just thank God Doreen was there.

75

Angela

'Angela Steele, we are arresting you on suspicion of the attempted murder of Evelyn Harris. You do not have to say anything unless you wish to do so, but what you say may be given in evidence...'

The rest of the words were lost in a blur as Angela felt her hands pulled behind her back, the sharp metal of the cuffs digging into her wrists.

They had come to her home and taken her down to the police station, the flash of blue lights from the police car prompting more than a few twitching curtains from her neighbours. It was unusual to see such a sight in her street, and Angela felt a flush of shame. At first, she had resisted, demanding to know what evidence they had to charge her with such an offence, but she knew it was pointless and the sooner she went with them, the sooner she could sort it out.

Jeremy Jackson was good. She'd seen him in court once

when she was assisting a partner on a case that had been brought to trial. She didn't know him personally either, which helped take the sting out of their meeting. He'd sounded intrigued on the phone and said he would be with her in an hour. True to his word, he had arrived just before lunchtime and they now sat opposite each other in a small, windowless room. Jackson's crisp suit was in stark contrast to Angela's own unkempt appearance, but she knew unless she was released on bail there was nothing she could do about it.

'Look,' started Angela, 'this is all just a misunderstanding. Evelyn is my birth mother. I recently found her and have been visiting most weeks. But the last couple of months I believe that she's been using drugs again. She's been claiming some strange things: that someone tried to kill her dog, that someone had broken in and moved her furniture around... that kind of thing. I even found drugs in her bathroom. This latest accusation is just another one of her delusional druggie benders gone wrong.'

Angela sat ram-rod straight, expectant.

'Well?' she asked impatiently. 'Are you going to get me out of here?'

Jeremy Jackson sifted through the papers in front of him.

'I'm afraid it's not going to be that easy,' he said eventually. 'Evelyn is in hospital in a critical condition. Not only has she multiple stab wounds but it looks like she's been tortured.'

Angela didn't reply. There was no way she was going to jail for this.

Jackson sat back in his seat, looking closely at her.

'What?' she asked.

'There's something else,' continued Jackson, his face unreadable. 'There's also an eyewitness.'

Angela sank back against her chair, her mind planning her next move. Leaning forward, she eyeballed her solicitor.

'Listen,' she said through gritted teeth, 'I hired you because you're the best. Now get me the hell out of here.'

76

Rosemary

The doorbell rang for the third time and Rosemary tried to ignore it, putting her head under the duvet and covering her ears with her hands. She hoped it wasn't Eileen again – she'd only just been round the day before with Mary. Why wouldn't they just leave her alone? She knew they had been shocked when they'd seen the state of her normally immaculate home. In their silence, Rosemary had heard a fly buzzing around the sink where the dirty dishes had been lying for goodness knows how long and she quickly ushered them out of the bungalow.

'Mrs Steele?'

Was someone now shouting through the letter box?

'Mrs Steele, it's the police. Can you open the door, please?'

The police?

Rosemary got out of bed and went to open the front door. There were two officers on the doorstep. She tried not to shake.

'Can I help you?'

'Mrs Steele?' asked the female officer.

'Yes?'

'I'm very sorry to trouble you. Would you have a few minutes? We just want to ask a few questions about the death of your husband.'

'He's… he's dead,' replied Rosemary.

The male police officer spoke this time.

'We know, Mrs Steele, and we're very sorry to have to bother you with this at such a difficult time. We would only need a few minutes. May we come in?'

Rosemary reluctantly opened the door and showed them through to the living room. It was a mess, as she'd told Betty not to come in for a few weeks, and she tried not to look at the thick layer of dust covering the television. She sat opposite them, her hands tucked under her thighs to keep them hidden. Why were they here? Had the doctor said something? Rosemary tried to remind herself that all the police knew was that she was a grieving widow, but the fear was clawing at her. She couldn't think straight. All she wanted to do was lie down and sleep. But she couldn't, and wouldn't be able to for the rest of her life.

'Mrs Steele, we're aware of your husband's recent death and, again, we'd like to offer our sincere condolences,' started the policewoman. 'As you may or may not be aware,' she continued, 'we've received a report from the paramedic who attended to your husband when you called 999. Unfortunately, this report only came to our attention now, but in it there are a number of statements recorded by the paramedic that you made and that we just need you to verify.'

Rosemary took the report, which was being handed to her to read. The statement was correct; he'd fallen on his way out to the garden. She'd only been gone a minute. He was on his way to the shed. And then she went completely still. *I didn't mean to do it.* She hadn't said that, had she?

'Could you confirm whether these statements are true?'

'Yes, yes, they're true – except that last sentence.'

'So what you're saying, Mrs Steele, is that you deny saying "I didn't mean to do it"?'

'Of course!' replied Rosemary, panicking. 'He was my husband – I loved him. Why would I push him? We'd been married over twenty years. We ran a business together.' She was aware she was talking too much but she couldn't stop herself. She had to get these officers out of her house. She didn't see them look at each other.

'He had cancer – his chemo made him slightly off balance. I only went away for a few minutes. I came back and there—'

'Mrs Steele.'

'And there he was – lying there. There was blood by his head.'

'Mrs Steele!'

'He'd fallen – he was on his way to the shed.' She was crying now, her hands flailing as if she were a puppet, before wildly combing through her hair.

'Mrs Steele!'

She stopped talking and looked up at the police officer. He no longer looked kind.

'You just said, "Why would I push him?"'

And Rosemary knew then her mistake.

'If he hadn't been going to the shed, it would never have happened. But he shut me down, and I had no choice.' She was sobbing now, her body heaving at the brief moment of relief for/ from? unburdening her secret. But as the police officers stood up to arrest her, terror took over and Rosemary crumpled in a heap.

77
Evelyn

Evelyn could smell disinfectant. Where was she? She tried to move but she was so comfortable she didn't try too hard. She was in such a nice, dreamy state, it reminded her of the cannabis she used to smoke when she was young. Oh, they were such wonderful times – anything felt possible and most of all, she was loved. It was a wonderful thing to be loved by a man like Jimmy; why had no one told her that before? Her mother had never talked about love and her father had been so handsome, so upstanding in the community. Everyone adored him. He worked hard, looked after his family, and always played with Evelyn when she asked. But then he died. It had happened at work – one of the machines had broken and a large piece of metal had fallen on him. It was instant – he didn't suffer, but still a terrible thing, and Evelyn so young as well. She never had the chance to say goodbye. But now, here was a man who loved her in a different way – who would protect her, care for her, yes – but who could also make her feel things she'd never felt in her life before. A single touch from Jimmy's hand and a whole new world had opened up to her. Evelyn sighed contently. She didn't want to wake up. She felt more at peace than she'd ever felt in her life.

The disinfectant tickled Evelyn's nose again. She'd smelt it before, a long time ago. When was that? Evelyn struggled to remember and felt herself being pulled back under, to the enticing bliss of sleep. But it gnawed at her and the medicinal aroma roused her memory. It was starting to annoy her now. Where had she smelt it before? As she felt the dark shadow of someone lean over her, she heard the distinct rustle of plastic. She'd heard that rustle before. It had caught her attention all those years ago because she'd associated it with a sharp pin prick, and as her mind relaxed, her past came back to her.

'All right, Evelyn, won't be long now,' a voice had said. 'I know it hurts but let's get this done and then you'll be free to go back to your life again. I've given you something for the pain – you should start to feel better soon.'

And she had. Whatever they'd injected into her had made her feel drowsy and she so wanted to sleep. Her pregnancy bump was so big. She'd been so cumbersome, it had been impossible to get comfortable. The pain in her stomach was lessening and Evelyn sighed in relief. She would sleep just for a few more minutes and then she would wake up and see her baby for the first and last time.

Evelyn could hear the wail of a baby's cry drifting further and further away and every cell in her body filled with adrenalin. The impulse was overwhelming and unexpected – her arms ached to feel the weight of her baby. But when she tried to get up, she realised she was strapped down. They would bring her baby back to her soon. They were most likely just cleaning her up. Oh, but she was so tired. She would just have a few more minutes of rest before they brought the baby to her.

Evelyn couldn't move. She wanted – no, needed – to move, but whether it was the straps, the drugs, or her overwhelming tiredness, her limbs were too dense to lift. Her stomach still felt heavy. What was going on? Evelyn felt herself being pulled under once again and this time did nothing to resist it. But in the corners of her mind, she heard a baby's cry again. And then she felt a second distinct prick in her arm and the drugs took over, dousing her subconscious with its satiating power.

'Good morning, Evelyn! Are you ready for a wash? It's a lovely day for you to wake up, Evelyn.' The voice came from very far away. Was it Brenda? It didn't sound like Brenda. Evelyn tried to respond but her lips wouldn't move. She'd heard the voice before. It was friendly and always gently coaxing her to wake up. But she didn't want to. She was so content. She would sleep some more. Just a few more minutes and then she would get up.

'Tough old bird, aren't you, Evelyn? I must have inherited my tolerance for pain from you.'

Evelyn's hand reflexed at the whispering voice – familiar but definitely not friendly.

'But now that you've had a taste of what my life was like, it's time to finally go. Goodnight, Evelyn.'

And then Evelyn remembered – the birth at St Anne's in-house maternity unit, the prick of the needle, the drugs, the unbearable tiredness. And – as she felt the choking pressure of the pillow on her face – she knew with absolute certainty that she hadn't just given birth to one daughter, but two.

Epilogue

Eight months later

Angela ran her fingers through her rich chocolate-brown hair, its silky softness just one of the many simple pleasures she enjoyed now. She'd had to admit, Jeremy Jackson had surpassed all her expectations, although, as there was no key witness any more, even the greenest of associates could have got an acquittal. Still, she'd been held for longer than she'd anticipated, and after she was released the very first thing she'd done once she'd got home was wash her hair. She'd stood under the shower in an almost meditative state, ridiculously grateful for the familiar sight of her expensive bottles of shampoo, conditioner and shower gel. The shimmering liquid, gliding from the bottle onto her hand, had the power to make her feel herself again, and she'd taken two or three showers a day in the week since she'd been released, savouring the privacy that had been lacking in the shared prison facilities.

Angela knew she still had a long way to go before her life was back to normal. Or whatever normal was these days. But she was strong and determined, and she would persevere as she always had. Even now, with the death of her father and her mother's hand in that, Angela knew that she had no choice but to just get through it. It would be the one-year anniversary of his death next month.

Sitting at her dresser, she finished brushing her hair, then opened her jewellery box and saw her silver bracelet with its hummingbird charm. It had been a gift from Mitchell. And while he was long gone, she'd kept it as she'd always believed it to be a symbol of good luck. She slipped it on her wrist, knowing that she would need all the help she could get.

The following day she was going to meet with her dad's solicitor for the reading of his will and she knew, from tomorrow, she'd be a very wealthy woman.

It had been Guy Fawkes the night before, and the next morning, having been up for most of the night, she arrived a few minutes late for the solicitor's appointment. After notifying the receptionist of her arrival, she sank gratefully into a chair in the waiting room, thankful to have a few minutes to compose herself. Rifling through her bag, she found a comb and gave her hair a quick once-over before smoothing down her jacket and spraying herself liberally with perfume. She could still smell the burning of the roaring fire in her nostrils.

Just at that moment, a door off the waiting room opened and a woman in her late forties, who she presumed was a secretary, appeared.

'Miss Steele?' enquired the woman.

She stood up and followed the woman through to the office.

'Miss Steele,' announced the solicitor, standing up and coming out from behind his desk, his hand outstretched. 'I'm Mr Bennett. Thank you for coming today. Before we begin, can I get you anything? Tea, perhaps?' The secretary hovered waiting to take her order.

'No, thank you,' she replied.

'Right, well, please take a seat and we shall begin.' Mr Bennett nodded his dismissal of his assistant, and finally it was just the two of them.

Sitting opposite the solicitor, the desk between them, she waited patiently as Mr Bennett went through the preliminary legalese of the will. Eventually he paused and looked up at her from his document. It was clear that the next part of the will would outline the inheritance. Mr Bennett coughed and took a sip of water before beginning.

Part 7. Gift of Residue. I give my Residuary Estate, all my properties and assets both moveable and immovable including my bank accounts, free of all taxes and death duties, to Angela Steele.

Placing the document down on the desk, he looked up at her once again.

'Angela Steele, do you accept this clause as beneficiary without question or challenge?'

Amanda looked the solicitor directly in the eye.

'I do.'

*

Monday, 6 November 1989

Dear Diary,

How ironic that it was Guy Fawkes the day before the solicitor's appointment? I've always loved bonfire night and it made it easy to execute the last step of my plan. Of course, I was counting on Angela getting quite a bit of inheritance – but everything to her and not a penny left for Rosemary? I'm not surprised Rosemary went for him! But then Angela always did get lucky – even her children's home was better than mine! Yes, she may have got the odd slap or two, but nothing compared to what I went through. The home ruined my life, but look what it got her: adoption, education, a career, a fancy flat. And where did I end up? On state handouts living in a small bedsit. Not any more, though – now it's time for the *new* Angela to make herself known, as I take on her identity. Finally, I will get to live the life I deserve.

Amanda.

Acknowledgements

There were many people involved in the creation of this book who I would like to thank. My gratitude goes to Luigi and Alison Bonomi for their unwavering support and to my editor, Sarah Ritherdon, whose feedback, direction and encouragement were invaluable. The copy-editing, sales, and marketing teams at Head of Zeus and Aria, including Melanie Price, Sue Lamprell, and Victoria Joss, always do a fantastic job and I'm so grateful for their expertise.

There was a fair amount of research required for this book and I'd like to thank Yvonne Spiller, Lexy James, Rebecca Platts, and Deborah Stead for taking the time to answer my questions.

My novel-writing journey started at the Emirates Airline Festival of Literature (EAFOL) winning the Montegrappa Novel Writing Award. Thank you to Isobel Abulhoul, Yvette Judge, and the whole team at EAFOL as well as Charles Nahhas of Montegrappa Middle East for creating such an opportunity for new authors.

Writing a book can be a solitary experience and I'm grateful to the many author friends who have generously shared their time, encouragement and advice including Rachel Hamilton, Jessica Jarlvi, and Annabel Kantaria.

To my readers, thank you for your continued support and reviews – without you, I wouldn't be doing my dream job.

To my parents, thank you for all the babysitting, which helped me get the book down on paper. And finally, thank you to my husband for his input, ideas, and endless patience and to Zane and Ryan who provide me with so much inspiration.